FALLEN

THE SHADOWS OF REGIA

BOOK ONE

TENAYA JAYNE

COLD FIRE PUBLISHING, LLC

TENAYA JAYNE

Other titles by Tenaya Jayne

Forbidden Forest

Forest Fire

Verdant

Dark Soul

Burning Bridges

Blood Lock

Lightning Flower

The Slayer's Wife

Cover design by Cold Fire Book Covers

Edited by Finish The Story.

Cold Fire Publishing, LLC

ISBN-10: 0-9986741-3-3
ISBN-13:978-0-9986741-3-1

This one is dedicated to Lacey's tattoo.

Characters from The Legends of Regia

Forest

Half elf, half shapeshifter. Skilled warrior, now the highest judge in Regia. Has the elven ability to become invisible at will. Can shape shift her full appearance, except her eyes. Carries a sword of obsidian glass infused with lightning. Mated to Syrus. Daughter of Rahaxeris. Mother of Tesla and Maddox.

Syrus

The vampire prince. Mage and master of the Blood Kata. Has the power of lightning. Can heal almost all wounds and illnesses. Gave up the throne, in favor of making Regia a republic. He works in the Obsidian Mountain, training other masters in the Kata. Mated to Forest.

Shi

Dryad princess. Died when her race was poisoned and existed for thousands of years as a ghost in the Wolf's Wood. Close friend and adopted mother to Forest. Mated to the late vampire king, Leramiun.

Netriet

Vampire. Thief. Murderess. Sacrificial messenger. Tortured by the leader of the werewolves, resulting in the loss of her arm. Possessed by a dark entity. Used as a pawn by Baal, a priest of the *Rune-dy*. Given an illegal, alien robotic arm. Finally, finds redemption in the love of her mate Merick. Mother of Melina.

Rahaxeris

Elf. Father of Forest. Former high priest of the *Rune-dy*. World jumper. Strong magical abilities, some unnatural. Loves his family but nothing else. Deadly. No scruples. No morality. On a constant quest for more knowledge and power.

Journey

Alien. Storyteller from the world of Illumistice. Has the power to look inside your heart and spin a *story* from your deepest desires. Can hypnotize you with just her voice. Gentle, and healing nature. Mated to Redge. Childless.

Shreve

Clone. Shapeshifter. Created by the wizards. Has Rahaxeris' DNA. Considered Forest's brother. Deadly fighter and weapons master. Lived as an outlaw. Redeemed through family love. His blood was the key ingredient in the blood lock that kept out the wizards before the war. Mated to Sabra. Father of Sophie.

Sabra

She-wolf. Became the leader of the pack through combat. Lost her sister to the insurgents. Mated to Shreve. Vicious in battle. Loves without restraint. Mother to her people, and Sophie.

Tesla

Daughter of Forest and Syrus. Half vampire. World jumper. Has the power of lightning in her hands. Can manipulate natural laws. Created her own mix of magic, science, and technology. Revered as a legend and the savior of Regia. Killed the wizard king. Mated to X.

X

Human. Necromancer. Cursed by a witch. Has the power to always know the truth. Helped Tesla save Regia from the wizards. The only human able to survive in Regia. Tesla's soul mate. Granted unnatural long life by the heart of the world. Works in Regia's government as an interrogator.

The Heart

Deity. Lives under the ground in the Wolf's Wood. No one had ever seen the Heart. All that can be seen is the manifestation. The manifestation is an immortal flame that burns in a circle of crystal trees. Speaks to few. Protected and served by the Dryads.

PROLOGUE

As the sun sets, jeweled colors flow through the sky like ribbons in the wind. Darkness falls, and the moon wraps you in silken bands of aquamarine light, disturbing your dreams. Don't be afraid. You might think you have wandered into a fairy tale. You are in Regia.

Step into the Wolf's Wood and lose yourself among the Dryads as you venture to The Heart of this world. Listen to the music of the wind as it chimes in the leaves of the crystal trees circling the flames of the manifestation. Watch the emotions of the world's heart in the shifting colors of the flames that never die.

Take off your shoes and breathe deep in the Dreaming Desert of the Vampire lands. The hallucinogenic Shadow Sand will show you your dreams. Or venture to the Obsidian Mountain where the Vampires train in the ancient martial art of the Blood Kata.

If you're looking for a little R and R you might enjoy the luxury of Kyhael where the Elves dwell in the clean straight lines and warm glow of the Bellis stone. While you are there, if you feel a chill under the surface, those are just the ghosts of the past. For once under the city of Kyhael were the priests of the *Rune-dy*: a sect of elves dedicated to perfecting torture and twisting science. Rest easy; they are no more.

In the mountains, the werewolves will welcome you in, but beware invoking their ire, for they are truly a pack, and they will kill you as a pack. Shake hands with an ogre, if you dare, and feel the power that throbs deep inside their palms. Power to open portals and forge deadly weapons.

You might come across a few nomadic shape shifters, but really, how could you know for sure? For they can imitate every race. Then there are the Halflings, whose parents dared to break convention and mate across racial lines. Of all Regians, the Halflings are the blessed *and* the cursed. Shunned by those who stick to the old ways and reject the mixing of the races. Halflings are the unpredictable ones, for you never know what power they may have.

Magic hangs in the air like dew. Many other worlds know of this place. Some have tried to breach the borders. Even the strongest of all, the Wizards, tried to conquer and claim the power of The Heart. They are all dead now.

Come with me. Let us stand on the sharp cliffs of the coast and gaze at the rose-colored waves of the Crystalline Sea as they beat the shore. Don't be afraid. You might think you have wandered into a fairy tale. You are in Regia.

ONE

City of Anue, Regia.

13 years after the war of the wizards

A rage burned in Erin's twelve-year-old heart, branding her with darkness. Rage at her mom for dying. Rage at her mother's family for not even bothering to show up to the funeral. Rage at her own powerless state. Her soul wept. She'd cried an ocean, but her eyes were dry, empty shells now.

"Mom..." she whispered, pinching her eyes shut tight. "Mom, I just wish you could hold my hand once more."

Erin put her hands together and imagined her left hand was her mother's.

Cold swept up her back as she realized she was an orphan. Her dad still lived in a technical sense only. He breathed, he spoke, his face was the same. He was there, and at the same time, he wasn't. The moment her mother had died, so had he. Erin watched it happen. The light went out of his eyes. His soul, forever tied to her mother's, left when hers left. There was no comfort she could offer her father. Witnessing him lose his destined life mate terrified Erin. The gravity of his loss seemed to dwarf her own, and Erin's grief was so severe it maimed her.

She raged at the injustice of reality. She was shunned by her mother's family because she was a Halfling. Cursed to suffer the stupidity of racism because her father was a vampire and her mother was an elf. But destiny had chosen to lock her parents together with the famous soul bridge shared by life mates. Destiny was a heartless bitch. Everyone said Regia had changed and now it was acceptable for the races to mix, and perhaps it had been worse before she was born. That didn't change the fact that her grandparents didn't even acknowledge her existence.

Erin leaned out her bedroom window, took as deep a breath as she could, and let it out slowly, gazing at the nearby homes that lined the humble street. Not one window was lit. Everyone slept. She was adrift in the dark quiet, and she would have to learn her own strength. No one else was going to hold her up. Halflings had to be tough, because the world would kick the shit out of you just for being mixed. She had to learn to kick back harder. How could she do that? She wasn't skilled or strong.

A faint rustling startled her. She pulled back into the

house and used her elf DNA to turn invisible. Through the gap in the curtains, a hooded figure walked closely past her window and around the side of the house.

Creeping from her room, slowly she approached the front window and looked out. The figure was there, leaning down by the front door. The size and shape of the stranger let her know it was a boy maybe just a little older than herself. His hands caught her attention. A mark, like a medallion, the size of a coin, glowed on his wrist in a beautiful gold.

He placed an envelope and a white flower on the front step. The breeze snatched the envelope and lifted it up. He caught it, put it back down, grabbed a rock from the ground, and set it on top of the envelope and flower stem. Before he moved away a surge of warm light from his marked hand went into the rock. She watched him walk away until the shadows swallowed him.

Erin waited a few minutes just to make sure he was really and truly gone before opening the door. Clasping the envelope, flower, and rock to her chest, she locked the front door and sat down on the floor. She opened the envelope and gasped. A small fortune of silver coins and a simple note spilled out into her hand.

I'm so sorry for your loss. I know money fixes nothing and cannot soothe your pain, but I have nothing else to give you.

It wasn't signed.

She put the note and money on the kitchen table before taking the flower and rock to her bedroom. She sat on her bed, brought the flower close to her face and inhaled its sweet fragrance. Kindness from a stranger. It touched her battered, broken heart. She pressed the flower inside the book on her bedside table. She didn't want to lose it.

Erin climbed into bed, the rock clutched in her hands. It glowed *very* faintly—the same gold as the mark on the stranger's hand. What kind of power was imbued inside? She instantly and inexplicably attached strong feelings to the stone. Lying face up, she put the stone over her heart. There was something about it...the tightness that held inside her chest for the last few days, eased. The stone made her feel better, healthier, and oddly enough...luckier.

In the years that followed, rumors spread about the benevolent, anonymous person who left help to those who needed it the most, and there was always a stone that the recipient kept and considered lucky. Erin listened to the rumors and would argue with any skeptic that indeed the generous stranger did exist.

Sometimes, in the dead of night, if she had a hard time sleeping, Erin got up and snuck out. She lurked in the shadows, invisible, just watching and hoping she might catch the gift giver in the act. A desire to know his identity only grew through the years and she had more than a few fantasies about him. Even though she didn't know his name, had never seen his face, or heard his voice, she loved him. Just that such a person existed gave her hope.

TWO

Paradigm, Regia

20 years after the war of the wizards.

Maddox left his date in the dancing crowd and stepped outside for a moment of fresh air. In the dark courtyard of The Academy, he leaned against the castle's wall and sighed. The after-graduation party was well under way, but he wasn't even halfway drunk yet. Always the center of attention—where he liked to be— there still were times, like right then, that he needed to be alone. No doubt, his best friend, Kendrick, would find him soon.

Maddox pulled his lighter and a joint from his pocket. The end glowed happily in the dark as he inhaled the head-spinning smoke and held it in his lungs. On his second pull, the door opened.

"Dude, why are you out here?" Kendrick asked, coming out.

Maddox blew smoke in his face and held up the joint. "Fresh air. Wanna hit?"

Kendrick took one drag and handed it back. "I'm not even close to being wasted. The party punch sucks."

"Did you expect better?" Maddox asked incredulously. "This is a school-hosted function. The music isn't bad though. The punch will work on the panties, don't worry."

"Thank goodness for that. Not all of us are superstars and have hordes of women throwing themselves on us the way you do."

Maddox smirked and took another drag. "Don't complain. I know picking the carcasses clean of my discards is one of your favorite pastimes."

Kendrick chuckled. "True. Most of the time the poor girls think I can get them back in your good graces. They will do *anything* for that. If it wasn't weird, I'd ask you to teach me. You're such a slayer."

Maddox pulled his face like he'd just swallowed something sour. "Eww... Anyway, my gifts can't be taught."

"Are you going back in or cutting out?"

"Haven't made up my mind. Neely is boring me. She can't dance. I hate that. Such a turn off."

"So?" Kendrick snorted. "She's got a great rack. Are you really not going to hit that?"

"I already have, yesterday. It wasn't that great. Once was enough. If I leave now, she'll get the hint."

"You think?" He scoffed. "She's got stars in her eyes when she looks at you. You know she'll show up on your doorstep tomorrow, begging."

Maddox pulled more smoke into his lungs and rolled his eyes. "Well, that will be more fun than taking her home tonight. Feel free to wipe her tears and whatever else. I don't give a shit."

Kendrick held out his fist. Maddox bumped it with his own and threw the joint to the ground.

"See you tomorrow, brother?"

Maddox nodded and began walking away. "Not before noon, or I'll kick your ass."

The music faded behind him as he walked through the school grounds and out. He grimaced since no one could see him. He shouldn't be so cruel, he knew that, but it was like a drug. It made him feel powerful...afterward however, the guilt was heavy.

He looked at his watch, the face shivering under the touch of his fingertip. He scrolled through his messages for a second, and then unfastened it and put it in his pocket. The watches most Regians used were all designed by his sister, Tesla. She'd taken her inspiration from Earth's technology and added her own flare to it. Everyone was connected as they chose, but Regia's version of the Internet was a product of Tesla's singular mix of science and magic. Nothing had to be charged. No equipment kept things running.

Now that his watch wasn't hiding the portal embedded in his wrist, he touched the gold medallion on his skin, opening a gateway to the outskirts of Anue. He wanted to walk a bit before going home. He relaxed in the dark solitude as he strolled, his hands in his pockets. His rangy frame cast a very thin shadow across the ground. He looked around and smiled. He'd missed this place. Anue had grown from a small town into a medium-sized, racially diverse city. And since he'd spent over half the year living at school, he didn't get time to spend there. That could change now that he'd graduated.

Memories of his past nightlife in Anue came into his head and caused him to scowl. He didn't want to analyze his character, it would just make him feel guilty. At least no one ever found out about his good deeds. He wove through the empty back streets, unconsciously moving toward the low-income area. He stopped in front of the shabbiest house he'd ever seen and smirked. Why not? Just for old times' sake.

He fished out a few large coins from the bottom of his pocket and put them in the mail box. The sum was enough to feed the family for a month. He began to walk away and stopped after three strides. He'd forgotten something. He bent over and picked up a stone from the ground. He tossed it in the air, caught it, and went back to the house to place the stone in the mail box with the coins. He never knew exactly why he did this, but he always had, ever since the first time, when he'd just needed a rock to keep the letter from blowing away. After that, it was just an odd compulsion he indulged.

He turned the direction of home and walked a little faster than before. Thumping music floated on the air a few streets over. He followed the beat to the house having the party and looked into the open front window. His eyes devoured the scene for a moment before he backed away and continued home. He smiled to himself as he opened a portal to home. Yeah, summer slumming was going to be good. The townie girls he'd glimpsed through that window were hotter than the snooty school tail he was used to.

He landed in the garden, under the shimmery magic dome of security that also had been created by his sister. Had he landed outside the dome, it would have opened for him when he touched it because it was designed to recognize his DNA. There was an invisible code panel on the back side of the property for trusted friends and family members to use. The dome made the house and the surrounding garden invisible to outsiders.

He was happy to be home. Nothing about it ever seemed to change. The stone house had been his mother's before she mated with his father, Syrus. And even though Syrus had been the vampire prince, and they could have lived in the castle, been the king and queen, they left all that and lived here, in privacy and comfort. It had been their choice to change Regia from a kingdom into a republic. And even though they weren't king and queen, no one in Regia had as much power and influence as his parents. Maddox was proud of his heritage. His mother, Forest, was the Hailemarris, highest judge, a powerful politician, and a badass warrior. His father was The Sanguine Mage, the only mage in the world for the last century and the highest level of master in the vampire martial art, the Blood Kata.

The windows were dark, but the porch light had been left on for him. He quietly opened the door and went to straight to his room. He sighed deeply, relaxing all the way. He hadn't been home since the last school holiday a few months ago, and he didn't mind acknowledging to himself that he'd missed his mom and dad, but mostly mom. The time was coming for him to move out, he was too old to live with Mommy and Daddy now. Problem was, he didn't know what he wanted to do or where he wanted to live.

He hung up his jacket, stripped down to his boxers, and threw on a T-shirt from his dresser. He held the fabric up to his nose and inhaled. It was always the same smell. Home. He flopped onto his bed and stretched out. He could have still been at the party, taken Neely back to his dorm room, but he was happier where he was at the moment. Disappearing without a word just added to his mystique. He couldn't let any girl think she could catch him, not even for a moment. He closed his gray-green eyes and yawned. For a few hours, no one could touch him. No one could stare and try to get close to him. Fame had its perks *and* its drawbacks.

He woke slowly to the feeling of his mother's hand smoothing his hair off his forehead.

"Hey, Mom." He blinked and smiled up at her, his heart swelling. She was the same as she'd been since he was a small child. Fierce, vibrant, and so lovely. She'd broken so many racial barriers—for herself and others. Not least of all himself and his sister, since they were more mixed than most, having a vampire as a father and a half elf-half shifter as a mother.

"I'm glad you're home. I missed you," Forest said.

"Missed you, too."

"I didn't think you'd be back last night. I hoped, but I thought the party would keep you away."

"Meh. There are always more parties. There's only one you, and I wanted to see you and Dad before you took off on your vacation. Congratulations on winning the election again, by the way, Madam Hailemarris. I read about it in the news."

She arched one eyebrow, beautifully stern. "I read about you, too. In the junk society section."

He rolled his eyes. "Don't worry. Most of that stuff is total bullshit."

"I certainly hope so…" She frowned for a second, then tapped him on the nose. "You're all grown up now. Twenty years old. Geez, that's weird to say…I'm relieved you graduated; you let your grades slip so far this last year. Have you thought any more about a career field?"

He flashed her his most charming smile. "I just want the summer, Mom. Just this one last summer to do nothing without you getting on my back about it. I promise, once the fall rolls around, I'll get my ass in gear, do something useful, and act like a man."

She softened and smiled. "Okay. I'm going to hold you to that. Now get up, your dad's made breakfast."

Maddox stalked out to the kitchen, yawning again and embraced his dad. Syrus hugged him briskly, slapping him a few times on the back. "Son."

Maddox smirked. "Dad."

The three of them sat down at the kitchen table and ate together.

"So, when are you guys leaving? Where are you going again?"

"Earth, and we leave this evening," Forest answered.

Maddox looked at his dad. "Got your vampire sunscreen?" he teased.

"We'll mostly be in Alaska, smart ass. No sun. The rest of the time, I'll stay in during the day."

"Don't forget to pack your portable coffin, dad."

Syrus chuckled. "I seem to have misplaced it."

After breakfast, Maddox showered and got dressed. He stood in front of his full-length mirror and considered which belt would look best. There was a knock on his door.

"Yeah, come in."

He knew it was his dad before he opened the door by the way the knock sounded. Syrus came in and shut the door behind him. He offered no preamble.

"I'm worried about you, Maddox. You're in the media a lot, and it's not...*flattering*. In fact, most of what's said about you makes me really angry."

"You shouldn't listen to celebrity gossip."

"It's not just the gossip. The pictures of you and your *friends* say enough." Syrus sighed and wrung his hands. "I get it. You're not that different from me when I was your age. *Regia* is different, now that your sister spreads her technology everywhere, and you have the public eye more than I ever did, but I had the same kind of power and attention you do. You're taking the easy way. I get it." He repeated. "You seem...lost. Only focused on fast girls and partying."

Maddox pursed his lips, unsure what to say. He couldn't bullshit his dad; Syrus saw through him.

"I didn't ask for this kind of fame. I feel like the whole world is trying to eat me alive in very small bites. What defense do I have against it except to be an asshole? How can I protect myself?"

Syrus laid a hand on his shoulder. "It doesn't matter what other people think of you. What matters is what you think of you. You're in charge of your path, son. *You*. I know the heart of you. And this is not who you are. Have you considered the consequences of your actions at all?"

He hung his head, the weight of his father's disapproval falling hard on him. "I will, sir... I'm sorry if I've shamed you." The words almost choked him as they came out.

Syrus crossed his arms. "When your mom and I get home, will you consider coming back to the Obsidian Mountain?"

"No." He shook his head, keeping his eyes down so he could get the words out. "I'm sorry, Dad. That's not for me. You already know I won't ever amount to much in the Kata. I'm not fast enough to make the level of master. All the badass genes in this family were used up before I was born."

"I just thought I'd ask. You're a very skilled fighter, Maddox, you just hesitate too much. It's my failure. I never could get you out of your own head when you were fighting."

Syrus walked around him, picked up one of the belts laid out on the bed, and handed it to him. Maddox scowled as his dad fluffed the top of his dark hair.

"There, that's better." His dad's voice was snide. "Now you're all set for another day of womanizing."

"Hey, It's the one thing I'm really good at."

Syrus snorted and shook his head. "One day, the right woman will come along and knock all the stupid out of you."

"Very doubtful. Why would you think that?" he demanded, near panic at the thought.

Syrus laughed darkly. "Because that's what your mom did to me. Trust me. I know."

After he was dressed, Maddox became antsy. He wanted to hang out with his folks, but they were making him uncomfortable. Their eyes held too much judgment. He pinged Kendrick to meet him in a few hours and decided to take off.

Forest stopped him by the door. "Where are you going?" Her voice was sad, and it brought him heartache.

He scrambled to come up with a reason that wouldn't hurt her feelings. "Uh...I thought I'd go see Tesla."

It worked. The hurt left her eyes, and she smiled before kissing him on the cheek. "That's good. Tell her we'll stop by before we leave, won't you?"

"Of course."

"You'll be back to say goodbye, right? We leave at sunset."

Maddox hugged her hard. "I'll be back."

He exhaled and then scowled to himself as he shut the front door behind him. He put on his sunglasses, shoved his hands in his pockets, and made his way out of the garden. He had no choice but to drop in on his sister now. At least she'd probably make him coffee. He just hoped X wasn't there. He touched the mark on his wrist and sent himself to Tesla's property.

Tesla and X lived in an awesomely odd house, far out from civilization. Not that he blamed them. They were the most famous people in all of Regia, but neither of them wanted the spotlight. The world revered them as the saviors from the wizards. Maddox had grown up knowing the incredible history of the wizard's war, but he hadn't lived through any of it. According to everyone, Regia had transformed since then. Everyone looked to Tesla to solve problems and make the world as safe as possible. Maddox could hardly imagine the medieval type place Regia had been before the war. Now it was tech rich and a total mash-up of off world stuff.

He approached the house nestled in the sharp rocks of the eastern hills. Tesla and X's home was a modern masterpiece of architecture. It jutted out from the rough landscape in sleek lines. The roof and entire east face of the house was one seamless expanse of glass, so you were both inside and outside. The sky filled their house at all hours, and their view was both serene and striking. On the top floor, you could see the edges of the Wolf's Wood, the defiant outline of the Lair, and all the way to the Crystalline Sea.

The invisible shield over their property shimmered as he came close, and it opened a door-sized hole for him to step through, the magic-science recognizing his DNA. He walked up the sharp stairs to the huge front door and knocked. Tesla cracked the door and smiled.

"It's the manwhore, also known as my baby brother." She opened the door wide for him. "Come in, Maddie."

"Ugh, don't call me that. I'm not five."

"Could've fooled me."

Tesla wore a plain white shift of a dress with her long black hair swept up in a ponytail. Jealousy poked at him immediately, as it usually did around her. It didn't matter that they shared the same parents, had the same blood. He was, and always would be, mundane compared to her. Veins of red light pulsed on her hands in time with her heartbeat. Lightning lived inside her, as it did in their father. She was perhaps the most powerful being in all of Regia. No one else could create things, or jump worlds quite like she could. It was as if the natural laws of their world or any other didn't apply to her.

And she was married to a human. The only human ever to survive longer than a few minutes in Regia. Of course, the term *human* applied very loosely to X. Cursed by a witch, X didn't age, had a magical ability to always see the truth, and could pull your soul right out of your body with just the touch of his hands.

He looked around. "Is X here?"

"No. He's at work, coward." She smirked.

"I'm not afraid of him," he argued.

"Uh huh. You don't like that you have to be honest around him, cause he always knows when you're not."

"Geez, first dad and now you. Everyone's picking on me today."

She grabbed his forearm, stinging him with her lightning covered hands.

"Ow! Shit, that hurts."

She laughed and pulled his watch off before he could stop her. "I thought so," she said smugly, touching the mark on his wrist. "I figured you still had this."

He half-scowled half-smiled. "It works," he said, trying to sound flippant.

"Does it still glow in the dark?"

"Yeah."

She gave him a genuine smile. "How old were you, seven?"

"Six." He let down his guard for a second. "It's still the best birthday present you ever gave me."

"I made it glow because you were afraid of the dark. You know that, right? It was meant to be a night light as well as a portal."

He hadn't ever realized that. "I guess you loved me more back then."

She tsked and rolled her eyes before looking at his watch. She touched the face. The glass rippled like water under her fingertip. "This thing is solid, but I've got a new prototype that won't roll out to the public for another few months. Want one?"

"Hell yes…Wait, you can transfer my contacts, right?"

She gave him a dirty look. "Give me a break, Maddie. Of course."

He held his hands up. "Hey, my watch is my black book."

"Sure, Skank. I get it. I'll transfer your contacts. I know all about your bad reputation."

"Don't hate, old married woman. I've worked hard for my bad rep."

She raised one eyebrow. *"Work?"*

"Yep." He gave her his smarmiest smile. "I really put my back into it."

Tesla made a gagging sound and shoved him lightly. "Disgusting."

He shrugged, relaxing in the familiarity of his sibling's company. "Can I have some coffee?"

She smiled easily. "You want the blood infused stuff?"

He nodded.

"All right."

He followed her to the kitchen. The glass ceiling soared high over his head, letting in all the cool late morning sunlight. He sat on a barstool and propped his elbows on the massive rock slab that made the kitchen island.

"Oh, I was supposed to tell you, Mom and Dad will be by later to see you before they take off on vacation."

She nodded as she moved around, starting her coffee maker. "So, how is my public transit system holding up?"

"No idea. I haven't caught one of your public portals in a while. I'm too recognizable. It's a pain in the ass to use things like that when you get swarmed at the hub. I know everyone else loves them though."

"That's nice to know. I need to check them soon for maintenance. But I have to do it in the dead of night. If you think you're too recognizable, you should walk a mile in my shoes."

"I bet. I still wish I had your hands though."

She pinned him with a sharp look over her shoulder. "No, you don't".

"Sorry. You know what I mean."

She turned to face him fully and braced her hands on the island. "Do I? You have no idea the agony that lives in my hands. I'd cut them off if I didn't feel a responsibility to use my power to help and protect everyone. You have it so damn easy. You should be grateful." She sighed and shook her head. "I get you. But it's nonsense. You've always envied me, and I've always envied you."

"Why would you envy me?"

"My childhood was fast and furious, and it caused Mom and Dad a lot of heartache. You were normal. They got to relax and play with you. I was already grown, so I saw clearly how much joy you brought them, just by being normal. Before X, I hated myself for being such a freak. You think you're nothing special, but you're wrong, Maddie. I know there's something about you, it's subtle." Her eyes slid out of focus. "I've tried to put my finger on it for years, but all I could ever come with was… *lucky*. It's like your birthright was to be blessed or something. I don't know…Nothing bad or painful ever seems to stick to you."

He harrumphed. "Being lucky? That's far from impressive."

She poured a mug and handed it to him. "Such a brat. I'll get your new watch. Be right back."

"Wait! Can I come? I want to see what craziness you've been making in your workshop."

"All right. Just don't touch anything."

Maddox stayed longer than he'd meant to, and as he left, his new watch pinged with three messages from Kendrick. He scrolled through them quickly. One had a picture of a girl he'd never met with a caption: You like? This is Selena. Ran into her this morning. Haven't seen her in years. She's blossomed hot. And she's crazy for you. Biggest fangirl ever. She begged me to talk to you about her.

He made the picture bigger and looked at the girl. His eyebrows shot up. She was a full-blood elf and very choice.

He messaged Kendrick back. Bait taken. Give me her number.

Nope. **Kendrick wrote.** Come pick me up first.

Fine, but you better be ready to roll.

THREE

The sounds of kids playing and fussing came from under the heavy door. Erin sat at her small, file-stacked desk, wishing she had the time to go play with the children for a few minutes. Their precious voices spurred her to focus on the paperwork. The faster and harder she worked, the better chance she could give them to be adopted quickly.

The light coming through the window was intense as the day come close to ending. The colors of the sunbeams began to change to the deep jeweled tones of evening. She glanced up, realizing it was already past quitting time. But she ignored the time and bent her head to her task. She was close to finishing reviewing the file, and it wasn't like she couldn't desperately use some overtime anyway.

A soft, familiar hand touched her shoulder. She looked up into the magenta eyes of Journey.

"It's time."

"I know," Erin said. "I'm almost done."

"Leave it, honey. I'll finish it. You run home and have dinner with your father...is he feeling better?"

Her heart sank at the question, but she didn't have the strength to answer it fully. "Somewhat. He doesn't get enough blood to stay strong. Insists he doesn't need it. He's looking old beyond his years, and he's starting to act like a cranky old man to go with it."

Erin stood and got her bag from the peg on the wall. She turned to the door and stopped with her hand on the knob, looking back. Journey smiled knowingly at her. Years ago, she'd given Journey permission to openly read her heart at any time. As a Storyteller, Journey could see right into you and hypnotize you if she wanted with nothing but her voice. Unnerving at times, but she never would use it against you, only for your good.

"Thank you so much for my job. I know I'm a slow learner. I'll get the hang of everything in the next few days. Promise."

Journey chuckled and shook her head. "No such thing. You're learning very quickly. You only started three days ago. Stop acting like I'm doing you a favor; I want you here. You're like a daughter to me. And you have the heart for this work."

She stepped forward and wrapped Erin in a warm hug. Erin closed her eyes, absorbing the love the Storyteller had always given her. After her mother had died, Journey stepped in and guided her into womanhood.

Erin worshiped her and didn't know what she'd do without her.

She gave Erin a gentle shove toward the door. "Go on home. I'll see you tomorrow."

She hurried out of the Onyx Castle and down into Halussis to the closest hub where she could grab a portal to Anue. She got into the line, crossed her arms, and looked down.

"Hey, Red." A guy behind her called. "Hey you, girl. Halfling."

She looked up then and glanced over her shoulder.

The guy smiled at her and waved. "What's your name?"

"Tired from a long day at work and not in the mood. That's my name."

He came closer. "Sorry. That was dumb to yell at you. I just wanted to meet you. You're really beautiful."

She rolled her eyes. "Beautiful for a Halfling?"

"I only called you that to get your attention. I'm not prejudiced. I agree with Maddox— *Halfling girls are the prettiest*."

Erin turned on him then. "You're quoting Maddox? Wow. Let me just melt into a puddle right now."

The guy frowned, scanning her face, then he smiled. "Oh, you're special. You obviously don't have Maddox fever like every other girl I know. Run away with me now! What's your name?"

She narrowed her eyes at him.

"Okay," he persisted. "I'm Jaris. I usually catch this portal. If I see you again, and I promise not to quote Maddox, will you tell me your name?"

Erin's lips twitched and she almost smiled. "Maybe." The line moved.

"Since we're stuck here for a moment, would you tell me your thoughts on the whole social phenomenon?"

"What? Regia's most famous family?"

"Yeah."

"I think all of them are amazing, except *him*. I mean, what has he done? His sister and brother-in-law saved the world, his father has trained the most decorated and revered masters of the Blood Kata, and his mom is Forest...so yeah, she's the coolest thing ever, and she's humble and does such great work for Regia. And then there's Maddox, who never does anything except seduce feather-brained girls and wear that signature look of disdain for everything. And yet everyone falls all over him and hangs on his every word, even though he never has anything good to say." The line moved up. She was next.

"Have you met him?"

"No. And I don't want to." She snapped.

Jaris blew out a breath. "I repeat, run away with me." He smiled broadly.

He was cute she decided, even if he had started with the most ass backward approach she'd ever seen.

"What's my name?" he asked.

"Can't remember," she lied.

The portal opened behind her. He put his hand theatrically on his heart like she'd wounded him.

"Jaris," she said, smirking as the end closed over her. She giggled to herself in the rushing blackness before it dumped her out in the center of Anue, only a block from home.

She strode up the path to the front door. The house was starting to look worn down since her dad's health had begun to decline. No one could seem to figure out what was wrong with him. Something beyond his constant depression was causing him to deteriorate fast and he didn't care to fight. The bills were piling up, and it was her responsibility now to take care of paying them, since he couldn't. The stress of watching her father dying and trying to hold everything together sewed tight stitches around and around the edges of her heart.

"I'm home," she called as she came through the front door.

"You don't have to shout," Nathan grumbled from the kitchen table. "I might be ill, but there's nothing wrong with my hearing."

She put her bag down, came over to him, and gave him a kiss on the head, testing his temperature along with showing him affection. His red hair was streaked with white, and the lines on his face seemed to deepen every day. He shouldn't look so old, he was still a fairly young vampire. She was going to lose him soon. That was reality, despite how hard she might hold on, how much she struggled to work hard and to show a brave face. Death was starting to crouch in the corners, getting closer. Erin had no weapons to battle against it, and death was deaf to her plea.

"Did it happen today?" he asked the same question every time she came home.

"Nope. Didn't find my destined life mate today. Maybe tomorrow," she said as she brought him a blanket and covered him up. "I did meet a guy at the hub just now though. I might see him again. He wasn't half bad."

He smiled warmly and grabbed her hand. "Not half bad, huh? That's something you can build on."

She snickered. "None of my friend's fathers want them mated, and you've been pushing me toward it ever since I began growing breasts."

He looked at her intently. "I'm not going to be around much longer, Erin. I want to know you're taken care of."

She shook her head. "So old school. I can take care of myself. And you've got lots of life left to live."

"I want you to know the ecstasy of the first eye contact, the gravity of the first touch. You don't understand the singular joy of finding your destined life mate, sweetheart," he said emphatically.

Or the agony of losing them. She bit her tongue so she didn't say the words aloud. She patted his arm. "Okay, Dad. But you know it will happen when it happens, or not at all. I might not have a destined life mate. Not everyone does."

The door burst open, making both Erin and her dad jump in alarm. Her best and oldest friend, Selena, came running in, a storm of giddy energy coming all from her.

"Erin! Oh my gosh, I have to talk to you!" She rushed up to her and grabbed her arm.

"Sheesh! Okay, calm down."

Selena bounced up and down. "I can't calm down! Please! I need to talk to you in private!" She dragged Erin to her bedroom and closed the door.

"Okay, what the hell is it?"

Instead of answering, Selena put her hands over her mouth and squeaked, bouncing on the balls of her feet.

"What?"

"Okay," Selena said as though she couldn't catch her breath. "All of my dreams are coming true!"

"Really. Wow, that's news," Erin said dryly.

"This morning I ran into Kendrick."

"Who?"

Selena waved her hand. "His dad and my dad worked some contracts a long time ago. Haven't' seen him in years. Honestly, if you kept up with current events you'd recognize his name."

"Why? Who is he?"

"Only Maddox's best friend!"

"Oh, hell. I think I see where this is going."

"Erin, *he* called *me*! *Maddox* called *me*! Kendrick said he'd introduce us and then only a few hours later, Maddox called me! He asked me to be his date to a party tonight! Can you believe it? I never...*What?* Why are you looking at me like that for?"

"If it didn't violate some kind of unwritten friend code, I'd slap the shit out of you! Have you lost your mind?"

"I thought you'd be happy for me. He's all I've ever wanted, and I never thought I'd get the chance. You have to help me decide what to wear."

"He's all you've ever wanted for the last six months. Can't you see what a jerk he is? I don't care how good-looking he is, he's an asshole."

"You're wrong. He's just misunderstood."

Erin laughed humorlessly. "What happened to my *smart* best friend? I'd like her back now."

"Do you have any idea how long I've stared into his eyes?"

"What are you babbling about?"

"His picture. I can see there's more to him. He's good. Everyone just wants to put him into a little box and make him what they want him to be." Selena argued.

"Do you hear yourself? You're doing exactly what you're accusing other people of doing. You've created some imaginary version of who you think Maddox is, and you've never met him. You see a prince who will give you a happy ever after. I see a spoiled, self-satisfied punk who will trample your soft heart under his designer boots. But regardless of either of our perceptions, he's a real person and you don't know him. You've painted him as the hero when he's probably the villain."

Selena put her head in her hands and exhaled. "You're right. I've lost it, but...how can I not go? I want to go. Maybe I'll be the one."

"No, honey. You'll just end up as one of the many."

"But if I show him my heart..."

"He'll just break it."

Selena began pacing back and forth. "You're my best friend. Don't you see more value in me than all those other girls?"

Erin came up to her and cupped her face with both of her hands. "You *are* special, Selena. I don't want you hurt. We promised each other as girls, remember? We promised to always protect and look out for one another. That's what I'm trying to do."

She nodded and looked down. "I see what you're trying to do and I appreciate it but—"

"*But* Maddox has asked you out, and you're going with him?"

Selena shrugged and nodded.

"I figured as much...Fine, I'll help you figure out what to wear."

Selena's eyes lit up, and she kissed Erin on the cheek.

Erin pointed sternly in her face. "Will you at least promise me you won't have sex with him? Please?"

Selena looked away.

"Promise!" Erin demanded. "You can't have a real chance with him if you're so easy."

"Okay. You're right. I promise."

Syrus came up behind Forest, wrapped his arms around her waist, leaned down, and kissed her shoulder. "Come on. He's not coming back. He forgot."

She nodded slowly and sighed. "Yeah. I know it's silly for it to hurt my feelings that he forgot. I know it's not a big thing. He's in a dumb time of life. A selfish time. It's not a big deal."

She toyed with edge of the ribbon on Maddox's graduation present. She pushed the long thin box to the center of the table and turned in Syrus' arms. He stroked the back of her hair.

"He's going to be all right," he reassured her.

"How do you know?"

"I just do. He's still the same Maddox we raised under this mask he's wearing. He won't wear it forever...Come on. Let's go. I need you, Forest. Just you and me for a while."

She looked up into his handsome face and smiled. "Why do I still like you so much after all these years?"

"I get better with age." He grabbed her ass with both hands and hauled her up so she wrapped her legs around his waist. "Now, we're leaving. I will carry you if I have to."

"You don't have to, but I kinda like it."

He kissed her deeply and then set her down. They picked up their luggage and the portal Tesla gave them to use for their vacation. Before they left, Forest made sure to leave the light on for her son.

FOUR

Kendrick and Maddox laughed stupidly at one another as the illegal, off world drugs they'd snorted took full effect, making them silly.

"I feel like I'm forgetting something," Maddox said, lying back on Kendrick's bedroom floor, his head swimming.

"You're forgetting to call that girl, the one you always refuse to hook me up with, even though you never mess around with her either."

"Who?"

"You know, that fierce blonde whose mom has that freaky robotic arm," Kendrick said.

"Oh, Melina."

"Yeah, that's her. Melina."

Maddox chuckled. "I don't mess around with her cause she's my oldest friend. Anyway, you've got no chance, dude. She'd chew you up and spit you out."

"I'd enjoy that."

Maddox snorted. "No you wouldn't, trust me. She's kicked my ass before, and it's an experience I never want to repeat. Anyway, she hates you."

"Why? She's only met me once."

"I dunno. Ugh, I swear I'm forgetting something."

"Did you forget to call Selena?" Kendrick offered. "You'll look stupid if you don't have a date tonight."

"No, fool. You were only standing right next to me when I called her. Remember?"

"Oh, yeah."

Maddox sat up, rubbing his temples. "How much longer do we have?"

"About an hour. If you get lucky with Selena, you have to give me details. I've had a jones for her since I was twelve. I was going to ask her to go to the party with me, but when she saw me, all she talked about was you."

"*If I get lucky?* Please. There is no *if*. She's a sure thing."

"Where do you plan to take her?" Kendrick smirked. "Your folk's house? That will be hot."

"Oh, shit! My folks! I missed them. That's what I forgot. I was supposed to go back home and tell them goodbye before they left for vacation." He hung his head; it was beginning to throb. "I'm such a jerk."

"Ah, well. They'll forgive you. Hey, they're gone. Now you really can take girls there without it being weird."

"Yeah, great," Maddox mumbled miserably.

"Speaking of which, I've been thinking. Why don't you and I get our own place? Get a few anytime girls as roommates."

"Anytime girls? What are those?" Maddox asked.

"What do you think? Girls ready for it anytime and know that's their place. Ones that don't whine for a relationship or fidelity, shit like that."

"Whoa, I think you just passed me up on the asshole scale there, Kendrick."

"Hey, we'd be totally upfront about it with them. They'd know what they were getting into."

"Yeah...I don't know. Us sharing a house, maybe. Having our own little harem is taking it a bit too far."

"Getting a little self-righteous aren't you? King of the one night stand."

"Whatever," he huffed, rubbing his head again.

Kendrick punched him in the shoulder. "Come on. Get some water or something. Sober up a bit, and we'll go get your girl for tonight."

"Okay." He got to his feet, the room only slightly spinning.

Erin loosely braided Selena's light blond hair and teased out a few tendrils around her face. She was wearing a sexy, light blue slip of a dress that made her blue eyes pop. Erin couldn't help but feel a little jealous of how gorgeous her friend looked. Her skin was flawless porcelain while Erin was plagued with freckles across her nose. She was all warm tones, red hair, and hazel eyes while Selena was fair and her ears were beautifully pointed.

"Thanks, Erin. I'd be a wreck without you. My heart hasn't stopped galloping since he called me. I'm so nervous."

"Stop that. How can you show him what you're really like if you act like a squirrel?"

Selena laughed and then took a deep breath. "You're right. Are you sure you don't want to come with us? There will be dancing. You look so sexy when you dance."

"The dancing is tempting, but the company of Maddox and his entourage is a *hell no* for me."

"Are you really going to deny how hot he is?"

Erin huffed. "No. He's beautiful. I see what you see, but then he opens his mouth or acts like he's better than everyone, and it just ruins it for me. I wouldn't touch him with a ten-foot pole."

Selena's thin, stylish watch pinged. "Oh gosh. It's him. He's on his way here."

"That's my cue to leave," Erin said grimly.

"Wait! You really don't want to meet him? Just briefly?"

"Nope," she said, making the 'p' at the end of the word pop.

A knock sounded on the front door. Selena gave Erin a wide eyed plea.

She squeezed her hand reassuringly. "Remember, no sex, and don't act like a squirrel."

"Got it. Thanks."

Erin escaped into the bathroom and locked the door to avoid having to meet Maddox. She pressed her ear against the door to hear. They didn't say much. He complimented Selena on how beautiful she looked and asked if she was ready to go. A chill went into her stomach as the front door shut, leaving her alone in Selena's house. She knew what she needed to do. She rushed home to throw on a dress and get to that party, so she could look out for her friend.

"I'm going out, Dad!" she called as she came through the front door and headed to her room.

He waved dismissively at her. "Have fun. Keep your eyes open for *the one*."

Erin ignored his advice, went to her closet, and grabbed her nicest dress, it would have to do. She wasn't going to be looked at anyway. The red halter maxi was made of cheap material, but it was cut perfectly to her body and the color matched her hair. She took her hair down, textured it a little, slicked some gloss on her lips, and headed out. She checked her own, old, and inconsistent watch to see if she could reach Selena. No luck.

Her sense of urgency ground to a halt as she walked to the portal hub. What was she doing? She hesitated and then shrugged, continuing on. Maybe she didn't need to look out for Selena, but she could at least see what the party was like. Just morbid curiosity she guessed. Regardless, something was driving her to go. It felt important.

The portal threw her out close to the main square of Paradigm. She heard the music. Dressed up people were walking with urgency toward the music. She followed them. Her heart sank as she reached the place. A line formed outside, and a bouncer wasn't letting anyone in unless they were on his list. *Well, so much for that*. She turned away to go home.

"Hey, Red!"

She looked around and saw Jaris bounding up the street at her. She smiled.

"Jaris. Hi."

He grinned wide. "You remembered my name. That's almost as great as running into you again. Will you tell me your name now?"

"Erin."

His smile grew bigger. "Erin. I like it. You look amazing! I'm assuming you're going to the party? I'm surprised. Maddox is here, you know."

She blushed a little and blew out a breath. "Yeah. That's my problem. He asked my best friend to come with him tonight. I just have a bad feeling about it. I tried to talk her out of it, but she's got...what did you call it? Maddox fever. I just hoped I could sneak in and keep an eye on her, but I'm not on the list, that's for sure, so I was just going to head home and—"

Jaris held up his hand. "I can get you in. The bouncer is my cousin."

"Well, that's handy. Thanks!"

"No problem. I only ask one thing in return."

She scowled. "What?"

"Dance with me. Just once."

"Deal. One dance."

"A *slow* dance."

She chuckled. "Don't push it."

He held out his hand. She took it, and he led her straight up to the bouncer. He looked down at them, winked at Jaris, and nodded for them to go in.

"Nice work, cuz," the bouncer said as they passed.

Erin blushed and smiled. It felt nice to be next to someone so obviously proud to have her on his arm. A heavy door swung open for them, and she was immediately enveloped in the dense atmosphere and music of the party. Free-floating twinkle lights hovered near the ceiling, moving and connecting to one another like molecules, changing color as they mixed. The whole place was dark aside from that. The dance floor was in the center, full of people moving to the heavy beat. Tables and booths were around the edges of the huge open room, where people sat drinking or making out. The whole thing was a little frightening but it looked fun, too. She could clearly see the dangers in the shadows under the vibrant surface.

Jaris leaned close and shouted so she could hear. "Your friend will be up there." He pointed to a raised area clearly set aside for VIPs, where she saw Selena sitting in the back of a large booth, tucked under Maddox's arm. Selena had a smile plastered on her face as the other people in Maddox's inner circle laughed, talked, smoked, and drank. Her heart sank. She could see it was everything she feared. Selena was nothing but the girl on his arm for tonight. He'd replace her in two days. A week tops.

"There are bodyguards there and there." Jaris pointed to a couple of guys standing at the entrance to the area Selena was in. "If your friend sees you, you could probably get up there. Wanna try?"

She was about to say yes, then Maddox leaned over Selena and kissed her. A pang of rage and disgust she couldn't account for hit her in the stomach. She turned away to keep from screaming. She didn't want his filthy hands on her friend.

Jaris grabbed her arm. "Hey, are you okay?"

"This was a bad idea. I shouldn't have come here. I want to leave."

"What about our dance?"

The music changed just then, the tempo slowing. She took in Jaris' expression and caved. "All right. This song. That's all."

He pulled her close. She sighed, forcing herself to let go of her dark emotions and rested her chin on his shoulder, closing her eyes. She did love to dance. Jaris wasn't as confident in his moves as she would have liked, but at least he didn't step on her toes.

Something about Selena bothered Maddox. She seemed a bit too innocent for him. Just the way she held herself and responded to him made him wish he hadn't asked her to come with him. She was beautiful but...

He took a drink and shook himself. It didn't matter. She was doing her job, making him the envy of the guys around him, and he could tell he'd been right about her. She was a sure thing. He'd have no problem getting her out of that dress later.

Kendrick and Selena talked about some of their personal history, knowing each other as kids. Maddox didn't care to listen. He leaned back and let his gaze roam over the room. The floating lights drifted up and down over the heads of the people dancing. His eyes caught on a redhead, his stomach swooping, and goosebumps slid out on his skin. All he could see was her profile, but damn if that wasn't the most amazing promise of pure beauty he'd ever seen.

Why didn't he know that girl?

He stood abruptly.

"Is something wrong?" Selena asked.

"No." He walked swiftly toward the short staircase that led to the dance floor, his eyes still glued to the girl. He couldn't afford to lose her in the crowd and felt a wave a panic that he might.

"I wouldn't advise it, sir," the bodyguard said as Maddox tried to shove past him.

"Just move!" he barked.

As soon as he hit the dance floor, he was swarmed with girls all trying to touch him and get him to dance. He tried pushing through them, keeping his eyes on the redhead. A girl slid her hand into his front pocket and groped him. He turned on her.

"Really?" he demanded angrily.

She smiled up into his face, a naughty glint in her eyes. "I'll give you everything you could ever want, Maddox."

He sneered. "You think you're on my level? As if. Now get away from me, slut."

He looked back for the redhead. Damnit. Of course! His gaze darted around. He couldn't see her anywhere. He'd only taken his eyes off her for a second.

He turned back and climbed the stairs again, the bodyguard moving back into place, blocking the girls still trying to get to him. He hoped getting higher would allow him to spot her again and he'd send someone to go get her and bring her to him instead of trying to wade through the crowd.

He swore under his breath as he continued to scan the dance floor. She'd vanished into thin air. Losing the redhead and being sexually assaulted soured his mood. He plunked back down next to Selena and Kendrick.

She leaned in close to him. "Who were you chasing?"

"A ghost," his tone was clipped.

"Did I do something wrong?" she asked.

His mood continued to plummet. He reached for his drink and downed the rest of it. "No. I'm sick of this." He gave her his smolder. "Let's get out of here. Alone. Just you and me."

Her eyes widened, and she pulled back a little. "I don't know...I..."

"I can hardly hear you. How are we supposed to get to know each other in this kind of a setting?"

He toyed with the ends of the hair framing her face before tucking it behind her ear. She flushed and looked down. He waited, watching her internal battle play across her face.

She looked up again, her bottom lip caught between her teeth, and nodded. He took her hand and pulled her to her feet.

"She's all yours after tonight," he said into Kendrick's ear as they headed for the door behind the protected area.

Kendrick smirked and raised his glass in a toast to Maddox.

In one hour, Maddox was back at the party, without Selena. He sat back down next to Kendrick, grabbed a shot off the table, and tossed it back.

"Where is she?" Kendrick asked.

"I dunno," he sighed. "I sent her packing when I was done with her."

"Shit, that's cold. Even for you. Oh well, it will make it easier for me to comfort her. Was she good?"

Maddox rolled his eyes and shrugged. "Meh."

"What nasty bug crawled up your ass?" Kendrick asked. "I thought you were into her."

"I was, until I saw something better."

"So why did you screw her?"

"Because I'm pissed off, and I could." Maddox spat.

Kendrick held his hands up. "Okay. So tell me about this piece of tail that's better."

"A redhead...in the crowd. I don't know her, but I will—I can promise you that. I'm going to find her."

Kendrick chuckled. "Since when have you been into redheads?"

"Never, until now."

"Maybe she's a shifter."

All the blood drained from Maddox's face. "Damnit, I didn't think of that."

"Hmmm...Mystery Girl. I like it. I'll help you track her down, shifter or not. Here." He slid another drink toward Maddox. "Knock that back; it's awesome."

He picked up the small glass and eyed the pink liquid inside. "What is it?"

"Syrup. Off world import. It will fuck you up fast. I promise."

"Perfect." Maddox swallowed it all.

FIVE

Jaris persuaded Erin to grab a drink with him at a cute little bar after they left the party. What started as a chance encounter morphed into a date. Jaris was quickly rising in her estimation. He was polite, funny, and totally respectful. She didn't drink much, and he didn't try to get her to drink more. She found it easy to talk to him. Like she could say anything. Be herself.

"So you're a V-E?" he asked.

"Yeah. Although I thought the current term was Vampelf."

He snickered. "You don't get out much, do you?"

"Guilty as charged." She smiled.

"I like that about you."

"Uh huh. So you're just a V?" she teased, knowing full well he was a full blood vampire.

"I'm actually an ogre. A short one."

She giggled. "It's getting late. I should go home now. Check on my dad. He's not well."

"I'm sorry to hear that." He pulled her chair out and held her hand as she stood.

She shivered as they walked to the hub. The summer night had turned cool.

"Here." Jaris draped his jacket over her shoulders.

With that one simple move, she decided she would see him again if he asked. The hub was empty. She stepped up to the open portal and turned back to him. "I'm glad I ran into you. Good night."

The portal closed over her. In a few seconds, she was back in Anue. The portal shivered behind her, and then Jaris stepped out of it.

"Jaris, what are you…Oh! I'm sorry I still have your jacket." She made to take it off.

He shook his head. "I wouldn't feel right if I didn't walk you all the way home. Make sure you're safe."

She blinked at him and then smiled. "This way."

He reached for her hand, and she gave it. They walked in silence the rest of the short way.

"This is me." She stopped at the front stoop, thankful he possibly couldn't see her blush in the dark. He probably lived in a much nicer place.

"What a great front porch," he said. "My aunt has a porch like that. I love sitting on the swing on summer evenings."

Her heart gave a little tug. She would definitely go out with him again if he asked. She slid out of his coat and handed it to him.

"Thanks, Jaris."

"Can I have your number? I'd really like to see you again."

"I'd like that, too."

He moved closer. "I don't want to seem too forward..."

She smiled and reached around his neck, pulling him closer. He kissed her, just once, softly.

"Wow," he breathed. "Thank you."

"There should be more guys like you. You could give first date lessons to the shmucks of the world."

"I'll try to wait an appropriate amount of time before calling you, so I don't seem desperate for your attention. I totally am, but I don't want to *seem* that way."

She giggled. "My watch is rather sad. I'm just warning you. If I miss a call, I'm not blowing you off. I just didn't hear it. See?" She held up her watch.

"I see what you mean. That thing is pretty beat up."

"I'm saving for a new one…" She felt awkward, half turned to the house, but indecisive. "Kiss me again?"

He did, a little harder than before, making her heart speed up. Then he pulled back and kissed her hand.

"Goodnight, Erin."

"Goodnight."

He stood there and waited for her to get all the way inside and close the door. The house was dark and quiet. She peeked out the front window and watched him walk away before squeaking and turning in a circle. She basked in the moment, still a little flushed, when a quiet cry hit her ears and her thoughts came back down with a hard bump.

She rushed to her bedroom and found what she hoped she wouldn't. Selena was there, curled up on her bed, crying. Erin closed the door and sat down next to her and rubbed her back.

"You were right, Erin. About everything." Her voice shook with tears.

"What happened?"

Selena just wailed.

"You had sex with him, didn't you?"

She sat up and nodded, wiping the tears from her cheeks. "I'm so stupid. I knew I was being stupid."

"So why did you go through with it?"

She exhaled and shook her head. "He was so charming. He seduced me. Then he was cruel. He got what he wanted, then he turned mean. He treated me like a whore."

"You acted like one," Erin snapped. "What did you think was going to happen?"

"I just wanted a chance to show him my heart."

"He can't see your heart when your skirt is up around your waist."

Anger flashed hot in Selena's eyes. "At least I don't fantasize about a ghost who left me a rock...I'm sorry," she wailed. "You're supposed to be on my side."

Erin hugged her. "You're right. I'm sorry, too. So, he's the bastard I figured him to be... Did you get anything out of it, at least?"

Selena's expression changed, and she nodded in a bemused kind of misery. "Well, *those* rumors are true. He knows what he's doing in the bedroom, I'll give him that. The physical part of it was amazing, the emotional was terrible. I wish I could rewind the whole night and undo it."

"I'm so sorry, sweetie. Why don't you stay here tonight? Tomorrow we'll have a girl's day and you can move on."

Selena wiped her eyes again. "Okay. Can I borrow some pajamas? I want to burn this dress."

"No problem. Let's go to sleep quickly, and when you wake up it will all be behind you."

In the middle of the night, Selena and Erin woke to the pinging sound of Selena's watch. She was tucked beside Erin in the narrow bed.

"Oh, hell," Selena whispered as she checked her message. "It's Maddox."

"What does he want?" Erin snapped.

"It says: I'm sorry for the way I treated you. There was something else bothering me, and I took it out on you. Will you let me explain? Meet me now?

"The nerve," Erin hissed.

"Yeah," Selena agreed halfheartedly, and then she squirmed.

"Selena?"

"What?" her voice was defensive.

"Don't even think about it."

The next second she was jumping out of the bed. "I'm sorry. I have to go. I'll always wonder otherwise."

"You're killing me!"

"I'm sorry. I can't help it. Just go back to sleep. I'll see you tomorrow."

"Damnit, Selena…Please be careful. *Please*."

"I promise. I just want to hear him out. I don't have stars in my eyes now. I'll be careful."

Erin put her pillow over her face and screamed into it after Selena left. The idiot. Well, she was determined to ruin herself. She was doing it with her eyes open. Erin tossed and turned. She got up and grabbed the rock from the top of her dresser and laid it against her chest. Her heart eased under the comforting feel of it, and she finally fell back asleep, but she was plagued by nightmares.

Erin woke in a cold sweat before dawn. She got up and dressed quickly. She tried to message Selena. Failure notice. Stupid antiquated tech. She headed out quietly, so as not to wake her dad, and went straight to Selena's house. Since Selena lived alone, Erin didn't hesitate to bang on the front door. The fool deserved to be woken harshly. And if Maddox was there, she'd plant her fist in his pretty face, just for the hell of it.

There was no answer.

She knocked more and she kept knocking. Nothing. Erin bit down on her lip and tried again to message Selena. Was she with the asshole at his place?

Maybe she was just sleeping too hard to wake. Erin went around the house— maybe the back door was unlocked. She walked into the backyard and stopped short. Her lungs stopped, half full. Her heartbeat filled her ears, slow and labored. Something invisible pressed hard into Erin as her eyes absorbed death. So cold. She held still for the length of one second. One second, she silently beheld Selena laid out on the ground. Her skin was ugly pale and looked hard, like she was carved from stone. Erin had never thought about what life really looked like until that second, now seeing the devoid, confronted with the blank abyss in Selena's eyes.

As if in a dream, Erin moved forward slowly when she was really trying to run. Reality of this horror broke free inside her and she screamed.

"No, no, no." She held her friend to her chest. Selena was so cold, her limbs stiff. Erin rubbed her arms. "Shhh...It's okay. I'll warm you up. I'll warm you up."

Both her wrists were cut. And letters were carved into her forearm, *Maddox*.

"You wouldn't do this, sweetheart. You wouldn't kill yourself over him. This isn't possible...This isn't possible...*Help!*" She screamed. *"Someone help me!"*

Help came. Erin stood back, her eyes tunneling, as she went into shock. People moved around her impossibly fast. Their bodies and voices blurred as her consciousness curled into a ball deep inside, rocking and crying.

"Erin? Can you hear me?" a familiar voice and face swam into her vision, drawing her out. "Erin?" she blinked. It was Redge.

She collapsed against him, weeping.

"I'm going to take you home now. Journey will stay with you, and when you're ready, I have to ask you a few questions. Okay?"

She nodded, shivering violently. "Selena wouldn't kill herself."

"Don't worry about anything right now. I'm going to handle this case myself. Trust me. We will find out what happened."

He picked her up and carried her home. Her vision clouded over. She heard her dad's concerned voice, but she didn't understand the words. Redge laid her down on her bed and covered her up. Humming filled her ears and drifted into her mind, unwinding her. Journey sat on the bed next to her and hummed in her hypnotic voice until Erin passed out.

Maddox woke in the afternoon with the worst hangover of his life. He squinted up at the ceiling of his room and closed his eyes again. No more off world imports for him. He didn't even remember coming home. He staggered out of bed, still in his dress clothes, his head throbbing sharply and his heart heavy. The memory of the way Selena looked when he told her to leave assailed him. He was so sick of himself. His father was right. He was lost.

The house felt so empty without his parents there. He missed them. He needed them. He sighed as he stalked to the kitchen and poured himself some blood. He drank it slowly, afraid his stomach would pitch. The blood cleared his head and eased the hangover. He set the empty glass down and spotted the present on the table.

He opened the card. *Happy graduation, Maddox! The power infused inside is your own. We used your blood. The reaction was interesting. We love you, son. —Mom and Dad.*

He grimaced as he opened the long box, feeling even lower and more worthless than ever. The katana was sleek black. He lifted it up. It was like his mom's only the style of it was totally different. The blade was obsidian, but the power inside it was gold and cascaded down the length of the blade in precise designs and not wild red lightning. The plain black tang fit his hands perfectly. He couldn't help smirking through his misery. *Sneaky.* Nice way to get him to practice more.

He took it to his room and looked for a good place to hang it on the wall. He got it up, next to the bed, decided it was time to clean the dirtiness of the night away and headed for the shower.

The remainder of his hangover faded as hot water and soap ran down his skin. Banging on the bathroom door startled him.

"Maddie!"

"Damnit, Tesla!" he shouted through the door. "You scared the life out of me."

"There's a shit storm out here with your name on it, so hurry up and get dressed."

Puzzled, he finished rinsing his hair and turned the water off. Wrapping a towel around his waist, he came out into the living room. It wasn't just Tesla. Redge was there, looking grim.

"Get dressed, Maddox," Redge ordered. "I have to arrest you on suspicion of murder."

"What?"

"It's just a formality that must be satisfied."

"What the hell?! I didn't kill anyone!"

Tesla grabbed Redge by the arm. "I can get X here in a second. He can question him. If you take him in, it's going to be all over the media."

Redge looked like he was thinking it over. "I don't care about any of that. A girl is dead, and I have to find out how it happened."

"Who? Who's dead?" Maddox asked.

Redge stared hard at him. "A lovely young elf named Selena. I believe you know her."

"Oh my gosh!" Maddox headed toward his room. "I'll be right out."

He shut the door and threw on jeans and T-shirt. His heart hammered as he came back out.

"You don't think I killed her, do you?" he asked Redge desperately.

The hard edge on his expression eased, and he looked at Maddox the way he normally did. Redge was as close as an uncle to him and had been his whole life.

"No. I don't' think that. I *can't* think that, but there is evidence that points at you. And since you are in the public eye, there will be plenty of speculation that can't be helped."

"I don't give a damn what's said about me. I didn't do it. You have my full cooperation."

"Okay. Let's go to Fortress."

"Is that really necessary?" Tesla argued.

"Yeah, it is, I'm afraid. He's going to have to talk to Kindel as well as X, and he'll have to give samples to forensics. I have to take him."

"It's okay, Tes," Maddox reassured her. "I didn't do it. I have nothing to hide."

She didn't look reassured as she pulled him into a tight hug. "I can get Mom and Dad back. It might take me a few days to track them, it won't be easy, but I can do it."

"No." He shook his head firmly. "I don't want them dragged into this. It's fine. I'll be cleared in no time."

She exhaled heavily. "Okay. If you're sure."

"I am."

"I need your watch, too," Redge said to Maddox.

He took it off and handed it over. Redge pocketed it before he pulled out a set of handcuffs and locked them around Maddox's hands. The metal purred and stretched out, lacing in between his fingers.

"What's that?" Redge asked pointing at the mark on his wrist.

"Personal portal. Birthday present from Tesla."

Redge looked at her. She nodded in agreement.

"Would you?" Redge asked Tesla.

She tore the air open for them. They landed in Forest's office. Maddox relaxed slightly in the comfort of his mom's office. It made him feel safer. Kindel and Ena were there, looking serious.

"Hey," he said quietly.

"It's a bad day, Maddox." Kindel shook his head.

"Yeah," he agreed, thinking of Selena. "Really bad."

"Ena, mark it down that Maddox surrendered quietly, of his own free will, and has promised to cooperate," Redge instructed.

She sat at her desk and began scribbling.

"Put this into evidence." Redge handed Maddox's watch to Kindel.

"When do you need me?" Kindel asked.

"X is first. Then I'll bring him to the lab."

"That's not necessary. I already have his DNA on file. I'll run it against the physical evidence on the body," Kindel said.

Redge put his hand on Maddox's shoulder and directed him down the hall and a flight of stairs. He didn't need direction, but Redge didn't let go of him. He kept reminding himself to breathe. The few people they passed in the halls stopped and stared. Just before they got to X's office, Redge stopped a clerk in the hall.

"I need you to come in here with me."

"Sir?" the clerk looked puzzled.

"Just stay back and watch. I need a witness."

The man's eyes darted between Redge and Maddox. "Yes, sir. Of course."

"You are not to leak anything to the media of this, unless I ask you to. You are to witness and keep silent unless otherwise directed, by me and *only* me. Got it?"

The clerk swallowed and nodded. "Yes, sir."

X's office was a cold, grey box of a space with two chairs a plain table and nothing else. X wasn't there, but Fluffy paced along the wall. The demon turned his red eyes on Maddox and grunted. Maddox sat down, and Fluffy came up to him, the edges of his frame hazy like black smoke.

"Hey, Fluffy. It's good to see you. Circumstance notwithstanding," he said easily.

"It's been a while since you came here." The demon's voice was mild, but it still held the resonance of hell. "I'm of no use, today. You're far from scared of me."

X came through the door then, an irritated expression on his face as he looked at a file Maddox could only assume was his. X sighed, closed the file, sat down, and looked directly into Maddox's eyes.

"Did you kill Selena?"

"No."

X leaned back in his chair and looked up at Redge. "He didn't do it."

Redge sighed in unmistakable relief. "Good."

"So," X said, his eyes pinning Maddox again. "What happened?"

"I only met Selena last night. She is...was...friends with my friend Kendrick, who arranged the date on her request. We picked her up at her house and went straight to Paradigm."

"We?"

"Me and Kendrick."

"Okay, then what?"

"Not much. I took Selena home for an hour or so, then I came back to the party alone. There are plenty of witnesses who can verify that I returned."

"You took her home? Meaning?"

Maddox sighed. "We had sex, and then I told her to leave, that I was done with her. She left. That was the last I saw of her." The looks on their faces frustrated him. "Yeah, I'm a bastard. But I didn't kill her. Why would I?"

Kindel poked his head into the room and handed a slip of paper to Redge.

Redge looked at it for a moment. "Your DNA is all over the body."

"Of course it is!" Maddox shouted. "I just told you I fucked her! Consensually as well, since I'm sure you want to know."

"Hmm…" Redge continued to look at the paper. "You messaged her in the middle of the night, asking her to come meet you."

"No, I didn't."

"Your watch says you did. Very close to the time she was killed."

"It wasn't me! I was hammered. I don't even remember how I got home last night. Someone else must have messaged her from my watch while I was passed out."

"What were you on?" X asked.

"Uh…I don't remember. It was pink."

X looked at Redge. "We need a toxicology report on him. If he drank Syrup, there's no way he had the physical strength to kill anyone, let alone the frame of mind to stage it to look like a suicide." X looked back at Maddox. "Was there anything else? Do you think she was capable of suicide?"

"I don't know. I didn't know her. She was really upset when she left though."

"You think she was *this* upset?" X slid a few pictures from the file across the table at him.

He didn't want to look, but he didn't have a choice. The images went straight into his brain and burrowed there. Her cut wrists. His name carved into her skin. Had he really hurt her that badly? He knew she was too innocent for him, too soft. He never should have touched her. He sat back and looked away.

X stood. "Okay. I'm finished. He's telling the truth. We just need to know what he drank so that can satisfy the girl's family. My integrity has never been questioned, but in this case..."

"I know," Redge said grimly.

"What are you talking about?" Maddox asked.

X gave him a furious look. "People will say *I* lied and cleared you because you're my brother in law, and that Redge and Kindel compromised as well because they work for your mom!"

The realization hit Maddox hard. "Oh shit."

"Yes, exactly. Your bad behavior will cast shade on the entire family." He snatched the file up and headed for the door. He stopped, his hand on the knob, and turned back. "Stop breaking your sister's heart," he half yelled. "It's lucky for you that you didn't kill that girl. I'd throw the book at you! And good riddance!"

Maddox blew out a breath, feeling like X had just run over him. "Geez..." he said quietly.

Redge touched him on the shoulder. "Come on. To the lab. We need to know what you drank."

He waited in the lab while the tech ran his blood. It only took a few seconds, then the report was handed to Redge. He glanced at it for a moment then he unlocked the handcuffs on Maddox. "All right. That checks out. You're free to go."

Relieved but dejected, he stalked for the door.

"Maddox?"

He turned back.

"Just a little advice. Keep your head down for a few days. Don't go out in public."

He nodded, looking at the floor. "I'm sorry. I'm really sorry."

Redge squeezed his arm. "I am, too. Think about living up to your heritage, okay?"

Maddox nodded again and sent himself home. When he got there, he realized he'd left his watch. Tesla was pacing the living room. She rushed to him and pulled him against her.

"What happened?"

He was suddenly exhausted. "I've been cleared. I can't talk about it now. I just want to be alone for a while."

She kissed his cheek. "If you need me, I'll be here."

"Thanks." X's harsh words came back to him. "I'm sorry, Tesla. Sorry for what I've put you through."

She hugged him tighter. "I love you, Maddie."

It was the first time in a long time being called that didn't bother him. It felt warm and comforting. She held on to him for another minute, then she left.

Slowly, he walked to his room, feeling disconnected from his body. Never again, he swore to himself. No more parties, no more easy girls, no more substance abuse. He turned and stared at himself in his full-length mirror. Self-loathing spread through his veins. Without thinking, he slapped himself in the face again and again. He inhaled as deeply as possible and let it all out in a roar of rage at his reflection before punching the mirror. It shattered and sliced his knuckles. What had he done?

Maddox wept.

Tesla didn't go home after she left Maddox. Her portal dumped her out in Kyhael inside the *Rune-dy's* old headquarters. The *Rune-dy* was no more. That sect of elves dedicated to perfecting torture, twisting science, and pushing to finding other worlds had all died, except one: her grandfather, Rahaxeris, who had been the high priest for many years.

She exhaled in the familiar space that was now just a library, her first lab, and Rahaxeris' apartments. He strode around the corner and smiled at her. His smile terrified most people, but she'd never feared him. He was always the same, as if caught in eternal youth. His golden hair hung straight to his shoulders, and his eyes were still the same signature red of the *Rune-dy*. He clasped her in a hug against his tall, angular frame, his sharp hands patting her back.

"How is Maddox?" he asked.

"Not good. He's been cleared. I just don't know what to do for him."

"He has to grow up."

She sulked. "He drives me crazy. He's been so self-destructive lately."

Rahaxeris chuckled. "Wonder where he gets that? He's not as bad as you were."

"Do you think you could…"

He raised one very severe eyebrow and shook his head. "I stay out of the public eye. I always will. It's better for everyone that way. Besides, Maddox and I are not close. Not like you and me, and being close to you has been a… rough journey."

She giggled. "I'm sorry, but that was a long time ago."

"Feels like yesterday to me. All my grandchildren give me headaches…except Sophie. She's perfect."

"I haven't seen Sophie in a while. Does she come here often?"

He frowned. "Hmm...it's been more lately."

SIX

For three days and nights, Erin lived in a haze of tears and grief. Finding Selena dead had scared her psyche. She barely slept and her nightmares were terrible. The only thing heavier than the grief was the guilt. Why hadn't she stopped Selena from leaving that night? She should have wrestled her to the floor. She should have begged her to stay. She'd still be alive...if only...

On the morning of the fourth day, she was awakened by the gentle touch of Journey's hand on her shoulder. She caressed Erin's cheek and hummed for a moment, sending waves a peace into her heart.

"The funeral is today, Erin."

She sat up and reached for Journey. She held her and rocked her like a small child while Erin cried yet again.

"I've brought you a black dress to wear, in case you don't have one."

"I need flowers." She sniffed. "Blue flowers, the color of Selena's eyes."

"That's lovely, sweetheart. We'll get some on the way."

Erin thought about the finality of a funeral and collapsed in on herself. "Selena wouldn't kill herself. She was my best friend. I know she wouldn't! Maddox killed her. He has to pay."

"Shhh...Maddox didn't kill her. Perhaps someone else did, but it wasn't him."

"No. He did it. I know he did."

"He was investigated. There was nothing. Your own account collaborated his story of the events of that night. I think you should accept that maybe she did choose to end her life."

"No. He's a liar. Everything about him is a lie." Erin ground her teeth.

Journey shook her head but didn't argue anymore. "Come on. Wash your face. Get something to eat. I'll wait for you. We can go together."

Erin slid the black dress on and didn't bother to look in the mirror. She checked on her dad before leaving. He was pale and unable to get out of bed. She stopped short as she opened the front door. Jaris was there, dressed in a black suit, with a handful of flowers.

"Hey," he said quietly.

She sniffed and then ran into his arms.

"Who's this?" Journey asked.

Erin backed away from him. "This is Jaris. He's a friend."

He looked at Journey, his eyes widening. "The Storyteller," he said with awe. "Wow. It's an honor to meet you."

"What are you doing here?" Erin asked. "Did you call? I missed it if you did."

He tore his gaze away from Journey and looked at her. "I sent you a few messages, but when I heard the news about your friend...I just thought I'd come and see if you needed, or wanted me to be with you today. A willing shoulder, you know."

She grabbed his face and kissed him hard, her tears falling on his cheeks. Her lip trembled as she pulled away. "Thank you."

Journey cleared her throat and gave Erin a sad, knowing smile. "I'll see you there?"

Erin nodded. Jaris wrapped his arm around her shoulders protectively. "I'll take care of her," he assured Journey.

"Okay." She squeezed Erin's hand quickly before walking past them and away.

She rested her head on his shoulder. "I'm sorry. I hardly know you, but it means so much that you came. I feel safe with you."

He didn't say anything; he just led her off the porch and down the street. The funeral was held outside in Anue's memorial gardens. A white marble memory stone was already set up for Selena, and it pulsed with pale light. On this day only, the stone would collect memories of Selena, transferred from everyone who chose to touch the marble while it was illuminated. From then on, anyone passing through the memorial garden could touch Selena's stone and would see all the good memories her loved ones had left behind.

There was an emptiness inside Erin. A ravenous hole that devoured her from within. All through the funeral, her mind kept returning to Selena, cold and lifeless on the ground. Left behind like trash when she was so special.

Maddox.

The image of his name carved on her skin twisted Erin's heart around and around. A scorching hatred for him spread through her like a disease. He would pay for this.

Selena's parents came over to her, embraced her, cried on her. She could barely stand it. The guilt crashing back on her again. She wanted to use her elf blood and disappear. Long words were spoken about Selena. Erin closed her eyes, and let her mind drift, refusing to listen. All too quickly, it was her turn to come forward and touch the memory stone.

Her hands shook as her broken heart spilled from her eyes. She held her breath, walking up to the stone. She didn't want to do this. She couldn't... but she had to.

Just one memory. She could only leave one. Which one was the right one? Erin hesitated, then she knew. It had to be her favorite one, nothing else would be adequate. She closed her eyes and exhaled, her fingertips connecting to the marble.

She watched the memory in her mind.

Erin jumped, just about to get into bed as a pebble hit her window. She looked out and instantly opened the glass. Fifteen-year-old Selena climbed through.

"What are you doing?" Erin whispered.

"I had to tell you something."

Her heart sank. She knew Selena's parents had not been happy they'd become such close friends.

"My mom and dad sat me down and got all serious, telling me I shouldn't be friends with you anymore."

"Because I'm Halfling?" Erin asked.

"Yeah," Her eyes were burning. Erin had never seen her look like that. Selena didn't get mad, ever.

"I listened quietly. Then I told them to take their racist asses back to Kyhael if that's how they felt, where they could live among all the other snobby Elves...Then I told them, I'm not giving you up. You're the best friend I've ever had."

Erin hugged her tightly. "Thank you! I don't know what I'd do if you weren't my friend anymore."

Selena was shaking slightly and blew out a breath. "I've never talked to my parents like that..." She giggled. "You should have seen their faces."

"I'll always be there for you. No matter what. You and me against the world."

She opened her eyes abruptly, feeling that she was being watched. She pulled her hand away from the stone, glancing around when she spotted the source of her feeling. Across the outdoor space, a guy was looking speculatively at her. Studying her. Frowning at her. She shivered under his dark gaze and pulled closer to Jaris.

"Who's that?" she whispered.

"Who?"

"Straight across, looking at me."

The two guys stared each other down. Jaris scowled and wrapped his arm around her shoulders in a possessive move. This seemed to amuse the other guy a little. He nodded and turned away.

"That's Kendrick. High society prick and—"

"Maddox's best friend," she finished angrily.

"Yeah. Old money. Prominent elf society of Paradigm. His mother is Catarina. I think she's a big wig in Fortress, but I'm not sure."

The funeral was over, and people were beginning to disperse. Erin's gaze followed Kendrick. Red clouded her vision, and she came after him. Jaris followed her.

She marched right up to his back and shoved him in the shoulder. "Hey you," she said aggressively.

He turned, bemusement on his face. "Can I help you?" he asked, one eyebrow raised.

"Kendrick?"

He smiled. "You know my name, but I don't have the pleasure of yours."

"Erin." Her voice was clipped. "Selena's best friend."

His expression turned sympathetic. "I'm sorry. It's such a terrible tragedy."

"You saw her the night she died. You were with her."

He straightened. "I was questioned at Fortress, you should know, since I can see the blame in your eyes. I had nothing to do with her suicide. It happened hours after I last saw her."

"What about Maddox?"

"What about him?"

"I...he..." She tried to form the right words.

Kendrick reached out and took one of her hands. She looked at him, slightly shocked he would touch her.

"I understand. You're distraught. True, Maddox took her to a party that night, but that was all. He decided she wasn't the one for him. So, maybe she couldn't take the disappointment. It wasn't his fault."

"But..."

"His name was carved into her arm, right?"

"Yeah."

"He's not stupid. If he killed her, do you really think he'd write his name on her? It's ridiculous."

She exhaled, frustration running all through her.

"You have such beautiful hair, Erin," Kendrick said. "Such a rich red."

She frowned at him. "What?" Was he hitting on her?

"Were you at the party that night?"

"I was, just for a few minutes."

He smiled. "I thought so... Mystery Girl."

"What?" He wasn't making any sense.

Kendrick released her hand and took a step back. "It was nice to meet you. Too bad it's on such a sad day."

"Did you even care about Selena?" she demanded.

"Very much. If you'll excuse me." He turned and walked briskly away.

She turned to Jaris. "Wow. He's... The rich really are different, aren't they? He was polite, yet..."

"A scumbag?" Jaris offered.

"Exactly. Did you hear him call me Mystery Girl? What the hell was that?"

Jaris shrugged. "Do you want to get out of here?"

She looked back at the dispersing crowd, her heart weighed down. "Yeah."

"Do you want to get something to eat or just go home?"

"I want to go to your place."

His eyebrows shot up. "Um...okay."

"I don't want to go home. I just need to be somewhere I have no memories for a little while."

"That makes sense."

Jaris lived in the middle of Paradigm in a modest flat, typical of a young man just starting out on his own. She immediately relaxed when she came through the door. It wasn't nasty or smelly, just a little messy. Normal. He apologized for the mess and began to pick up.

"Leave it. You weren't expecting company. I crashed on you. I like it like this. It's real."

"Well, make yourself at home then."

She plopped on his couch and exhaled. He took off his suit jacket and sat down next to her. She snuggled into his side and fell asleep. She woke up groggy with her stomach rumbling. The flat was going dark as the evening matured. She sat up and rubbed her eyes. She was alone. Jaris had covered her up with a fluffy throw. She stretched.

"Jaris?"

No answer. The flat was quiet. Where had he gone? Her feelings smarted a little that he'd left her alone. She stood and folded the throw. The door opening made her jump.

"Hey. You're awake. I didn't know if I should leave you, but I thought you might be hungry," Jaris said. "I got takeout."

She looked at the bag in his hands. The smell of greasy junk food filled the flat. "I'm starving."

"Good, cause I bought a lot." He laid the food out on the tiny table. "I have blood if you want some. You look a little weak."

"Thanks. I'll run away with you now."

"What?" He smirked.

"At the hub, when we first met, you asked me to run away with you. Remember?"

"Hmm. Yes. I was being dramatic. I'd be content if you'd just agree to be my girlfriend."

"You're asking for exclusivity?"

He smiled brightly. "Not asking, just hoping." His face fell suddenly, and he shook his head. "Sorry. The timing is wrong. It's a bad day."

"Ask me again sometime."

"I promise you, I will."

They ate together, and it was like their date—they gelled easily. He distracted her from the emptiness still eating at her insides. The night grew late.

"Do you need to check on your dad?" he asked. "Is he still sick?"

"Are you trying to get rid of me?"

"Not at all. I was hoping you'd think me heroically romantic if I showed concern about your dad."

She chuckled. "Sucker."

"I do honestly care."

"I know. You're a good guy."

"But not too good, right?" he asked. "I have my bad boy side."

She walked to the window and looked out at the lights of the city. He came up behind her. She turned, caught in his arms. She wanted to spend the night. She wanted to ask, or just make a move on him. She hurt so much she wanted him to put her back in her body.

"Jaris." Her voice betrayed her thoughts. "Ask me to stay."

He blinked down at her for a second then he shook his head. "No. I can't take advantage of you like that. Not today, when you're so raw emotionally."

"Wow…I…"

He kissed her gently. "I would love for you to stay the night, soon. But now, I think I should probably take you home."

She pulled tight into his chest. "I'm glad you yelled at me at the hub. Even if it was far from smooth. You're quite tolerable."

He chuckled. "That's my main goal in life, being tolerated, especially by sweet and gorgeous females like yourself."

He took her home, kissed her goodnight and left. Her dad was asleep, the house quiet and dark. She stood in the doorway of his bedroom and listened to his breathing for a few minutes. She went to her room and closed the door. Since she'd found Selena dead, she'd felt it, but part of her had shut down. *I am alone. I lost my best friend.* She would never be able to hear Selena's voice again. They would never laugh together, cry together, nothing together ever again.

She thought of the people in her life that loved her and mattered. The few she had were wonderful, but none of them were her best friend. Erin hadn't realized the preciousness of that place in her heart that only Selena could fill. That place would forever be desolate. Some things cannot be replaced.

The hate inside shivered and expanded. *Maddox.* He'd stolen from her. She would not let this pass. She'd cut his black heart out. Perhaps that would ease the ravenous hole eating her up.

In the dead of night, Maddox left the house, a hood shadowing his face, a knife in his belt, and a spade in his hand. He walked through the woods, searching. The night was warm, but he was frozen inside. He couldn't have shown his face at the funeral, but he had to do something to pay his respects. Even though nothing he could do would ever be adequate. The idea of doing nothing made him sick.

Finally, the moonlight fell on the type of sapling he was looking for. He crouched down and dug it up, careful to not damage its roots. He opened a portal to Anue's memorial gardens. Looking around, making sure there was no one there, he moved forward to Selena's marble stone. He knew it was hers because it was still illuminated.

Maddox dug a hole next to the stone and set the sapling in the dirt. Burying its roots, he pulled out his knife and sliced his hand. His blood soaked into the ground at the base of the young tree. The branches shivered and stretched out. It would grow, and it would flower, dropping white petals over her.

Trembling, he reached to touch the stone. His fingertip barely grazed its smooth surface, flashes of a bright memory filling his mind. He pulled his hand back, his heart fracturing sharply at the sound of her laughter as a child. He couldn't look at the memories of her.

Maddox picked up his spade and touched the tree once more, light from his hand sliding into the trunk. Light he didn't notice. The tree shivered again, a faint gold shimmer pulsing through the veins of the leaves.

"I'm sorry," he whispered.

He opened a portal home and left.

Kendrick came into his mother's study and sat down by the fire.

"So?" Catarina asked.

"The story will be all over tomorrow's headlines. Maddox will fall from grace."

She smiled. "And then so will his mother...Thank you for your help. You did well, son. Keep to the course. We're far from finished. I've worked too long to get close to Forest. Deceived and flattered until I gained her trust. We will see this all the way through. I *will* be the next Hailemarris."

"Yes, Mother."

SEVEN

Melina got up before dawn. She threw on a sweater and headed outside to watch the sunrise from the cliffs overlooking the sea. She sat on her favorite boulder and smiled to herself, inhaling the smell of the water. She knew she was spoiled. That was how things should be. No, she wasn't rich. But she'd been raised in the most beautiful location and she had the best parents in the world. They didn't tolerate stress or drama. They pushed it back and beat the shit out of it if it tried to come close. She'd grown up knowing the value of a peaceful existence, and she intended to guard her own peace just the same as she ventured out into the world to find her own life path.

Her watch pinged. She scowled and ignored it. It pinged again and then again. Growling, she looked at it, her eyes bugging as she read the morning news. She usually didn't give a flip about the news, but she set her watch to inform her whenever someone she knew personally was mentioned. Her watch pinged over and over in rapid succession as the story immediately went viral. She scrolled through for a moment and then looked away. She got the gist.

"Damnit, M," she muttered.

She got up and walked back to the house. Her parents were only just getting up. Both of them were already reading the headlines. They gave her a knowing look. She nodded.

"I have to go."

Merrick grunted and looked back at the streaming news. Netriet shook her head as she read.

"Go on. Try to keep out of sight. Don't get caught by the cameras if you can avoid it," her mom said, framing Melina's face with her uneven hands. The heat from one and the cold from the alien robotic hand was normal and comforting to her, it was how her mom had been her whole life. Blond and beautiful, Netriet was also slightly frightening to some. And in truth, she could tear heads off with one swipe of her robotic arm.

"I'll be careful."

Melina quickly combed her hair, threw on some jeans and her boots. She headed out, realizing it was going to be one of those days she was trained to avoid. There were very few people she would wade through shit for, but Maddox was one of them.

Since they lived in a rural area, she had to run a few miles to get to the closest hub. She didn't mind. Full blooded vampires could run fast and far without breaking a sweat. The portal kicked her out in Anue. She ran the rest of the way, out to the wooded fringe of the city, where Forest and Syrus' land began. Surprisingly, she didn't spot a crowd. It was true that the house was hidden by a dome of magic, but that didn't mean people didn't know it was there.

She circled around the back and found the invisible hand scanner. She placed her palm flat on the air. It was solid, and it shimmered under her skin. It opened to her. She crossed under the protection, still in awe over what Tesla created.

The garden was empty and quiet. She walked up to the front door and pounded on it. "M! Answer the door. Don't force me to kick it in, dumbass!"

The door swung open. She narrowed her eyes at Kendrick and shoved him aside. "What are you doing here?" she demanded.

"Doing what friends do. Trying to be helpful in a dark time. Despite your obvious displeasure at seeing me, not sure what I did to deserve your ire, I'm thrilled to see you again."

She didn't answer and marched to Maddox's bedroom. He was sitting cross-legged on his bed, leaning against the wall, looking disheveled in a pair of flannel pajama pants and a T-shirt. The smell of fragrant smoke hung heavy in the air. He glanced up through bloodshot eyes, looking like he wasn't really seeing her.

She spun on Kendrick. He was standing too close behind her. "That's your idea of helping? *Drugs?*"

"Yeah, it is. He needed to relax."

She turned back to Maddox and pointed at him. "I'll get to you in a minute, after I take out the trash."

She faced Kendrick and stepped up to him. He didn't see the fire in her eyes, too preoccupied looking at her breasts.

He blew out a breath, "Oh, sweetheart. You should stop denying the chemistry between us."

"Leave," she ordered.

"No way." He put his hand on her shoulder. "I care about Maddox as much as you do."

"You're about to lose your hand."

"I'll risk it." He slid his hand up to her cheek. "Look at me."

She laughed and then plowed her fist into his stomach. He coughed, doubled over. She grabbed his hand and twisted it around behind him.

"Ahhh!" he shouted in pain.

She directed him easily out the door, shoved him off the porch, and locked the door behind him.

Maddox was standing, watching her from his doorway. "You are meaner than a damn snake."

Her expression softened, and she went to him, wrapping her arms around his waist. He sighed and slumped against her.

"I've missed you," he admitted.

"You know where I am. It's your own fault if you miss me."

He kissed her temple.

"Why do you still hang out with that douche? He's no good."

He let go of her and ran his hands through his hair. "I know. But he's fun."

She shook her head. "You've had enough fun, M. Have you seen what's being said about you?"

"You mean all of Regia speculating whether or not I murdered a girl? Is the whole family corrupt and letting me get away with it? And if I didn't kill her, what the hell did I do to make her kill herself?"

"Yeah. That."

"Seen it."

"And?" she demanded.

"And what? *And* did I kill her?" he snapped.

She scowled. "*And* what are you going to do about it? *And* don't treat me like I'd even think that for a second again or I'll throw you off the porch, too."

He gave her a miserable smile and stalked back to his room. She followed him.

He flopped back on the bed, his hands on his head. "I don't know what to do."

She sat on the bed next to him and grabbed his hand. "How can I help?" she asked quietly.

He pulled on her hand until she laid down next to him. He closed his eyes and sighed as she wrapped her arms around him. "I love you, Mel," he said quietly.

"I know. I love you, too."

"How come we aren't in love with each other? That would make everything perfect."

She chuckled. "We tried that once, remember? We were thirteen, fourteen years old?"

"Something like that. I screwed it up, didn't I?"

"No. It just wasn't right, you and me, like that. It didn't work for me. You either."

"I wish it did."

"You're just saying that because you're hurting and I'm comfortable."

His lips curved up. "You? Comfortable? That's funny."

"Well, you're comfortable with me," she said. "Why do you make me worry?"

"Sorry. Truly. I'm done. With all of it." His voice slowed as he relaxed against her. "I don't know how to stop everything I've been doing, but I want to."

"You could change your friends to start with." Her voice took a stern edge. "And stop using, please. Process your damn feelings instead of just anesthetizing yourself with substance and hurting every girl that comes your way before she can hurt you. I know that's your deal... I know what *she* did to you."

He was silent.

"Are you listening to me?" she demanded. "M?"

He answered with a quiet snore. She scowled and shook her head as she got up off the bed and looked down at him. "You're impossible." Her voice was quiet. "Fine, sleep it off. I'm leaving."

Before she left, Melina scrawled a quick note and set it on the pillow next to his head.

If you need me, call. I'll come back.

The sky darkened, and thunder began rumbling overhead as Melina made her way home.

Erin hadn't slept. Her grip on reality loosened until she just let go completely. She consumed the day's news, obsessed with every word that questioned if perhaps

Maddox was guilty. A loud thump drew her out of her room.

"What was that? Dad?"

He wasn't in the living room or kitchen as he usually was during the day. She went to his room, her tired heart speeding up.

"No, Dad!" she rushed to him, terrified he was dead.

He'd fallen out of bed. She grabbed at him. His skin was damp and cold, but he looked up at her and gave her a weak smile.

"Sorry, hon. I'm not myself today."

On a push of adrenaline, she hefted him up back on the bed and covered him up. "What hurts? What can I get you?"

He just shook his head feebly. "I can't eat anything. It's okay, Erin. I only have days left."

"I'll get you anything you want. I think I might know someone who can get me some human blood."

"That's illegal, Erin." His voice was feeble, but he managed to sound stern. "Don't you dare. Stay away from blood smugglers. You haven't tried human blood have you?" he demanded.

She shook her head. "No, Dad. I promise." She held her wrist next to his mouth. "Please, you need blood. Take mine. You'll get better."

"No."

"Stop being so stubborn! You know I can out stubborn you any day of the week. I'm like Mom, remember?"

A faint smile lifted the side of his mouth, his eyes full of memories. "You are, so like her. If she were here, how would she coerce me into doing what she wanted?"

Erin blinked. It was a challenge. He was daring her to try. "She'd bargain with you."

"That's right."

She worried her bottom lip between her teeth, contemplating. What was it her father wanted most?

"I kinda have a boyfriend. If you drink some of my blood now, let me give you some strength, then I'll invite him over so you can meet him."

He smiled a little bigger, but his breathing was labored. "A dying man cannot make promises, but I'll try." He sank his fangs into her wrist.

She exhaled in relief. He took a few pulls and then sank back on his pillows. "So, what's this young man's name?"

"Jaris. He's a vampire. He lives in Paradigm. He's one of the nicest guys I've ever met."

He reached up and touched her cheek. "I'll hang around to meet him."

"Is that a promise?"

"We struck a bargain. A deal's a deal. I feel a little better; I'm going to take a little nap now."

"Okay, Dad." She leaned over and kissed his head.

He closed his eyes. She sat there watching him breathe for a while. Each time his chest rose was a relief; every time it fell there was that one moment where she felt unsure he would breathe again. And then when he did, she questioned would this be the last breath? Or the next? She wasn't sure what to do. There wasn't enough money for the physician to come back. Not that they'd done any good the last time. No one knew what was wrong with him. She touched his forehead to check his temperature again. His eyes opened in thin slits.

"Stop staring at me. I gave you my word. I won't die today. Why don't you go see your young man for a while?"

She frowned at him.

"Go on. Let me rest. I can't relax with you staring at me like that."

She sighed and left the room, leaving the door cracked. Thunder shook the house, and rain began to pour suddenly. She pinched her eyes shut as the sound of dripping bounced lightly around the room. She looked up. The roof was leaking. *Drip. Drip. Drip. Drip…* Each drop was like a weight on her back, and her back was already fractured. Her dad was dying. Selena was dead. She felt so alone. Life slid barbed wire through her hands. She couldn't hold on. The harder she tried the more painfully it sliced into her.

The foundation of her mind cracked. This was where she broke. Right there. Right then. The only strength she had left came from hate.

She latched onto the loathing with her fingernails and teeth. Her eyes blazed as she went to the kitchen and grabbed a knife. It felt so good in her hand. Just so damn good. She walked out the door. Rain pelted her face, soaked through her clothes. Her vision tunneled as her stride ate up the muddy ground. She walked right out of the city to the rural fringe, where she knew her target lived. She would cut out his heart. She would carve her name in his skin.

EIGHT

Thunder woke Maddox. He lay in bed and stared at the ceiling for a while, listening to the rain. He saw Melina's note and felt guilty for passing out on her. He didn't deserve her as a friend. His head was clear of the junk he'd put in his system with Kendrick. He got up and changed out of his pajamas pants. Since he still didn't have his new watch back, he strapped an old one over his mark.

Half of him was relieved to be alone, the other half was desolate. He paced around the house, his mind circling everything he wished he could forget. He thought about Selena. *I'm sorry. I'm so sorry.* He figured he was cursed to be haunted by her for the rest of his life. Why had she been so stupid? Why did she put such a value on him? He was worthless.

Maddox wished he could shed his skin and be someone else. He would have looked in a mirror and tried to use the small amount of shifter ability he had to change his appearance, but he couldn't stomach the idea of looking at himself. His own eyes condemned him.

The perimeter alarm sounded. He glanced out the window. He couldn't see anything out of place. He opened the door and stepped outside.

An odd scratching noise came from beyond the rock wall around the garden. Frowning, he stepped out into the rain and walked toward the gate. He should ignore it, he told himself, but he continued on anyway.

The noise stopped.

"Maddox!"

His heart lurched. The resonance of the voice that shouted his name tore something inside him. He pushed the vines covering the open gate aside and looked to the outer barrier a few feet away. She wasn't looking at him. She was looking away, her head thrown back. *It's her.* That was all he could think. *It's her.* The girl he'd lost in the crowd. He'd know that red hair anywhere.

Her shoulders shook as if she cried. He was transfixed. He couldn't say anything to her. He moved closer to the barrier. She wailed. He touched the dome. It shimmered and opened silently.

"Hello."

She jumped and spun on him, a knife in hand, raised...

Time ended. The fabric of the universe tore, as did he. Her eyes connected with his, and he ceased to be. He was dissolved. A bridge of light and spirit connected her heart to his. Her hands to his. A million golden threads of fire tied her to him and him to her. No thoughts, no identity, nothing but the connection existed, and it was insane with starvation.

The knife in her hand shook as she tried to strike but couldn't. Tears and rain ran down her cheeks. She bared her teeth and slowly lowered the knife to his chest. He didn't move, his mind blank and on fire. Her eyes rolled back in her head for a second. His hands grasped her above the elbows. First eye contact had bound them. The first touch was something else.

The second his skin touched hers, her eyes snapped back to his, alight with the soul bridge between them. The knife slashed at him, but it never broke the skin. She cut his shirt open. Then she was in his arms. He pulled her backward through the garden gate. Nothing could stop it. Nothing. Choice did not exist in this moment. The threads pulled tighter and tighter until it was unbearable. She tore at him and he tore at her until he was inside her. Light and fire slid along every vein as they became one. They couldn't get any closer, and even then it wasn't enough. *More, still more!* The connection demanded, the threads pulling tighter.

The raindrops hitting their bare skin turned to steam. When she arched and cried out, he felt himself die and be reborn, his body shattering under the force of pleasure. The pulling eased, but it didn't vanish.

Panting, eternity lived between one heartbeat and the next as they looked, stunned, into each other's eyes. Destiny had spoken, and they were powerless against its verdict.

As her breathing slowed, her eyes went oddly hollow, and tears built layers along her bottom eyelids and then spilled over. She trembled in his arms and shook her head.

"No…" Her whisper was agony. "Not this."

The knife was still in her hand. They'd joined body and soul, and she'd held the knife the whole time. He took it from her hand, not knowing what to say.

Her head fell back, her face to the sky. "No!" she screamed.

The next second she slumped against him, unconscious. He carried her into the house, leaving the shreds of their clothes strewn on the ground.

Maddox laid her on his bed and covered her up. She was his destiny. His life mate. His soul was forever tied to hers. And he didn't even know her name.

Freezing and burning up at the same time, he threw on some pants and climbed, shirtless, onto the bed next to her. He leaned back, propped on his elbows, and stared. Had that really just happened? His mind flashed through it all, not sure of the amount of time that had passed outside. The rain, her eyes, the feel of her skin, and the knife shaking in her hand as they'd had each other in a fit of unreasoning need. He hadn't chosen it.

He'd had no control. He couldn't wrap his brain around it, but his body confirmed it. Her heart burned inside his. He felt its beating inside the walls of his own heart.

Shivers covered his skin. He rubbed the heel of his hand over his aching chest. The heat trembled under the surface. The bond had its own needs, like a separate entity, possessing him. It made him touch her. He had to. He *needed* to.

Still unconscious, her breathing hitched, and shivers covered her skin the second he ran his fingertip down her arm. Whoa, that was an amazing response. Even unconscious, her body lit up under the faintest pressure of his caress.

His...

He frowned. Was she crazy? She'd acted crazy.

He tried to compare the level of sexuality they'd just shared in the garden to anything else he'd ever experienced. His mind strained. He'd been with so many casual partners, and yet they blurred in his mind. He barely remembered their faces or their names at all. What had she done to him? He wasn't the same. Having her was unlike anything he'd ever felt or done. No physical pleasure in the past could compare to being inside her.

She moaned and rolled to her side. She was waking. He rushed to his parent's room and grabbed her some of his mom's clothes. Her eyes pinned him as he came back in the room, and again, they filled with tears.

"No!" she screamed at him, holding his blanket to her chest. "This cannot be happening!"

His heart collapsed. Nothing had ever hurt as much as the look in her eyes. "I'm sorry."

"Sorry? *I hate you! I came here to kill you!*"

She pulled her knees up to her chest, covered her face with her hands, and sobbed. What should he do? He wanted to hold her, comfort her, but he figured she wouldn't accept it. It would just make things worse, if that was possible. He didn't understand. Girls came up to him all the time, just to look in his eyes to see if they were possibly his destined life mate. He'd found her, and she acted like he was planning to torture her or already had. He didn't even know her. Why would she hate him?

He took a deep breath, trying to steady himself. *Slowly. Approach slowly.* The way he might a small, frightened animal. Maybe she'd been a virgin until a few minutes ago and the experience was too harsh and terrifying for her.

But that didn't seem right, she'd been ruled by the pull as well. She fought, not to get away, but to get closer, to have more. She'd touched him as much as he'd touched her. And she'd cried out in pleasure, not pain. Nothing about her body's response was in doubt.

He came one step closer.

Her head shot up, fury in her eyes.

"Here," he said quietly, holding the clothes out to her.

She snatched them from his hand. He left the room and shut the door before she had the chance to order him out.

He paced, staring at the closed door. It seemed to take forever. Dressed, she burst from his room, looked for the front door, and headed right for it.

"Wait!"

She stopped, her hand on the knob and turned to him, her expression caught between fear and fury. Then she jabbed her finger at him. "Don't tell anyone about this!" Her voice was sharp.

Under the hurt, a spark of anger ignited. He took a step toward her.

"Stay away from me!" she shrieked.

"I'm not going to touch you. But it's not your choice who I tell about this."

Her mouth fell open, and all the color drained from her face. "Please." Her voice shifted from sharp to quiet desperation. "I'm begging you. Please, don't tell anyone about this."

He hesitated, shoving his hands in his pockets. "Why? What did I do to you? Why did you want to kill me?"

"*Do*. Present tense."

"Why?"

Her bottom lip trembled. "Selena…. She was my best friend."

"Oh gosh…" His voice was barely audible.

Her eyes held him in a well of despair. "You killed her."

"I did not!"

"You're a liar!"

He moved toward her. She pulled the door open, trying to bolt. He grabbed her arm, pulled her back, and slammed the door. She pressed her back against the door, looking at him fearfully. He didn't think how to do what he did next. Instinct led him. He grabbed her hand, forced it open with his thumb, and held her palm flat over his heart.

"Look at me," he ordered.

She did, her eyes round.

"I did *not* kill Selena. I swear."

The bond shivered and stretched between them. There was no way to be dishonest like this. No way to hide. Her hand against his heart, the boundary of flesh was nothing, she was inside him, a part of him.

She closed her eyes and nodded, tears sliding down her cheeks again. "Okay, damn it. I believe you. Let me go. I still hate you!"

His grip on her hand eased, and she jerked it back.

"So what happens now?" he asked, aching to touch her again.

"I don't know. Just leave me alone. Don't look for me. We can pretend this never happened, and we never have to see each other again."

As soon as she said it, he knew that was impossible. Was it necessary to say it aloud though?

"Okay." He backed away so she could open the door.

She frowned at him as if he confused her and opened the door. She hesitated, looking torn.

"What?" he asked.

She rubbed her arms like she was cold. He felt it in his own arms and hands, the longing to touch. She wanted to touch him. Or she needed to.

"It hurts," she said quietly.

"I feel it, too."

He held his hand out to her, hesitantly. She looked at it and flinched. He shrugged and dropped his hand like he didn't care, but he felt sick. She took a tentative step out the door.

"What's your name?" he asked.

She turned again and faced him, her eyes confused and hurting, but she no longer looked like she was going to start screaming and throwing things at him. His heart ached like it was filled with nails. She was the most beautiful thing he'd ever seen. She surpassed every other woman without question.

"Erin."

Erin. It was perfect. It suited her completely, and he'd never met anyone else with that name.

"It's beautiful."

Her eyes flashed angry again. "Don't!" she snapped.

"*What?* Don't what?"

"Don't flatter me. Don't compliment me. Your silver tongue won't work on me. I'm not one of your whores."

He wanted to shout at her. No shit, she wasn't his whore. She was his mate! He sighed and didn't answer.

"Are we done?" she asked.

"I don't know. Are we?" he challenged.

"Are you?" she shot back.

"No. Hell no, I'm not done with you. But I'll leave you alone, for a while. You know where I am. You don't have to tell me where you live. I'm sure I can find you even if you tried to keep it secret. Maybe once this pull starts to make us deranged and we can't stand it, we'll talk again."

"And until then?" she asked.

"I don't know. You tell me."

"I have a boyfriend." She lifted her chin defiantly.

"And?" He was successful in sounding glib, but her words made him burn.

"Damn you, Maddox!" She exploded, charging at him. "You've ruined my life! I wish you were dead! I want my friend back! Why did you touch me? Who said you could?" She slapped him in the face, *really* hard. The next second she was clawing at him like she wanted sex again.

He grabbed her wrists and pulled her against him. "Shhh..." He held her tightly.

She groaned, holding him like a lover one second, fighting to get away the next.

"I didn't do this to you, Erin. And you didn't do it to me. It just happened. We didn't choose it."

"I don't want it."

"I don't want it, either," he lied. "Let's just try to get through the next few days, okay? Without hacking holes into one another, please. I won't tell anyone if that's how you want it."

She pulled back and looked into his face. "Thank you...I...I'm sorry for striking you just now."

She reached up to touch his abused cheek and hesitated. She shook her head as if she could shake her thoughts clear. "I have to get away from you. It's like a war inside me."

"Go." His voice was quiet.

She ran out the door and into the rain. He watched her go, his soul splintering. It went against everything inside him to stay there. He should go with her, make sure she got home safely. He had to protect her...even from himself?

He closed the door, leaned against it, and slid down to the floor. His eyes burned with tears. He should be happy. He'd found his mate. That was supposed to be joy and ecstasy. Instead, he hurt so badly death seemed preferable.

Erin. He didn't know anything about her, but she was his. Did Destiny make mistakes?

He wished his parents were there. He needed some guidance about this. They were life mates. They would know what he should do. Growing up, watching his parents, seeing how amazing it could be to have a life mate.... He didn't want to lose her. It could be incredible for both of them.

Patience. Give it time...

He hit his forehead with his knuckles. What was he thinking? She'd come here to kill him. Not tell him off. End his life. So, he'd convinced her he didn't kill Selena. That had been her best friend, and no matter how he looked at it, some of it was his fault. How did they get past that? Was it even possible?

And she had someone else. Someone she actually loved. He thought about this faceless guy, and the rage was instant. Erin was his. *His mate.*

He leaned his head back and closed his eyes, everything about her filling his mind. Everything about taking each other in the rain, every detail came back, and he blew out a breath. That had been crazy. He couldn't walk away. She'd destroyed him with her body and claimed him with her soul. It wasn't a one-way street. She said it hurt. Did it hurt her the way it hurt him? If he wanted her, surely she wanted him in return.

It hadn't been complete he suddenly realized. They hadn't kissed even once...the thought of kissing her mouth sent a wave of sensation through him. He fixated on the memory of her lips for a while, their shape, and color. He sighed. *Patience...*

So much she had against him...this wasn't going to be easy. He smiled to himself miserably. That just made him want it more. He was sick of things being so easy. His hands already hurt with the ache to touch her again. How long could she hold out? How long could he? The longer they stayed away from each other, the better it would feel? He wanted to find out.

NINE

Erin ran from the house, through the gate, and back out into the real world. She'd come there in a fit of insanity, ready to commit murder. She left in a state of shock and confusion, in different clothes, no less, her hips, and abdomen aching from their joining. She stopped and looked back as the dome closed over the property behind her.

Where was she going? Her soul was back there. He held it. It lived there, under his skin.

She continued to walk away, very slowly. Her mind tripped along the information like walking over uneven ground. Maddox... Of all the girls to get him, it just *had* to be her! She was the only one who didn't want him.

She stopped under a large tree and leaned against the trunk. The rain still came down, but too much churned inside her to notice the cold. She could see the house. It had been hidden from sight before. Now she could see it, and the magic that covered it. The dome held her back before—would it now? She wanted to test it, just curious. She took a step toward the house and stopped. Nope. She wasn't going back there.

She leaned against the tree and stared at the house, trying to process. Tears filled her eyes again. What kind of madness was this? It was a mistake. Nothing about it was right. Why would Destiny pair her with the one person she truly hated? He hadn't killed Selena, but it was his fault she was dead. He was the personification of everything she hated about men. He was the poster child of cruelty and conceit.

Okay, she was going to analyze it pragmatically... right now. Really. *Oh, come on*, she pleaded with her brain as it blurred with the memory of them together in the garden. Goosebumps covered her, head to toe. Shivers pricked and rolled inside her body as well. She closed her eyes, flushed with heat. What had they done to each other? It was equal. It hadn't been him taking, as much as she would have liked to blame him, she couldn't. He wasn't in any more control than she had been.

She blushed, even though she was alone, remembering she moved first, cutting his shirt off him. How could she go on now? Physically anyway? Nothing would be able to rival that experience sexually, ever again, no way.

She frowned and shook her head. That was wrong. Sex was the wrong word...The physical act was an extension of their souls mating, their bodies conduit for the light and heat they shared.

She pushed off from the tree and continued home, his words in her head. *Let's just get through the next few days...*

She didn't realize how different she already was. Her spirit had been so fractured with grief before. Now she was stronger, replenished, changed. All kinds of pissed off, heartbroken in a new way, and ashamed of herself. She must have some type of serious character flaw to be punished like this.

The rain eased to a drizzle as she rounded the corner to her house and her watch pinged. She stepped up on the porch and checked her message, hoping it was Maddox, swearing it better not be him either—and how had he gotten her number?

It was Jaris. Her heart sank twice. First, and stupidly, because it wasn't Maddox, and second because she felt like a cheating slut. She wanted Jaris. He was the one her conscious brain had picked. His message was an invitation. He wanted to see her again. She wanted to see him. What would that be like? She had to tell him the truth.

Ugh. Her stomach twisted at the thought. She'd begged Maddox not to tell anyone. How long before people knew anyway?

Fear gripped her as she considered what it would mean for her once it was common knowledge. Her life would transform in a way she certainly didn't desire. People would notice her. Her picture would end up in the media. She would be a part of celebrity gossip. All the love and desire Maddox had from the public would mean she would become the most hated person ever. He was uncatchable, and she was the one who had him.

She'd throw him back, if she could.

Wait! Erin shook herself, angrily. What was she thinking? She wasn't stuck with this. She could reject him. That was her way forward. That was exactly what she was going to do.

A devious smile parted her lips. She had the power. This was how she would exact revenge for Selena and all the other girls Maddox had treated badly. She would reject him, but not yet. Not until she had tortured him and broken him down to nothing. He would be humiliated and left behind, just as he had done to Selena.

It wasn't a curse. It was a gift of revenge.

For one second only, she faltered on the thought of rejecting Maddox. It was as simple as making a committed choice. Everyone knew that. All you had to do was *truly* decide to shut off your mate's access to your heart and it was over. But everyone knew that was also only just the beginning. Legends and stories as old as Regia itself told of the pain of such an action and that you never actually recovered. As if you cut yourself a mortal wound that killed you slowly every day by small degrees. There were also stories that all of that was bunk. Erin tended to think the latter was true because she wanted to, but also because she knew someone who had rejected their mate for love of another.

She pushed off from the porch and headed to the memorial gardens. She stopped and stared at the young tree next to Selena's stone. That hadn't been there before. The leaves danced as the rain fell on them. She touched it gently, immediately recognizing the sensation and the color deep inside. It was the same as her stone. She sat on the wet ground, her heart filling. The gift giver had planted this tree for Selena.

It touched her bruised heart. She wished she knew who it was. It was odd to care so deeply for someone whose identity was unknown. For so many years, the phantom of this anonymous person had comforted her. *Thank you so much. I love you. I've always loved you.*

She placed her hand on the ground in front of Selena's memory stone and sighed.

"Hey, Selena…You'll never believe what happened to me," she said quietly. "It's so bad, but I'm going to use it to avenge you."

Anxious energy filled Maddox. Everything was just wrong. Erin should be with him. He figured when other people found their life mates they told everyone they knew it had happened and not to expect to see them for a while. And they would have some time to be alone and get to know each other. That would be natural. Natural for the lucky people whose life mates didn't hate their guts and basically ran away screaming.

He didn't know what to do, but he had to do something. If he stayed busy maybe that might help.

He cleaned the whole house from top to bottom, but that was menial, and his mind spun on Erin the whole time. Should he go look for her? No, he shouldn't, but he wanted to. It would be so easy. He could probably find her with his eyes closed. Was she thinking about him at all? If she was, it was probably just clever ways to hide his body.

He put on a hoodie and stood by the door, indecisive for a while. He didn't have to talk to her. Didn't need to bother her. He just wanted to know where she lived. She knew where he lived—it was only fair.

His watch pinged. Was it Erin? Did she even have his number? He frowned, disappointed it was Kendrick.

Has your watch dog left? Damn, I want her more than ever. Never had a girl almost break my wrist before. It was hot.

Melina's gone. He couldn't think of anything else to write.

Hey, guess what? I think I found Mystery Girl. I was going to tell you before, but I forgot, and then Melina showed up and kicked me out.

His stomach swooped. He didn't want Kendrick anywhere near Erin. When? Where?

Is this her? Cause if not, I'm going to call *I saw her first.*

A picture of Erin came attached to the message. It must have been at the funeral. She obviously wasn't aware someone was taking her picture, and some guy had his arm around her. He pinched his eyes shut and tried to not grind his teeth.

That's her. And *I* saw her first. *Mine.* **He typed.**

I don't know, Dude. This one might be a unicorn for you. I talked to her. Selena was her friend. She's no fangirl. In fact, she's nothing like your usual palate. Wholesome. Don't think she gives easy. Just my observation.

Maddox groaned. He didn't want to tell Kendrick, but he also really wanted him to shut up about Erin. He decided he couldn't tell him. Kendrick wouldn't keep it to himself. Even if he swore not to tell, he would.

Whatever.

What? You don't want to chase her down now?

No. Like you said, she's not really my type. Leave her alone. She just lost her friend.

?????? The Hell? Who are you, and where's Maddox?

I mean it, Kendrick. Leave her alone.

Watch it. Where do you get off giving me orders? You don't want her. Don't tell me what to pass on.

Shit. How did he get him to drop it and forget her? Are you partying tonight? **Maddox typed.**

Dead scene everywhere tonight. Nothing happening. We could start something. I send the word you're coming out of hiding, and it will happen.

The idea was repugnant. He didn't want to party. He wanted to be with Erin. That wasn't going to happen, but getting wasted with the same people as always wasn't even close to second. But...if he was hammered would that take the edge off this pain?

He shook his head. No. He wasn't ready to be in public. The stories about him were running wild and would continue for at least another few days. He was going to continue to do what Redge told him and keep his head down.

Yes or no? Kendrick asked.

No. Too soon. The headlines were only this morning.

I can bring some shit over. Cheer you up. Kendrick offered.

No thanks. I want to be alone.

Fine. I'll send you pictures of what you missed. Especially the pics of Mystery Girl under me.

He ground his teeth again and took a deep breath. It didn't matter what Kendrick said. He wasn't going to get anywhere near Erin.

Later.

He took his watch off and put his hood up before going out. He'd walk for a while and see if he could catch the direction that would lead him to her.

The storm had blown over, and the moon was bright, its haunting aquamarine light shooting down sharply in between the shadows. It was unseasonably cool. He jammed his hands in his pockets and let his connection to her pull him. She didn't feel that far away. It was too far for his taste, but it seemed she was maybe in Anue and not Paradigm or Halussis. He wandered the empty streets and suddenly stopped dead. She was here, he felt her.

The cream colored house was small and run down, but it still had a measure of charm. He knew this place. The irony made him smile. Did she remember it? That had been the first time he'd ever left an anonymous gift for anyone in the middle of the night. She'd been his first one. Not that he'd seen her at all.

He remembered so clearly, for some reason. Her mother's obituary had caught his attention, and it stung his young heart. He hadn't known what else to do, but he left her a sympathy note, some money, and a flower.

He stared at the house for a few minutes before looking down and walking away. He picked up a rock, tossed it in the air, caught it, and wandered to the low end of town. This was all he knew to do to make himself feel better. His wallet was too full. He'd find somewhere to relieve the burden of its contents.

Frustration simmered under Kendrick's cool exterior. Maddox wasn't playing along with his plans, at least not at the moment. He considered how to improvise to please his mother and keep things moving forward. Tonight would have to be minimal damage. Tomorrow night would be a killer, whether Maddox did what he wanted or not.

He moved all the most damning pictures he could find of Maddox in his own watch and sent them to his media contact. Whatever they chose to use would be edited so it looked like the pictures were new, right after Selena's funeral. It would break first thing in the morning and keep the spin going.

TEN

Early the next morning, Melina found herself yet again banging on Maddox's front door. She hoped it rattled a nasty hangover. He deserved to suffer, and she was going to serve him some more pain as soon as he opened the door.

The door swung open, and he stood there, clear eyed with an anxious look on his face that fell the second he laid eyes on her.

"Oh, hey, Mel. Come in."

Taken aback she scowled and walked in. "Were you expecting someone?"

"Uh...no."

"Didn't look that way."

"What are you doing here?" he asked. "It's pretty early."

"I...The news..."

"I haven't looked. What now?"

"Oh, you know, just really ugly stuff. Pictures of you and your friends partying last night. They're saying you're a heartless bastard who celebrated right after Selena's funeral and disrespected her family and her memory."

"What?" He pulled the headlines up on his watch and grimaced. "This is bullshit. I didn't go out last night. Those pictures are from months ago."

"No one will believe you. There are accounts of your actions last night by witnesses."

"Yeah. Paid off liars." He looked into her eyes. "Someone's creating this."

She crossed her arms.

"You believe me, don't you?"

"Yeah. But only because I can see you're clean."

He looked back at the headlines. "Who do you think would do this?"

She laughed darkly. "You have as many enemies as you do admirers, M. Brokenhearted exes. Jilted boyfriends of girls you stole away from them. Just psycho fans. Could be anyone. They're not saying you did anything criminal; it's just really bad optics. Regardless, do you have an alibi?"

"No. I was alone."

"I'm going to have to start babysitting you. We'll have to go out and be seen doing nothing but wonderful stuff. Make sure this shit can be refuted by other eyewitnesses."

"You're so good to me, Mel. I don't deserve it."

She smirked. "Don't worry, I'm keeping an account. Your bill will come due."

He chuckled and hugged her. He thought about telling her about Erin. He needed to tell someone. And she would keep his confidence. It wouldn't be breaking his word to Erin to not tell anyone if he shared it with Melina.

"Something happened to me yesterday. I need to tell someone about it. Will you promise to keep it secret?"

She nodded.

The rain slid down Erin's shoulder blades in thin lines. Shivers lifted on her heated skin as Maddox's hands smeared the water over her back. He blurred, came into sharp focus, and then blurred again. His eyes trapped her. Nowhere to hide. He saw everything in his beautiful, brooding, grey-green eyes. She tried to push him away and saw her hands only pull him closer. Leave me alone...I hate you. Touch me more. Fill me up. Take me higher...I wish you were dead.

Erin woke on a moan. She lay in bed for a few minutes, staring at the ceiling, on the verge of tears. She rubbed her hands together trying to massage the pain away. All the incredible light and heat that ran along her veins ached now. She would do her best to ignore it. She could manage through it. Perhaps it would ease over time if she didn't see Maddox again.

Erin pressed her hands to her lower abdomen. She felt bruised inside. The shame came back as she remembered she'd told Selena not to be with him because she'd just end up as one of the many. But what was she?

No. she wasn't one of the many. She was *the one*. She *was* special to him, whether he liked it or not. What they shared was spiritual and beyond either of their control. She groaned and rolled her face into her pillow. She wanted to see him. And she never wanted to see him again.

She got out of bed and went to her dad's room. She sat on the bed next to him and put her hand on his.

"Dad?"

He roused and blinked at her. "Hi, honey."

She touched his forehead and felt his pulse. "I think my blood helped a little. Do you feel well enough to get up? I'll make you breakfast."

"No. I still feel too weak...When are you going to invite your young man here, so I can meet him?"

"Madd—uh, I mean Jaris. I told him you were too sick."

"We had a deal, Erin. Invite him."

"Okay, Dad."

"I just wish this guy was your life mate."

She bit down on her lip. "Me too."

She almost told her dad about Maddox right then. The words were right there, pushing in her throat. Should she? Then he could die feeling happy, and she'd never have to tell him she planned to end it. But she'd have to introduce him to Maddox and she'd have to act pleased….

Nope.

She got her dad some water and went to get ready for the day. She'd go to Halussis and check in at work, even though Journey had given her time off to grieve. And she'd go to Paradigm and drop in on Jaris.

She laid out her clothes and abruptly realized she hadn't showered after she came home last night. Maddox was still all over her.

She went straight to the bathroom. The water hitting her skin took her right back there. Back to the garden in the rain. She closed her eyes against the memory, but that only made it sharper. She needed him. She'd suffer through it, and she'd deny it, but she needed him. She hoped he was suffering as much as she was.

She got out and stood looking at the clothes she'd laid out on the bed. Today she was going to look hot, or as close as she could come to it. Jaris would want her.

She put on the one pair of jeans she knew hugged her just right and a flouncy, green, sleeveless top. She tousled her hair, put some big hoops in her ears, and finished with a pair of heels.

"I'm going out, Dad. I'll be back in a..."

Her words died off as she strapped on her watch. The headlines slapped her in the face. She looked at the pictures of Maddox and saw red. Incensed, she marched from the house.

Melina listened and didn't interrupt. He left out the details, wanting to keep them to himself, and he was sure Mel would have stuck her fingers in her ears anyway and shouted, "*TMI!*"

"What do you think I should do?" he asked.

"Hmm...I'm not sure. I have some ideas, but I need to meet her before I can tell one way or the other. You want to keep her, I'm assuming?"

"Yes. Of course."

"You're willing to fight for her?"

"I am."

"She held a boyfriend over your head…There may come a time to do something like that to her. Not yet, perhaps."

"What? Get a girlfriend? I can't do that."

"Not a real one… Me. I'll be your stand-in."

"Why? What good would that do?" he asked, confused.

"Jealousy is a great teacher. She wants to run away. She wants to deny your connection. She doesn't want you, but I'd bet anything she doesn't want anyone else to have you either. If you can arouse jealousy, she'll have to consider why she feels it."

Maddox shook his head. "I don't think she'll ever feel any such thing. She wants me dead."

Melina shrugged. "Still might be worth testing."

He looked up, his muscles tightening.

"What?" Melina asked.

"She's coming right now. I feel her getting closer." He stood and went toward the front door.

Melina grabbed him and pulled him back. "Oh, no you don't. Sit down. I'll answer it."

"Why?"

"Just an experiment. Humor me. Let me take her measure. Follow my lead, and don't contradict me. Sit," she ordered again.

He snorted and sat down on the couch, shaking his head. "I don't know why I trust you so much. Just please don't scare her away."

Melina crossed her arms and leaned against the door, waiting. In a moment, a loud knock sounded on the other side, but Melina didn't answer it.

"What are—"

She put her finger to her lips in a shushing motion.

Erin knocked again, louder and longer. Still, Melina didn't move. He stood. She jabbed her finger at him, a stern look in her eyes. He frowned but sat back down. Erin knocked again. Melina sighed, ran her fingers through her hair, and opened the door.

"Hello," Melina said vaguely.

Erin's eyes were blazing, but she blinked and took a step back. "Um…Who are you?"

"Who are *you?*" Melina shot back.

"I'm…um. Erin. Is Maddox here?"

"He is." Melina didn't budge to let Erin in.

"I need to talk to him."

"What about?"

"That's between me and him." Erin's voice went hard and chilly.

Melina shrugged and stepped back so Erin could come in. She stalked into the room and stopped short when their eyes connected. Damn, it hurt. Like a punch to the brain straight through his eyes. He forced himself to hold still, but it was difficult. He wanted to grab her and hold her until she absorbed into him. She was so hot. So damn beautiful, and she was dressed to entice. Had she done that for him? Or to torture him with what she wouldn't let him touch?

One thing was for sure, she was flaming mad.

"How could you?" she demanded.

"What?"

"How could you act like that last night? I know you're a self-centered ass, but don't you even have one ounce of respect or decency?"

He stood up then. "You're talking about the headlines."

"That didn't happen last night," Melina said, coming to stand next to him. She wrapped her arm around the back of his waist.

Erin's gaze fixed on Melina and there was a stronger rage that flashed there than the previous one.

"Someone is trying to taint the public's opinion of me, Erin. Those pictures weren't from last night. I wasn't with those people."

"Where were you then?" she demanded.

"He was with me," Melina said smugly.

Everything Erin was feeling hit him in the chest. Anger, confusion, jealousy, sorrow. He put his hand on Mel's shoulder and looked into her face. "Give us a minute."

She nodded and walked past Erin and out the front door. Alone, they stared at each other. Too much played across her face. The confusion and hurt in her eyes surprised him.

"I'm sorry about the media. A friend asked me to come out and party last night, but I turned him down. I would never do anything to be disrespectful of...Selena. At least not intentionally. I promise."

She rubbed her forearms and looked down. He felt her emotions shift. He was thankful for this. Thankful he could tell her the truth and she accepted it because the connection laid everything open.

"Okay." She sighed. "I'm sorry for...barging in on you like this...and your company. Is she..."

"What?"

"Never mind... I don't have a right to... I mean, I don't care. I...I'm going to see my boyfriend in a few minutes anyway."

"Lucky guy."

She looked back at him and flinched. "Are you mocking me?"

"No. I think he *is* a lucky guy. I want to kill him for it, but I don't think that will enhance your opinion of me."

To his shock, she smiled, somewhat wickedly. He quirked an eyebrow, but her expression shifted before he could ask her why she was looking at him like that. He didn't want to play games with her. She could play all she wanted, but he wanted to be honest.

"I dreamed about you."

She swallowed, and he felt her panic. It urged him on.

"You look incredible, Erin. I don't like it. I don't want anyone gawking at you, and I know they will. I want you to stay here with me so we can start to get to know each other."

"You just want sex," she accused.

"Hey, if it happened again, I wouldn't object. Yesterday was mind-blowing. But I'd be more than happy to just spend time with you. I don't know you. I want to."

"Why are you talking like this?" she demanded.

"I'm just being honest."

"I can tell, and it's pissing me off."

He chuckled. "You want me to lie to you?"

"Yes! No, that's stupid. You're screwing with my...my..."

"Your misconceptions of who I am?"

She frowned at him. "Maybe," she admitted grudgingly.

"I'm hurting, Erin. Our connection makes me hurt."

"Me too."

"I know if you'd let me touch you, it would ease the pain."

She looked fearful and on the verge of tears. She licked her lips. It almost unmade him. He'd been obsessing about her lips so much.

She took a step toward him. "Just hands. For a minute."

He reached for her and clasped her hands in his. The first second was terrible. A stinging burn that vanished the next moment into ecstasy.

"Oh…" Shivers surfaced on her skin. "Holy shit." She breathed.

He kept his mouth shut, thinking similar thoughts on the sensation. After a minute, the feeling eased back into a pleasant hum.

"Please stay with me today, Erin."

"I can't." Her voice wasn't steady.

"I was going to visit my sister. You could come with me."

Her eyes rounded. "That's quite the carrot, Maddox. Meeting Tesla…that would be…" She shook her head. "I'd be terrified to meet a legend like her."

"She's just my sister. She's a brilliant, gifted, sweet, pain in my ass."

Erin laughed, making his heart swell. Then she shook her head again. "No. I can't. I wouldn't feel right about it."

"Why not?"

She looked away, her cheeks coloring. What was that about? If only he could hear her thoughts and not just feel her emotions. Feeling what she felt didn't let him know why she was feeling it.

Erin pulled her hands away roughly. "That's enough," she snapped. "I have to go. Jaris is waiting for me."

"Okay. Fine. We should exchange numbers before you go."

"Why?" Her tone was waspish.

He shrugged. "Just in case."

She pursed her lips.

"I won't bother you. I just want to know you can reach me if you need to. Okay?"

"All right fine," she caved. "I'll give you my number, but you won't be able to reach me. My watch is old and not very consistent. So if you drunk dial me, it will be a total waste of smarm."

He laughed. "Well, that's a real problem."

She lifted her wrist up to him, and he put in his number. She did have the junkiest watch he'd ever seen. He scrolled through and grabbed her number so she didn't have the chance to give him a bogus one.

She turned and headed for the door.

"Touching helped me," he said quickly. "Did it you?"

She turned back. "Yes. It helped."

"Will you come back tonight? Just for a few minutes? We could just hold hands again. I'm sure it would help me sleep. Take the edge off the pain."

"I don't know."

"I could come to your place if it's too much trouble for you to come here."

"No! No way! You can't come to my place."

"I know where it is."

"How?"

He rolled his eyes. "Erin, please. I could find you across the universe. You only live a few miles away."

"Stay away from my house."

"Only if you come back."

"Ugh! Fine!" She opened the door and walked out. "I hate you!" she yelled as she slammed the door.

A smirk lifted his lips for a moment, then he smiled broadly. "Yeah, yeah, run away," he said to the closed door. "You're mine."

Melina came back in after Erin was gone. "So?" she asked. "How did that go? You're smiling, so it must not have been that bad."

"She told me she hates me again, but she agreed to come back tonight...What did you think?"

"She was shooting daggers at me from her eyes when I touched you, so that's a good sign."

He sighed. "She's different."

Melina laughed. "Different than what you're used to?"

"Yeah. It's really appealing….I'm going to see Tesla, wanna come?"

"I guess so. I said I was going to babysit you."

He used his portal and took them to Tesla's home. His heart sank as soon as she opened the door. His mind was on Erin, and he'd already forgotten the bad press until Tesla gave him *that* look.

"It's a lie, I swear," he said quickly before she could flay him.

Tesla narrowed her eyes and then nodded, turning her attention onto Melina. "Hey, you. Haven't seen you in a while. Your reputation's going to get tainted hanging out with the manwhore."

Melina snickered.

"Stop calling me that," Maddox griped.

"The nickname doesn't apply now, Tesla," Melina said. "Now that he's found—"

He poked her in the side. "It's my news, isn't it? Shut your trap."

"News that negates your womanizer title?" Tesla gave him a scrutinizing look, then she jumped and grabbed him. "You've found your life mate? Is that it?"

"You're too smart sometimes," he grumbled.

"Well, where is she? Who is she? Why are you even out and about? You should be locked away somewhere with her."

"I know," he said through clenched teeth. "She hates me."

"What's going on?" X asked coming up behind Tesla, wrapping his arms around her.

"Maddie's found his destined life mate, and she hates him," she chirped it out happily like a little bird.

X just blinked at Maddox for a second, then he threw his head back laughing. "Oh, it serves you right."

"Thanks a lot, X."

X shook his white-blond head, chortling, and let go of Tesla. He kissed her and backed away. "I'd love to stay and hear more, but I've got to head into work for a while."

"I'll tell you everything later," Tesla promised him gleefully.

"If you're going to make fun of me, can you at least make me coffee first?"

"Oh, all right. Melina, do you want some, too?"

"Yes, please."

The three of them headed into the kitchen, where Tesla attempted to pick him clean of information. The more he told her, the more she quit poking at him and turned thoughtful.

"Have you told Erin about Bess?" Tesla asked seriously.

He flinched. "No...She hasn't given me the chance to talk to her hardly at all. It's nothing I'm looking forward to either. I'd rather not tell her."

"She needs to know," Tesla insisted.

Melina nodded in agreement.

"Well, as funny as this has been, I'd like to meet my new sister sooner rather than later. What can I do to help?"

"I need two new watches. One for me, one for her. I want them connected. She has the oldest watch I've ever seen. Can you make hers pretty?"

Tesla smiled. "No problem. Anything else?"

"A portal between her room and mine. One she can close on her side."

"So you want it to just be there, and I'll put a door she can use to keep you out?"

"Yeah. I want her to feel comfortable with it. In control of when she wants to let me in or not."

Melina socked him in the arm. "That's brilliant, M. No wonder the girls always fell all over you. You're seriously smooth."

"Thanks." He scowled, rubbing his arm.

Tesla gave him an approving nod. "I second that. Very good idea. Give me a few minutes, and I'll have your watches and the portal."

Maddox and Melina sat outside on the front stoop and chatted while Tesla worked her magic in her workshop. He stood abruptly, flame and sparks surging through his hands.

"What is it?"

"I don't know," he grimaced. "My hands and—" He hissed in pain, touching his mouth. "My lips, they burn." He cried out as his heart began to burn as well. "It's Erin, somehow." He inhaled sharply.

Mel grabbed his hands and looked sternly in his eyes. "Betrayal?"

He could hardly breathe. "She's with her boyfriend. He's touching her. He kissed her. Everywhere he is, I can feel it...it's burning me."

"That bitch. I'm gonna kick her ass. How could she?"

The pain began to drift away. He took a steadying breath and shook his head. "Thanks, Mel. For having my back, but don't worry about this."

"But she—"

"She's doing what she feels she needs to. I can't expect her to let go of someone she cares for just because I fell into her life."

Angry light still glinted in her eyes.

"Let it go," he said.

"Fine. For now. But she better watch it."

"Do you think it hurt her as well?" he asked.

"Let's test it."

The next second, Melina was all over him. He staggered back in shock as she held onto his collar and kissed him roughly.

"What the hell?" he exclaimed when she let go.

"Did it hurt?"

"Yeah. Not quite the same level."

Mel smirked. "Good. Then you know she felt that. It burned her. And I feel better cause I got some small piece of revenge on her for hurting you."

"Geez, you're vicious. Warn me next time you decide to jam your tongue in my mouth."

She smirked. "Not a chance. That shocked look on your face was priceless. And we can hold off messing around ever again unless your girl needs another reminder."

"I appreciate it, but I want her to give him up because she wants to, not because I'll burn her otherwise."

Melina narrowed her eyes at him. "Being valiant has its place, but remember, nice guys always finish last. You said you would fight for her."

"That's what I'm trying to do."

"Just make sure you don't fight too passively. She wants you to want her. Even if she won't admit it to herself yet."

"How do you know?" he asked.

"I would if I was her."

Erin gasped and pulled away from Jaris, fire scorching her lips. It was worse than before. It hurt when she first came to see him, and he gave her a kiss. But this time, he wasn't kissing her, and her lips burned a quick searing sting. Maddox? What was he doing to her?

"What's wrong?" Jaris asked. "Every time I touch you, you jump."

"I'm sorry." She took a step back from him and turned away.

"Why don't you tell me what's going on?"

Misery twisted inside her. It wasn't fair. Tears pushed behind her eyes. "Oh, I have the worst news. I didn't want to tell you, but I didn't realize it would be like this. Feel like this. You're going to hate me."

"I could never hate you, Erin."

"I guess we're about to find out." Her voice was bitter.

She turned back to him, her shoulder's squared. "I found my destined life mate."

"Oh…"

All the blood drained from his face. He sat down and put his head in his hands. She waited, the tears beginning to spill from her eyes.

"Congratulations…I'm happy for you, even if I'm sad for myself. I just found you…" His voice was desolate.

She sat down next to him. "No. I'm going to reject him. I want to be with you."

"*What?* That's crazy, Erin. I mean, I want you, but we did only just get together. You can't give up your mate for me…The agony—"

"It's Maddox!" she shouted.

"Oh shit."

"Yeah! Exactly! After the funeral, I just lost it. My dad is dying, I felt so alone, the roof started leaking. I snapped. I knew he killed Selena. I grabbed a knife and headed to his house. I was going to kill him. I couldn't get through the magic protections around the place, but he came out and…Oh!" She wailed and covered her face. "I hate him so much."

Jaris knelt in front of her and rested his hands on her knees. "Did he do it? Did he kill Selena?"

"No. But still, it's his fault she's dead, even if he didn't cut her up. I won't stay with him."

"So why haven't you ended it already?" he asked.

She sniffed, trying to organize her thoughts. Why hadn't she? She had a reason. "I want to make him suffer first. I want to humiliate him the same way he's humiliated so many others, and now I have the power to do it."

Jaris frowned and looked down.

She wiped the tears from her cheeks. "What? Do you think me heartless?"

"No." He shook his head. "I understand, but is he really as bad as all that?"

"What? You're defending him?"

"No. I just wonder if the person behind the public persona is more real. I don't want you with him. Not for a second. But until you end it, how can we be together? I thought infidelity was impossible with life mates."

She exhaled raggedly. "That's why I kept jumping when you touched me. It burns."

"I see...What can I do to help you through this time?"

"Can you come to dinner tonight? I made a deal with my dad. I promised to bring you to meet him. He wants to know someone will care for me when he's gone. I'm not asking that of you, by the way," she added quickly. "To take care of me. I can take care of myself. It's just the way he thinks of it. It literally is the request of a dying man. Please?"

"Of course, Erin. I'll tell him how I feel about you and that I'll take care of you."

"Thank you." She leaned down and kissed him. She tried to ignore the pain, but after a second, she broke away. The burning was too intense. "I should go. I need to check into work for a while."

"I'll be by at dusk?"

"That's great. Thank you for this, Jaris."

"Sure." He smiled, but there was only sorrow in his eyes.

She touched his cheek. "I'm so sorry. Will you give me a few days? I'll make it right."

He ran his hands through his hair and sighed. "I'll wait...but you have to tell me if your feelings for Maddox change."

"They won't."

Erin went to the hub and waited in line for her turn to go to Halussis. Her mind and heart tussled and fought while she stared at her feet. She still had some time off work, but she really needed to see Journey.

A memory of her and Selena waiting right where she stood now thrust into the forefront of her mind. Grief massaged deep into her shoulders, over and over its ghostly fingers rubbed deep into her flesh, leaving brittleness behind.

While he was still at Tesla's house, everything Erin was feeling hit Maddox in the chest. He clutched at his heart and gasped.

Melina grabbed his hand. "You okay? What's happening?"

He shook his head and walked away. "I'm okay."

He went back outside and took a deep breath. It wasn't what she was feeling that hurt him, it was that he could do nothing to ease it from her. If things were different, he'd go to her. He wanted to. The most he could do was to tell her later that he felt it and wished he could have helped...

Wait. He lifted his head. Was that really all he could do? She could feel his emotions just as he could feel hers. He could feel something for her, send it to her.

Trying to feel happy would seem callous, and he didn't think it would balance what she felt. It would just be a sharp contrast that would seem jerky. He focused, comfort. Comfort was about joining the person suffering, at least in his mind. Empathy and understanding. He'd never lost a close friend to death. But he had lost someone he loved because they weren't who he thought they were. That was as close as he could come to it. As much as he didn't want to rehash something painful, he focused on his memories of his ex-lover, Bess, and how he felt when he learned the truth of her betrayal. Not the anger, but the pain.

Since she wouldn't let him hold her hand through this physically, he'd have to spiritually.

ELEVEN

"Erin! Erin!"

She laughed as the kids swarmed around her, hugging her waist and legs.

"We've missed you!"

She sat down cross-legged on the floor, letting them pile on her. "Oh, I missed you, too."

Their smiles and cuddles were sunlight to her heart. She listened attentively to their chatter and played dumb games with them, forgetting her troubles for a while.

"It's time for your afternoon lessons, children." Journey came in.

They all groaned dramatically but obeyed and headed off to the school room. Erin wanted to run into Journey's arms, but she held still, in a state of apprehension as the Storyteller stared at her chest, a look of mild surprise on her face. Then she looked up into Erin's eyes and smiled.

"Congratulations on finding your life mate."

Erin grimaced. "You can see that, can you?"

"Of course. It's helping you through this hard time, you know. Your spirit is stronger."

"Can you see who it is?"

Journey smirked. "No. But he's trying to help you right now, sending you feelings to try and ease your pain...You're lucky. You have a very thoughtful mate."

Erin rolled her eyes. "He is many things, but thoughtful is not one of them."

"Hmm..." She gave her a funny look and gestured for Erin to follow.

They headed down the hall and through the door to Redge and Journey's apartments. "Sit down, Erin. I'll make you some tea."

She sat at the comfortably worn table. Redge came in and sat down next to her, grabbing a cookie from the plate in the center of the table.

"How are you?" he asked. "Didn't expect to see you for a few more days."

"I know. I just needed to be here for a little while. Life is upside-down."

"Is it your dad?"

"No. I mean yeah, he's not good, but—"

Journey came back and poured tea for all of them and sat down. "She's found her life mate, Redge, but she's not too happy about it."

"Why is that?" he asked.

"It doesn't suit. I'm going to reject him."

"Ah, well. I rejected my own mate, you know. Never regretted it for a second." He covered Journey's hand with his own. "Who is it?"

She pursed her lips. "I better go. I need to get home and check on my dad. I'll be back to work in the morning."

"No you won't," Journey said sternly. "Not yet. If you want to drop in, you're always welcome, but you aren't working for a while yet."

She scampered out the door.

Journey snickered when she was gone, and Redge crossed his arms.

"Who is it?" he asked.

"You'll never guess..." She paused for dramatic effect. "It's Maddox."

He laughed. "You're right. I never would have guessed that. Knowing Erin, I see why she doesn't want to keep the connection."

"I hope she does, though." Her eyes slid out of focus. "Everyone's heart has a different resonance. Like music. Until I saw their connection in her heart, I never would have thought mixing his resonance with hers would have worked, but now that I've heard it...it not only works, it's beautiful."

Redge nodded thoughtfully. "Not many could be strong enough to save him. She is."

"Yes. And he's worth saving. I hope she realizes that before it's too late."

"I can't even imagine doing what she's contemplating. I never connected to my life mate. I didn't meet her first."

"Yes. She wants to cut out her own heart because she's mad."

"Always was a long temper on that one, despite how warm she is."

Maddox and Melina went back to his place when the afternoon grew long. The portal hummed inside the smooth little black box on the counter next to Erin's new watch. Melina put it on her wrist for the third time, holding her arm out, admiring the look of the scrolling band against her skin.

"It's so pretty. I love how it snakes around my arm."

"So why didn't you ask Tesla for one for yourself?"

"I dunno." She took it off again. "I'd feel like a freeloader."

"You should feel like an ass." He smirked. "You know Tesla wouldn't even blink if you asked."

"I hate asking for things."

"That's because you're spoiled rotten and you like things handed to you so you don't have to ask."

She chuckled. "I'm spoiled? That's the kettle-pot calling."

He laughed. "You have that saying screwed up, Mel. But you're right—takes one to know one."

He flopped onto the couch and scrolled through his new watch, wondering vaguely if his other new one was still floating around Fortress. He sighed, deleting his list of skanks. Tesla had transferred all of his contacts again, even though he hadn't asked her to. He didn't want them anymore. His list went from overflowing, down to just family and a few friends.

Melina's company really helped distract him, but the hours since he'd seen Erin began to feel like months. His body ached all over, and depression invaded and took over.

"You okay, M? You don't look so good."

He rubbed his temples as they began to throb. "I feel sick. How long has it been?"

"How long since when?"

"Since I saw Erin?"

"All day...I think you're getting separation sickness."

"Figures," he complained.

"What are you going to do?"

"I can either go to her and beg, or I can get wasted."

Melina crossed her arms. "What's option three?"

"There is no option three." He closed his eyes.

"I bet we can get her to come to you."

"How?"

His eyes shot open as Melina straddled him. He grabbed her hips. "No."

She raised her eyebrows. "I bet it would work."

"I want her to *stop* hating me." He gave her a little shove, and she moved off him with a shrug. "If you keep doing this kind of thing, it's going to get weird between us."

She laughed. "Relax. I'm not into you. I love you to death, just not like that. I'm just trying to help. You should trust me."

"I do, but you're kinda crazy."

"Don't forget it either. And crazy isn't all bad. Okay, I *am not* going to let you crawl to her. So, wasted it is."

"Really? You don't object?"

"Oh, I object big time, but I'm not going to let you fly alone. I'll make sure you're safe when you can't see clearly or form full sentences. And this might work well on Erin, too."

"How?"

"No idea. We'll just have to see."

"Why are you doing this? I haven't been that great of a friend to you, especially in the last year and a half."

She shrugged. "I'm loyal. This whole saga is entertaining as hell, and I don't have anything better to do."

He lifted his watch up.

"You're not messaging that slime ball, Kendrick, are you?"

"I was going to. What? He always has the best shit."

"I will not tolerate his society. It's him or me. You choose. He won't look out for you the way I will. We can go out. Hit the clubs if you want, but just not with him."

He sighed. There was no way he was going to throw Melina over for Kendrick after everything she had done for him in the last two days.

"All right. You and me."

"Good choice, boy-o. I'm going to get changed into something killer. I suggest you do the same. This is a date. We need to be seen holding hands and looking cozy for the cameras."

"You're evil, Mel." He said it with deep affection, and she took it as the compliment it was meant to be. "I don't want to stay out too long. Erin said she'd come back tonight."

The skin was already growing cold as the blade sliced through the girl's arm. Trina, or Tracy, he didn't remember or care much. The only thing that mattered was she'd been with Maddox in the last month. Kendrick meticulously carved Maddox's name on her the same way he had on Selena.

He laid her out and surveyed the scene. Nothing about it was near as good as Selena because she'd still had physical evidence on her, but Maddox had stopped whoreing for the last few days. He figured he'd snap out of it soon, but Kendrick couldn't be idle until that happened.

He looked up at the darkening sky. All traces of the girl's overdose would be gone in two hours. That's when he could play anonymous tipper and call it in. His watch pinged. Kendrick's eyes widened with rage as he saw new pictures of Maddox, out and about without him, and Melina cozy on his arm, to boot. What the hell was going on? His insides writhed. Maddox never went out without him, and Melina was supposed to be his, and for once, he wouldn't accept a hand-me-down. She was perfect because Maddox didn't touch her. What had changed?

He enlarged the pictures, looking beyond them to figure out where they were...central Paradigm. Why would they be there? Maddox hated the regular night scene there. He narrowed his eyes. The only reason to go there was *to be* seen. What was he up to? Kendrick needed to finish up with the body and get over there. This was going to mess up his timeline and the false account of Maddox's actions and whereabouts he was going to feed the media.

At least Maddox was partying again, and that still made him look like a prick so soon after Selena's death.

Kendrick pulled the corked bottle from his pocket and opened it slowly. His mother had given him this bottle of illegal off-world stuff and instructed him how to use it. Holding his breath, he poured the dust on the body. The dust lit up, sliding over her skin and around her. A flash lit the space and died out. He walked away, confident the dust had erased any evidence he left behind.

Erin made dinner. Her dad was up in his chair, looking pale, but in better spirits than she'd seen him in very long time. Her hands shook as she set the table. She took a deep breath, closed her eyes, and let it out slowly. *It doesn't hurt that bad*. She told herself for the hundredth time.

What was it going to feel like when she rejected Maddox?

One hundred percent worth it, no matter how it hurt. Anything was better than being tied to him for the rest of her life.

The glass in her hand slipped. The shattering made her jump. A tremble quaked around her heart. Stress. Like any muscle overtired and overworked, her heart was warning her it had reached a danger point. She only had two choices. She could find Maddox now, or…

Erin ran to her room and grabbed the rock off her dresser and held it against her chest.

"You okay, honey?" her dad called.

"Fine. Just a minute. I need to change into something nicer."

Her pulse eased and relaxed. Relieved, she put the rock back and changed into a somewhat dressy blouse. She would be okay enough to get through the evening, but she realized she would have to keep her appointment to see Maddox before the night was over.

She looked at herself in the mirror and wanted to cry. What was she doing? Her connection to Maddox was new. How long could she manage like this? How much humiliation for him would satisfy her?

Unbidden, a wave of desire moved through her. Her eyes rolled back, and her mouth grew hot. She licked her lips, remembering connecting to him. Her mind blurred with it, and her body jolted. The physical memory was suddenly overwhelming. And her body began to rage with desire for him. Her cheeks heated in embarrassment. Could he feel this from her?

Her watch pinged. Damn it. Guess the answer was yes. She grimaced as she opened the message from Maddox.

Are you thinking about me, darling?

She whimpered, feeling she would die of embarrassment. *Pull it together! You can bluff your way through this.*

Nope. **She wrote.** This heat is all Jaris.

Her watch refused to play along. The message wouldn't send. Another message came through.

I feel you... and now I'm thinking of the rain.

She closed her eyes, shivers rising and falling through her body. Damn him.

A knock sounded on the front door. She took her watch off and put it in her sock drawer. There. Now he couldn't bother her—for a while at least. She only wished she had the time to splash cold water on her face. Erin shook herself and went to open the door.

Dinner was everything she hoped and needed it to be. Jaris was so kind and polite to her dad, and he seemed more energetic than he had been in so long. When it was time for dessert, Jaris' watch pinged. He looked at it for a moment, then he put his hand under the table in his lap. His watch pinged again and then again.

"I'm sorry," he said getting up. "Excuse me...Erin, would you join me outside on the porch for a moment?"

"What is it?" she asked, going out and closing the door behind her.

"I'm sorry, I just...After you visited me earlier today, I set my notifications to track you and Maddox."

"Oh. Okay. What's going on?"

He showed her his watch. She blinked a few times as she looked at the pictures of Maddox and the blonde that had been at his house that morning. They looked *together*. It cut a wound in her soul, made her feel sick, and sent a wave of relief through her all at the same time.

"What does it mean?" Jaris asked.

"I told him I'm not giving you up." She shrugged. "I guess he's got someone else he doesn't intend to give up either."

Jaris frowned, looking back at the news. "I don't know about this, Erin, it's screwed up. I feel weird about it. Your dad is dying, and all he wants is for you to have a life mate. And you have one. But here I am, pretending to be more to you than I am."

"It's not going to last!" she insisted. "Please."

She wrapped her arms around his neck. He pulled her tight against him and kissed her mouth. The pain was terrible, but she ignored it and tried to throw herself into the kiss. Would the pain ease the more she kissed

Jaris? His hands moved over her back, lighting her up everywhere he touched like flash paper.

Someone cleared their throat. She jumped and looked around, her stomach swooping. Maddox was there, arms crossed, casually leaning against the porch newel post.

"Forgive my intrusion, but I'm going to have to object to this."

"Why are you here?" she demanded.

Maddox glanced at her and then set his sights on Jaris. "She's mine, in case you were unaware…and I've grown tired of being burned today. Perhaps you'd be willing to not touch my mate again until tomorrow. I'd appreciate it."

Jaris straightened up and took a step toward Maddox. Maddox just quirked an eyebrow at him.

"Are you really that smug, or is it a cover?" Jaris demanded.

"Smug?" Fire lit Maddox's eyes. "You've got your hands on my life mate. I ask you nicely to stop. That makes me smug?"

"She was mine first," Jaris yelled.

"Yeah, cause that really matters," he mocked. "My claim is still stronger than yours."

"You don't deserve her," Jaris insisted harshly.

"I'm aware of that."

"Let her go then!"

"Hmm…no."

Jaris moved first.

"Don't do this!" she pleaded, but they were already in a shoving match.

"Stop!" She pushed in between them. "Just stop."

They both dropped their raised fists. She looked desperately at Maddox.

He frowned. "We have an appointment, Erin."

"I'll be there in one hour, okay?"

"Fine." His voice was clipped. "If you don't show, I'll come back. Fair warning."

"All right!" she yelled.

He walked down the stairs, and a portal opened and swallowed him. She turned to Jaris. "I'm sorry. I don't know what to say."

"Do you want me to back off?"

"No. Please don't."

"He said appointment. What does that mean?"

"The connection is making both of us sick, physically. Being near one another lessens the pain. We agreed to meet so it wouldn't be so severe that neither one of us would lose sleep. That's all."

"What are you going to do with him?"

"Nothing," she insisted. "We might hold hands for a few minutes, that's all. Trust me, that's all I can stand."

"Okay. I'll go back in and say goodnight to your dad, and then I'll be on my way."

"Thank you so much for this. It's all kinds of wrong. I'm sorry Maddox showed up here. All this just really sucks."

"Yeah...It's okay, Erin. You're worth fighting for."

They went back in. He said good night to her dad and left. She cleaned up the table and helped her dad back into bed.

"So, what did you think?" she asked as she covered him up.

"What was going on when you were outside? I looked out the window. Looks like you've got another young man vying for your affection. I thought that was going to get serious there for a second, until you broke it up. I was a little disappointed. I haven't seen a good fight in a while."

"Dad!"

He laughed weakly. "What? If it had come to it, my money would have been on the rangy one. He's been trained in the Kata—you can see it in the way he moves. What's his name?"

She shrugged. "Can't remember."

"Ha! You're a bad liar, girl. I don't pay attention to current events, but he looks like someone I've seen. Someone famous, I think. I'll make you another deal. You bring that other guy around to meet me, and I'll decide to get a bit better."

"Really not fair, Dad."

"Eh. Fair or not, what do say?"

"I'll think about it. Now you rest. I have somewhere I have to be."

He barked out a laugh louder than she would have thought possible for him. "You're juggling them, aren't you?"

"Ugh. Just rest."

"Okay. I won't wait up for you."

She scowled, turned off his bedside lamp, and left the room. She took stock of her appearance in the mirror for a second. *I don't care what he thinks of the way I look.* But she still found herself freshening up and slicking her lips with gloss before heading out into the night. She didn't want to be seen by anyone, so she pulled from her elf blood and went invisible before using her vampire ability to run really fast.

She got there in a few minutes and dropped the invisibility just outside the protective dome. It shimmered and let her through again. She crossed into the dark garden, it was lit only by the lights in the windows of the house. She stopped and stared at the house. She hadn't actually looked at it before. Erin blinked, an unconscious smile lifting her lips. The family was super rich, everyone knew that. But this was awesome in a real life way. Cozy and charming. This was where Maddox had grown up?

She didn't go to the door. Instead, she sat down on a bench next to a fountain. She hadn't looked at the garden before either, even though the location was forever burned into her psyche. The desire came back with the memory. She breathed deep and leaned back on the bench. She didn't fight against remembering. She just relaxed as Maddox took her again, right there in the rain, in her mind. There was no rain now. She looked up into the clear night sky as the dreamlike memory shifted through her. Her body remembered as clearly as her mind.

It's my memory. Nothing can change that.

Tears threatened again as she thought of Selena. It wasn't fair. If Maddox was to be hers, why did she have to share him with Selena or anyone else?

Erin shook herself, furious at her errant train of thought. The pain must be twisting her mind. Pain. She focused on the pain in her body. That's why she was here. *Just get your medicine and leave.* The connection was trying to manipulate her. She wouldn't let it.

The front door opened, throwing a band of light across her. Maddox walked out slowly.

"Are you coming in, or would you prefer to do this outside?"

"Is she here?" Erin demanded.

"Who?"

"The blonde."

"No. And her name's Melina."

"I don't care what her name is!" Erin snapped.

He held his hands up. "It sounds like you care."

"Fuck you."

"I'm ready for that. Seems you are, too. All that heat you've been sending me just now and earlier... Inside or out?"

She didn't budge and seriously considered bolting. This was a bad idea.

"I want to talk to you." His voice changed, no longer combative. "I'll make you something to drink."

She stood then and sighed. She wasn't afraid of him, and she needed to take control. She marched up to the front of the house and pushed past him. He closed the door. She instantly felt trapped. The connection reared up and was already trying to bring them together. She sat on the couch and looked down.

"I don't want anything to drink. Thanks anyway."

"Are you going to run away if I sit next to you?"

"No," she grumbled. "You wanted to talk to me? Talk."

He sat down close, but he didn't touch her. The proximity made her skin hum. Everywhere Jaris had touched her hurt again, only worse than before. She whimpered and leaned forward.

"Will you touch my back? It hurts so much."

His hand pressed flat against her shoulder blade. She cried out and then bit down on her lip. "Lower." She breathed.

He ran his hand up and down all over her back repeatedly. The pain turned to a dull ache, then faded and was replaced by warmth and light under the surface. It felt so good, she lost herself in it.

"I'm sorry," she said before she could think what in the hell she was saying.

"What?"

"Um...for burning you. I hurt both of us."

He took his hand off her and stood up. She looked at him, confused as he moved to a chair and sat across from her.

"I tried to burn you, too. Didn't you feel it?"

"What do you mean?"

"Earlier in the day. I assume you were with Jaris. He touched you? He kissed you?"

She nodded.

"I felt it all. I knew what was happening."

Erin put her hand to her lips. "Yes. I had a moment where it hurt worse, burned hotter on my mouth...So, I let Jaris touch me, and it hurts but it hurts you worse...You kissed someone else, it hurt you, but it burned my mouth worse."

"I was trying to test it. Sorry."

She shook her head. "No. That's okay. So, you and Melina are together?"

He sighed and looked away.

"It's okay. I saw the pictures from tonight, or were those fake like the headlines this morning?"

"Melina's trying to help me. She thought if we were seen by lots of people, then whoever has targeted me will have a harder time of it because I had my own witnesses of where I was...but that's what I wanted to talk to you about, or sort of. It's connected."

He wrung his hands together and grimaced.

"You okay?" she asked.

He dropped his hands. "Yeah. I just want to touch you again." He shook his head. "Anyway. I wanted to talk to you about Selena."

Her mouth pressed into a thin line, and her eyes burned. "Tread. Very. Lightly."

He stood and began to pace. "Okay, maybe a different angle...I don't fully understand why you hate me. Is it just what happened with Selena?"

"No. That's not all, but it would be more than enough."

He stopped pacing and sat back down, gazing at her intently. "Tell me. I'll listen. You are judge, jury, and executioner, Erin. Why do you hate me? Tell me all of it."

Her heart sped at the thought of laying into him without restraint, but she took a deep breath and tried to organize her thoughts. *Cold*, she schooled herself. *Be cold as ice.* "Why should I tell you anything?"

She gasped as a pang of heartbreak smarted in her chest. It wasn't hers. It was his. She gaped at him, recognizing for the first time she felt his emotions. Her lungs contracted around the feeling and arrested her breathing. She looked into his eyes. They were filling with tears. He turned his face away from her. She shouldn't do this.

"Okay, Maddox. You asked for it...Look at me."

He did, and the world seemed to live between his eyes and hers.

"I have always admired your family, as most Regian's do. All of them seem to... *bless* everything they touch, and as loved and revered as they are, all of them are humble, except you. You're nothing but a pretty face with an amazing heritage. That wouldn't be so bad on its own, but you are hurtful. You hurt the people around you for the hell of it, or perhaps it's more than that and you get off on hurting others. I don't know...It's like this fury behind your eyes. You're angry or something, and you have no right to be angry." She paused.

He frowned at her but didn't speak.

She continued. "I hate the way you treat women. The way you use and then throw them away like trash, with no respect at all. And then my dear friend has the misfortune to catch your eye. I warned her to stay away from you. I knew you'd hurt her. You did, and now she's dead. I know you didn't kill her, but it's your fault. That's why I hate you."

He leaned back, his expression turning contemplative. "Is there more?"

"Are you a masochist as well as a sadist? Isn't that enough?"

"It's enough, I just want it all."

She threw her hands up. Then she chuckled, the tension breaking inside her. "I hate your face. And your hands. And your body. I hate that you make me want you. I hate the way my body sang with you. I hate that I can't deny the appeal you have, just the way you look. And I hate that so many women have been with you. It makes me feel tainted." All the color drained from her face, and she put her hands on her mouth. "I can't believe I just said all that. Forget it please."

"I don't think I could if I tried."

She sat back down on the couch and stared at him.

"You want to hurt me, don't you? You want revenge?"

"Yes." She breathed.

"I see."

"I'm going to reject you, Maddox. I can't see any other way."

"My gosh…" He put his head in his hands. "You're serious."

"Completely."

He opened his mouth, closed it, and shook his head. "Why haven't you done it then?" His tone turned harder.

"I'm not finished hurting you. I haven't even started."

"So we're enemies then?"

"Unequivocally."

He smiled, catching her off guard, and causing her disquiet.

"Why are you smiling?"

His smile grew. "Was I?"

She got her feet. "See? This is why I hate you. You're terrible."

"Are you leaving then? Is your pain manageable?"

She hesitated. He stood and reached for her before she could think, taking her forearms in his hands. The pain was shoved back. She caught her lip between her teeth and fought to not moan. The only defense she had was to close her eyes and not look at him.

"You can hurt me, but I won't hurt you. I've done enough of that already. I'm sorry about Selena. I did treat her badly. I wish I could take it back... But you don't know me. You don't know my family...I believe in us, Erin. I have hope."

Her eyes snapped open. "I didn't think you a fool, but you are. Why would you say that?"

"I trust destiny doesn't make mistakes. So you go ahead and strike at me. I deserve it. I won't dodge my guilt, and I won't retaliate."

"What about Melina?"

"It's not quite as it appears...like a few other things you're so sure of. There." He released her and stepped back. "Same time tomorrow?"

"Fine." She glared.

"I have something for you."

"I'm not interested in gifts from the likes of you."

"Sure. You've made yourself clear how you feel. And it's not so much a gift as...a necessity I think. Hold on."

She sighed and held still as he walked into the other room. He was back in a second, holding a small box and a watch.

"This is for you," he wrapped the watch around her wrist. She was so taken with it she didn't even think to object. The band felt like a second skin and snaked around her wrist like a flowering vine. The surface of the face trembled and the words *Hello, Erin* swirled in the middle. She touched it, scrolled through it.

"I've never seen tech like this."

"It hasn't hit the market yet. I had Tesla make it for you today. It's connected to mine, in case you actually need me some time. And you can't delete or block me, so forget those thoughts. I can see you were already plotting."

"Okay. I'll keep it. Now I can at least respond with venom when you drunk dial me, like earlier."

"I wasn't drunk. Not from lack of trying. Getting burned repeatedly has a sobering effect."

He handed her the box. "Don't open it until you're home. It's a portal. It will connect your room to mine. Wait!" he grabbed her hand as she was about to throw the box. "You can close it on your end. I won't be able to come through it unless you open it on your side. Even then, I won't unless you ask me. My side will always be open to you."

"This is pointless."

"Oh? I thought it would make things more convenient for you. I can go where I want when I want. This way you don't have to come on foot for our next *appointment,* since you've made it clear you don't want me at your house...Just take it with you. You can think about it."

"I'll take it, but it will be a cold day in hell when I open it."

He shrugged. "It's yours. You decide what to do with it."

She narrowed her eyes. "I meant everything I said. I'm going to hurt you. It's not a game."

"Oh no? Sounds like a game. And just because I said I won't hurt you, doesn't mean I won't be making moves to achieve what I want. And here's my first move."

"What, the watch?"

"No," he wrapped his hand around her wrist and pulled her closer. "If I was the person you've accused me of being, I would take you right now."

Her eyes widened. "You wouldn't...I'd fight."

"You think so?" He moved in, his voice dropping. "I have the connection on my side. You're already lit up for me. You can't hide it, Erin. I feel it. Your body will tell me the truth, even when your mouth lies. If I was that person, I'd kiss you. I'd put my hands on you. You might fight, but I'd take you under in seconds, and you'd surrender. You'd fight me to give you more, like you did the first time."

She trembled, trying to hold herself strong. He was right. "You've made it all about you. Your choice. Your power. You can't ever have me like that."

"No. I *won't* ever have you like that. It's not that I can't." He let go and stepped back from her.

She headed to the door and stopped. "Bad move, Maddox."

"Go home." His voice was cold and he turned his back on her.

She closed the door behind her, but she didn't leave immediately. Fury slid molten under her skin. Was she in over her head with him? She faced the house again.

"I hate you!" she shouted at the door.

"Yeah, yeah," he called back from the other side. "You're mine."

Oh! She wanted to kick things. She marched home, burning in more than one way. She would make him pay for that tomorrow.

Maddox tried to analyze his time with Erin. As much as she'd driven spikes into his soul, she had let him know the truth. He had her reasons for hating him. That gave him a direction. But he didn't have much time. She was going to end it after she'd abused him. Panic licked around his heart at the thought of her rejecting him. He couldn't stop her, but he wasn't going to lay down and play dead. Maybe he'd done the wrong thing just then, but it was too late to take back.

He sighed and flopped onto his bed. If she was as good as her word, he was in for a few rough days.

His watch buzzed. Kendrick was calling. Not messaging but actually calling. He never did that. Maddox answered.

"Yeah?"

"The hell, man? You go out without me, and I have to see it in the media?"

"Sorry. Melina wouldn't let me contact you. I told you she hates you."

"I need to use that hate to tap into other things. But it looks like you lied about you and her."

He shook his head. Kendrick was pissed at him. He didn't know how much more negativity he could take tonight. "I didn't lie. It was just about optics. I'm trying to give myself alibies...Anyway, the only thing you're going to get if you pursue Mel is broken bones."

"Maybe you're full of shit and want her as your fall back."

"Mel would never be anyone's fall back. Anyway, I've got someone."

Kendrick was quiet for a second. "Someone new?"

Maddox hesitated. He wasn't going to tell Kendrick Erin was his mate, but maybe he should give him the heads up on her, that she might be around and was off limits.

"Yeah. Mystery Girl."

"You're lying!" Kendrick laughed.

"Okay. Believe what you want."

"You said you didn't want her."

"Are you nuts? You've seen her."

"Yeah. That's why I was confused when you said you were passing."

"I was just in a bad mood."

Kendrick laughed again. "You are my king. How in the hell did you swing that? She has a totally *not happening* vibe about her."

"Yeah, she does." Maddox smiled. "She's a bit of work, I can tell you. The challenge is a nice change. We're exclusive though. Keep your distance."

"Sure. Until you're done."

"I'm not going to be done with her anytime soon." *Or ever.*

"Sounds serious."

"Um hm."

"Have you hit that yet? You have to tell me."

Maddox frowned, suddenly disgusted by his friend, and he realized this was exactly the way they always talked.

"She's a game changer, Kendrick."

He groaned. "Oh, man. Don't do this to me. You can't mellow out. Your reputation has reached epic levels."

"Maybe it's time for you to step out of my shadow. I'll pass the mantle to you...Look, I'm going to go."

"Is she there now?"

"Goodnight." Maddox hung up.

He closed his eyes, but he was restless as hell. Sleep was going to evade him tonight. He let everything go and tried to just focus on Erin and what she was feeling. He sighed. She was still pissed. Their conversation replayed in his mind, and he found himself smiling unintentionally, particularly when he thought about her saying she hated that he made her want him. She'd admitted she was attracted to him. He hadn't expected that. He thought maybe she didn't like the way he looked and that was part of her initial violent reaction to their connection.

He realized he hadn't really told her anything like that yet. How gorgeous she was to him. That would change the next time she let him talk. He'd tell her everything he thought about her beauty. She would probably accuse him of using his charm on her to get his way. He'd have to think his way around that. What could he say to convince her how he really felt?

It couldn't wait. He would start now. She would fuss; that was fine. He'd wait till he had her alone to *really* tell her, but he could message her with small things now.

Just one thing, he decided, and he wouldn't respond to any caustic replies.

He thought about the usual things guys say. Things he'd said countless times to warm a girl up. None of that was going to be a part of this.

The rain... and your perfect skin... under my hands.

That was all. He sent it.

Erin sat on the floor in her room, trying to distract herself from her time with Maddox by looking over the overdue household bills. He unsettled her. She didn't have a handle on him at all. The way he acted, the things he said, it surprised her. She would never have thought he'd ask for her to tell him off, and then if there was more. It didn't matter, she reminded herself. She would be ending it soon. She shouldn't try to think her way clear. She would get her revenge for Selena and move on with her life.

Her new watch pinged. She read his message her eyebrows pulling down. *What?* She read it again. Nine words. A fragment of a sentence and he had her right back there in the rain. She considered what type of nasty reply she should send and found she didn't have the heart at that moment. She could think of nothing to say. Yet she had to say something. He was going to use that memory on her over and over because it was his ace....

Inspiration struck. Torture could take different forms. Oh, yeah. Two could play that game. *Careful, Erin, this game is dangerous.*

A storm...and your hunter's eyes...all over me.

She sent it, a dark smile on her lips. *Take that, player. I can take you back there, too. To something you will never have again.*

Her watch pinged.

Touché...Goodnight, Erin.

Running scared? **She messaged back.**

Hell, yes. Enjoying it though.

She hesitated then typed. Goodnight, Maddox.

A second after she sent it, she wished she hadn't. What the hell was that? Looked like flirting. Ugh. Her watch pinged again.

I was being sincere.

She pursed her lips and decided to leave it. No more contact tonight.

TWELVE

Redge looked at the dead girl. It wasn't right. The whole thing was staged. He glanced at Kindel.

"Should we get Forest back?" Kindel asked.

"Not yet."

"This is going to escalate."

"Yeah," Redge sighed. "I think this is just the beginning."

"We need to keep this quiet. Do you think Maddox is the ultimate target? Or just who they want to take the fall?"

"Too soon to know. The whole damn thing is sloppy, but it's almost as if..."

"Sloppy on purpose?" Kindel added.

"Yeah...This framing isn't about evidence. There is none. The perp is seeking the court of public opinion to destroy Maddox. They want this in the media. You want to go talk to him, or should I?"

"Let's keep this in the family. Tesla should do it. I need to get started working that dust, and then I need to go under...start catching the threads of this web so we can find the spider before any more girls die. If they want this seen and we don't show it..."

"We need a detail on Maddox, but he doesn't need to know it's there."

"Agreed."

Maddox woke in agony. Every inch of him, inside and out, felt bludgeoned. He lifted his hands and watched them shake for a second. Gosh, what was she doing to him? He didn't know it could be this bad. His stomach twisted with nausea, and cold sweat chilled him to the bone. He'd said he would take it. He'd said he wouldn't strike back. He had no idea what he was saying when he said that.

I'm sorry, Erin. He tried to send remorse to her, hoping she could feel it. Hoping she would acknowledge it.

She threw her hatred at him like a javelin. She weaponized her pain and stabbed him with it over and over. But it wasn't just her pain of losing Selena. She shredded him with her contempt.

He wanted to call her. Beg her to stop. Plead with her to ease up, even just a little. But his pride held him still. He wouldn't let her see how disarmed he was. She needed to do this to him. He'd take it in silence. He tried to mediate through it, wishing he had his father's discipline in the Kata.

Excruciation crashed over him. She was going to break him much faster than he'd anticipated. He rubbed his eyes, his vision clouding, his thoughts skittering in all directions. Someone touched him. He blinked, looking up into Tesla's face.

She put both of her hands on his chest, power sliding into him.

"Don't," he breathed. "It's all right. Don't try to shield me."

She sniffed, looking annoyed. The sensation from her hands shifted, filling him with a numbness.

"No," he argued again. "I have to own this."

She removed her hands and crossed her arms. "I don't think her hating you is funny anymore."

"It's okay."

"Hmm...what's wrong with her? Doesn't she know that hurting you only hurts her in return? And what's wrong with you? Why haven't you been able to convince her she's overjoyed to be with you? Where are all your smooth skills you've worked so hard to perfect?"

"My skill is exactly why she hates me. I can't work her."

"The hell you can't. Pull your head out of your ass."

He took a deep breath and sat up, the room only spun a little. "Mind your own business."

"I love you."

"It's nice someone does. I really did bring this on myself. Don't worry about it, Tes."

She huffed and left the room. In a second, she was back with a glass of water. It shook in his hand as he tried to drink. He sighed as the cool liquid slid down his throat, easing the nausea.

"What did you do to me?" he asked.

"Not much. I just numbed your heart a little. Is it some better?"

"Yeah. Some."

"Good, cause I have bad news."

He groaned. "I can't take it."

"No choice, Maddie."

"I'm serious, Tesla. I can't take anything else right now."

"There's another dead girl with your name carved into her skin."

He hung his head, tears burning his eyes. "Did I know her?"

"Yeah, Trish. You went out with her."

A stream of obscenities came pouring out of him. "I don't get this! She killed herself like Selena?"

"No. She was murdered. It was all staged. Someone is trying to frame you. It's good you were out with Melina last night. The murder happened while you were in public. I think it's important you keep that up. You need to be seen. And you need to act like nothing is wrong."

"You mean I need to act like a dick."

"Yeah. Redge is keeping news of the dead girl hushed up."

"I don't feel well enough to go out and play lothario. Look at me."

She pursed her lips. "You have a point there. Here." She held her wrist next to his mouth. "Drink my blood."

He frowned. He'd never drunk his sister's blood. "Um...why?"

"I can't stop what Erin is doing to you, but I can give you the strength to get through today. Trust me. My blood will fix you up."

He managed a weak smirk. "Cause you're so awesome? The elixir of life flows in your veins?"

"Damn straight. Just drink. Not much, or it will go from being good for you to damaging."

He bit into her wrist, her blood filling his mouth. He swallowed, his eyes bugging. "That is all kinds of wrong!" he exclaimed. Lightning raced through his body. He'd never felt stronger or healthier. Only one thing felt better…Connecting with Erin. "So not fair. I wish I just had some of what makes you…so awesomely freaky. Geez, Tesla. I feel like I could take on the world."

"Good. Cause you kinda have to now. You have a murderer trying to frame you and a vengeful mate."

He paced for a moment, looking at the floor. "Do I really have to go out tonight? I just want to be with Erin."

"What does Mom always say?"

He huffed. "*What you want is irrelevant.*"

"If this story about Trish comes out, we'll have to shift gears. You'll have to make a public statement. If that happens, you need to convince Erin to make your status public. She could protect you, just by standing beside you."

"She won't. And I am *not* asking."

Tesla shook her head. "I'll have to repeat myself. Pull your head out of your ass."

"Thanks," he said acidly.

"I'm going. Don't tell anyone about Trish."

"What about Mel?" he asked.

"She knows. I called her before I came here. I'm sure she'll be here later to play girlfriend again tonight. You really don't deserve her."

"I know it. I'm going to have to get her a really big gift or something...Thanks for the drink."

"Sure. Let me know if I can do anything. You can come stay at my house if you want."

"I appreciate it, but I'd rather suffer alone."

She gave him a quick hug, tore open the air, and was gone. Alone, he tried to think clearly. Tried. It wasn't working, but at least he wasn't out of his head, writhing in pain. The pain was still there, oddly scratching beneath the surface. Thinking about what the night was going to have to be like, he decided he needed to talk to Erin. He messaged her.

I need to talk to you. It's important.

It will have to wait till tonight. I'm on my way to see Jaris.

He ground his teeth as he typed. Something bad has happened. Because of it, I have to go out tonight and act the way everyone expects. I don't want to. It's not real.

That makes no sense.

It would if you'd let me talk to you.

Sorry. Jaris is more important than your trivial issue you want to try and manipulate me with.

He narrowed his eyes at her message and imagined slapping her ass. The mental image boosted his mood.

I'll be out with Melina tonight...unless you'd rather be beside me.

He stared at his watch. It took her a while to respond. Too long really. Was she thinking it over?

Nope. I'll meet you at your house for our appointment. That's it...You been feeling me today?

Yes.

How does it feel?

Like shit. How does it make you feel, Erin? You enjoying what you're doing to me?

Very much.

You're lying.

He waited. It took her too long again to respond.

Don't message me again today. I'll see you tonight.

He smirked. *You can't block me, baby.* It was time to move on her again. If she was going to see her chump boyfriend, she wasn't going to do it with her head clear of him.

Your hair…like gold burning flame…brands me forever.

Stop it.

I want you, Erin…I'll always want you. Even with a knife in your hand.

She didn't respond. He smiled. *Gottcha.*

A few minutes later, she made him pay. Jaris was all over her. Gah, he wanted to die. The burning was blistering, but it was nothing to the rage he felt. Erin was *his*. Even if it was only for a few more days.

His anger mixed with sorrow. No, she wasn't his, despite their connection. She wasn't his, and she never would be. He focused on his breathing. The burning stopped abruptly.

He waited for it to start again. Nothing. Remorse hit him in the chest. It was hers. She was sorry. He jumped at the opportunity and messaged her again.

It doesn't have to be like this.

Erin pulled into herself and read his message. Tears slid down her cheeks. Jaris knocked on the door she'd locked.

"I'm sorry," she called. "Please just leave me alone for a few minutes."

All day, she'd been after Maddox. Trying everything she could think of to hurt him and hating herself every second for it. She'd never sought to hurt anyone or anything on purpose. And yet, that was all that consumed her now. How could she hurt him more? And she was using Jaris at the same time to do it. But what would it say to Maddox if she stopped now? He would win. She couldn't let him win. After everything he'd done...it was up to her to make him pay. Why wasn't this job given to someone stronger?

Her thoughts and feelings went to war.

She splashed water on her face, her heart twisting with shame. She knew Maddox would be able to feel it. Her time with him last night came back into her head. He really could have coerced her into bed, *easily*. He knew it, but he didn't do it. He didn't want her to break it off. Why? Why would he want to be tied down to one woman at all?

She thought about the blonde, Melina. Her ego reeled back like it had been bitch slapped. There was no way she measured up to Melina. Not only was she gorgeous, she exuded a strong sense of self. Erin wasn't anything like that. She could understand why he would want Melina. She couldn't understand why he would want her. It had to be the connection and nothing more that made him say things.

The rain...and your perfect skin...under my hands.

Her heart trembled as she thought about his words last night. She'd never be able to forget them. She wasn't equipped to fight against him. She was just another stupid girl. Her heart and ego sank together. Her watch pinged again.

Erin...I don't know why you're feeling this, but I wish you weren't. I don't want you to feel like this. Not ever. No matter what you do to me.

She winced. Yep. Just another stupid girl.

Leave me alone.

She waited. He didn't respond. She sighed, pushed her long hair back away from her face, and unlocked the door. Jaris stood there, waiting.

"Oh, sweetheart." He pulled her into his arms.

She buried her face in his shoulder and cried.

"What's that bastard doing to you?"

"Nothing," she sniffed. "It's me. I'm striking at him."

"I thought that's what you wanted."

"It is. It was. I don't know. The reality is uglier than the idea."

"Ugly?" his voice took on an edge she'd never heard from him before. "How ugly were Selena's cut wrists?"

She shuddered.

"That's what I thought." He pushed. "Put some steel in your spine."

A chill swept through her. "Jaris...I just..."

"Maybe you weren't as good of a friend to her as you've claimed...He's getting into your head. You can't listen to anything he says. It's what he does, Erin. You know that. Don't wind up like Selena, or any of the rest of his throwaways. Don't listen to his lies."

She nodded. "Yeah. You're right."

She spent the rest of the day with Jaris, but she couldn't stand to let him kiss her again. It hurt too much, and all the pain she'd been heaping on Maddox now pushed back on her, sinking an ache down into her bones. The pain spread madness through her mind. She closed her eyes and saw Maddox. *I want to touch you. I want the rain. I want the world to go away. Nothing but you and me and no hate in-between. My heart living in yours and yours in mine. Destined. Who am I to know better than destiny?*

She shook herself. *No! No! No! Stop it. Just hold strong for a few more days. Then you can walk away and never look back.* Her watch pinged. She took a deep breath before reading his message.

I'll be at the Main Street Club in Paradigm by dark. Come. I want to dance with you.

What about Melina?

She will be there, but I don't want Melina. I want you.

"What do you think?" she asked Jaris, showing him Maddox's request.

He snickered. "Idiot." Then his eyes lit up. "Let's go! You and me. This is the perfect set up. You can humiliate him publicly."

Erin cringed inside. "I don't know. What would we do?"

"You could tease him. String him along. Let everyone see how gone he is over you, and then you can make a scene. Tell him off. Make fun of him. Let everyone see."

"I don't like to be the center of attention."

"He does. You can hit him right where it will hurt the most, in his inflated ego...You'll need something killer to wear. Like a little black dress. Something like that."

"I don't have anything like that."

He looked out the windows at the sky. We've got a few hours before it gets dark. Let's go shopping and grab dinner."

"I'm broke, Jaris."

"My treat. Come on. Let's go."

It was the most uncomfortable time Erin could remember ever having. Every fiber of her being pulled away from the thought of what she was planning on doing. Yet here she was trying on a black slip of a dress with cutouts at the waist and a slit so high up one leg it was lewd. It wasn't that expensive, but still...Jaris was paying for this. Everything felt wrong.

She stepped out of the dressing room, her cheeks burning. He didn't seem to notice. Instead, he grabbed her and kissed her hard on the mouth, holding her a little too intimately. Her skin burned under his touch. She pulled away, feeling dirty.

"Sorry," he said. "You in that dress...made me lose my head. It's perfect. You're a goddess, Erin."

"It's almost dark. I need a few other things, and I'll be ready. Just a few minutes."

He just nodded like he would have agreed to anything. She grabbed a pair of black stilettos and a gold bangle for her wrist to finish her look. She headed to the beauty counter. She sprayed some stuff in her hair, teased out some curls with her fingers, and put on a true red lip color from the samples. She turned to Jaris. He stared at her like he'd been bashed over the head.

"I'll pay you back for all this. Promise."

"Don't worry about it."

The night was pleasantly warm as they walked down the streets of Paradigm. Everyone they passed looked at her. She felt their eyes follow her. If her stomach wasn't squirming, she might have enjoyed it. She tried to hold her head up and exude confidence and indifference. Jaris held her arm possessively. He seemed ecstatic, as if her being on his arm made him the emperor or something.

She heard the music of the club the closer they came. *What am I doing? I don't want to do this. How do I stop it?* She pinched her eyes shut for a second. *This is no big deal. It's just a little salt in the wound. Think of Selena. Remember her wrists.* Her anger surfaced again. She embraced it like an old friend. She needed it now.

THIRTEEN

Mel sat on the floor painting her toenails a bright red to match her dress, humming along to whatever she was playing in her earbuds. Maddox scowled at his closet. He didn't want to look too overdressed, in case Erin showed up. She wasn't going to. But in case. He wanted to be able to breathe. And he was fantasizing about dancing with her. If only she would. It was a fantasy. She wasn't going to show, and if by some miracle she did, she wouldn't dance with him.

He put on a black suit jacket over his jeans, leaving his collar casually unbuttoned. He felt stupid as he fixed his hair, remembering his dad fluffing it on top the last time he spoke to him. Tonight was about nothing but protecting his family's reputation and keeping up his persona to aid Redge in his investigation. Secure your alibi. Keep things status quo...dance with your life mate, if only.

"So?" he said loudly to Mel to get her attention.

She pulled her earbuds out. "Huh?"

"Do I look, *normal*?"

She chuckled. "You mean do you look like a rich prick?"

"Yeah."

She winked. "Spot on, M…Just kidding. You look fine. No one's going to look at you and go, *hey, he's a killer! Or he's found his destined life mate!*"

"It'll have to do, then. Are you ready to go?"

"Almost. Do I look like your hot date?"

"You're a bombshell. But you already know that, don't you?"

She smirked. "I know." She looked at the new watch he'd given her. "I love this thing, M. It's not as feminine as Erin's, but it's still very pretty. You're lucky you got me something for my trouble tonight. Especially since Kendrick is going to be there." She shuddered. "I will stomp him to death with my high heels if he gets handsy with me. Don't try to stop me either."

"Hey, no means no, love…I uh…asked Erin to come tonight."

"Do you expect her to show?"

"No. I just wanted you to know, in case."

"If she shows, will you trust me again? Follow my lead?" Mel asked.

"I will do my best."

"Good. I won't badger you for drinking, so long as you don't go so far as to pass out or vomit."

He chuckled. "Thanks. I really want to drink. This was one of the worst days I've ever had."

He wrapped his arm around her waist and opened a portal for them to Paradigm. It dumped them out in the main square, thirty feet from the club. They were spotted almost immediately and swarmed by people taking their picture and asking questions.

Maddox kept his hand around Melina. She smiled smugly at them all and leaned suggestively against him. The same question was asked by numerous people at once. "Is she your girlfriend, Maddox? Are you a thing? You've been out together before. Is it serious?"

He just smiled and walked Mel into the club. People parted for them. Kendrick waved from the back, at the VIP table. Maddox felt Mel stiffen next to him as they walked over to Kendrick, and her smile grew fixed, her eyes cold. Kendrick put his fist out. Maddox bumped it with his own and slid into the oversized booth.

"What's your poison tonight?" Kendrick asked. "This place is so overrated. They stick only to the legal stuff."

"That's fine. Nothing strong tonight."

"What about you, Melina?" Kendrick leaned close to her, smiling.

"I'm not drinking tonight."

"That's a shame," he turned to Maddox. "So, where's Mystery Girl?"

He shrugged. "She might show. But this isn't really her scene. And her name is Erin."

"You still claiming exclusivity?"

Maddox gave him a warning look.

Kendrick held his hands up. "Hey, just wondering since you came in here with Melina on your arm. Mystery Girl doesn't mind that?"

"Erin," Maddox said through his clenched teeth.

Mel squeezed his arm under the table. He looked at her. "I'm going to get you a drink, M. I'll be right back."

She slid out of the booth and disappeared on the dance floor. Kendrick watched her go, his eyes fixed on her ass. He blew out a breath. "I really need that. You've got to help me out with her."

"Mel doesn't change her mind easily. That's on you."

The music was loud, the lights dim. People on the floor were calling to him, trying to get his attention. One girl was particularly loud, waving at him. He smirked at her and waved back while pictures were taken constantly. He reminded himself this was why he was here. He suddenly realized just how stupid his life was and had been for the last year and a half.

"Well, you made that girl's night," Kendrick laughed. "You should go ask her to dance. She'd pass out."

"You go ask her to dance."

Kendrick looked back at her, and he smiled. "You know, brother, I think I will."

He headed out onto the floor toward the girl. Maddox sighed, his eyes scanning the floor. He almost swallowed his tongue, and his heart stopped. Erin stood across the room looking at him. Her hair was like an ember in the dark. *I'm going to die right now.* The dress she wore...how much of her it didn't cover, sections of it cut out so her skin was there for everyone to see.

He stood up, walked to her, grabbed her hand, and took her straight out of there. The portal took them back to his room where he had her out of that dress in three seconds flat.

He closed his eyes and exhaled, still sitting in the booth, trying to school his thoughts. When he opened his eyes again, she was smiling darkly at him.

I surrender. He messaged her. You own me.

He watched her read his message. But it didn't make her smile or give him a saucy look. Instead, she looked at him with fear and shook her head. What? What did she want?

He started to get up.

Melina came back. "Where are you going?" she asked.

He pointed at Erin. Mel looked, her eyebrows raised. "Sit down, you fool. It's a trap."

"What?"

"Just sit down. Drink this." She handed him a glass.

He hesitated.

"Trust me, M. Please. This could go sideways fast. She has no idea what she's doing. She's not the type for this game."

"What game?"

She gave him a little shove, and he leaned back in the seat again, downing the drink she brought him.

"I asked her to come. She came. I want to dance with her," he argued.

"Yeah. You're blinded by her…her…"

He snorted, still staring at Erin.

"At a loss for words? She's so gorgeous, she's dazzled you, too."

"That's the point, Dumbass. She's done that to scramble your brain. To what end, I don't know, but it can't be good for you." She pointed aggressively at Erin. "*That* is bait. There's a sharp hook underneath."

"It's worth it."

She shoved him back again as he moved to get up. "Don't make me hurt you. I will."

He locked gazes with Erin again, trying to search her face. Then he spotted Jaris, looming close behind her. He whispered something in her ear. She nodded as he gave her a little push forward. Maddox exhaled. Mel was right. Damn.

What are you doing? He messaged her.

I thought you wanted to dance with me. I'm waiting.

"I see it, Mel," he said. "Thanks. Stay here."

She crossed her arms as he stood. "Eyes up. Brain on, M."

"Yes, ma'am."

He ignored the hands that grabbed at him and the voices that begged for his attention as he walked up to Erin. He stopped a few inches from her. She was trembling, and her gaze darted around at all the people looking at them.

"So cold, Erin," he said. "Haven't you done enough to me for one day?"

She looked down.

"Go ahead. Do your worst."

"No," she shook her head taking a step back from him.

He moved forward. "Will you dance with me?"

Her eyes rounded, and she glanced at the onlookers again. He came close and leaned down, putting his mouth next to her ear. "Say no. Make it loud so they can hear. Stomp out. It will be all over the society section tomorrow that I was rejected. You win."

She pulled back from him. "You're serious?"

He nodded. She worried her bottom lip between her teeth, and then she looked at Jaris.

"Dance with me," he said louder holding his hands out to her.

His breath caught as she did the exact opposite of what he expected and moved into him. "Okay."

He clasped her against him and turned her in a circle. She was shaking like a leaf as she braced her hands on his shoulders. He could tell she was going to bolt any second. His hands held her waist, his fingers skimming the skin exposed there. Their connection surged in the physical contact.

"You surprise me…" he said in her ear.

She pulled away from him. He let go. They stared at each other for a moment, then she turned and left the club. He held still and watched her go. People began asking him questions about Erin.

One guy thumped him on the shoulder. "I hope the poor girl doesn't go kill herself now."

Maddox scowled and pushed through the crowd and back to Melina. She stared at him, her eyebrows raised. Kendrick sat too close to her, trying to engage her in conversation.

He sat down, grabbed a shot off the table, and tossed it back.

"Not as expected," he said to Mel.

"Not at all," she agreed.

"What are you talking about?" Kendrick asked.

"Nothing," Maddox said.

His watch pinged.

Your house, in one hour.

I'll be there.

He took another drink, feeling conflicted.

Jaris' grip on her arm was beginning to hurt, not from the burn, but how hard his fingers dug in. They walked in silence for a block from the club and down an alley, then he lost it.

"What happened?" he demanded.

"You're hurting me."

He let go. "Sorry. I didn't mean to."

She rubbed her arm and looked down. "Nothing about that felt right to me. I couldn't do it. That's not me. I'm not built like that."

"He's getting to you. Isn't he?"

"No."

"Then let's ruin his night another way."

"How?"

"Spend the night with me."

"You mean…"

"Yes."

"I can't do that…it would feel like torture to me. I can't even imagine how painful that would be. It hurts so much just to kiss you."

He turned his back on her and walked away.

"Jaris?"

He stopped and hung his head. "I'm sorry. I'll call you tomorrow."

Erin stood still for a moment, all alone on the street. The dress against her skin felt wrong. Everything felt wrong. She walked slowly to the hub and caught a portal home.

"Dad? I'm home." She didn't say it too loudly.

He was dozing in his recliner, an open book on his chest. She sat on the armrest and touched his head. His temperature felt normal. He blinked and looked at her.

"Hey, honey. Finished with your date?"

"Yeah. The first one anyway."

He laughed. "You need to pick one." He looked at her dress, and his humor vanished. He frowned at her.

"I know," she said quickly. "Bad choice. I'm going to return it to the store tomorrow."

"You could bring the jealousy between your young men to a murderous rage wearing stuff like that. It's dangerous."

"I know. Well, I know now. You're right. How are you feeling?"

"Not too bad. A little better. Guess what I heard today?"

"What?"

"The gift giver is back. A few families have reported receiving anonymous gifts."

"I know," she smiled. "They planted a tree at Selena's grave. I wish I knew who it was. It meant so much to me, what they did for us when Mom died."

He patted her hand. "When are you going to bring your other guy around to meet me?"

"I'm going to end it with him."

"Oh...well. Try not to break his heart too badly."

"Okay, dad. I'm going to change clothes then I'll be heading out again for a little while. Do you need help getting into bed?"

"No. I'm fine. I can do it on my own." He pulled her down to kiss her on the forehead. "I love you."

"I love you, too, Dad."

She headed to her room, tears blurring her eyes. She carefully stripped out of the dress and folded it before heading to the shower. She felt dirty. She dressed in plain jeans and a T-shirt after she was clean and decided to not put on any makeup. She went invisible again as she walked out of Anue...to him.

She passed under the dome into the garden and took a deep breath of the summer flowers blooming in vines covering the stone wall. She sat again on the bench next to the fountain and leaned her head back. She was early. The house was dark. He wasn't here yet. Should she message him? Her heart strained, heavy and tired.

I'm at your house. I'm a little early.

I'll be there in a second. I just have to bow out of this bullshit circus first.

She looked up at the stars and waited for him to show to their *appointment*. Would he have Melina with him? She thought back through the crappy, weird day. Not once had she been burned by him touching someone else.

Lights came on inside the house. Guess he was home. She didn't budge. In a few minutes, the door opened, and he came out on the porch.

"Hey," he said easily. He wasn't wearing the suit jacket anymore. His collar was unbuttoned, and his sleeves were rolled up to his elbows.

"Hey," she answered. "It's nice out here. Do you want to come sit with me?"

He moved forward instantly. Their eyes connected as he walked to her and sat down. He reached for her hand. She gave it. The connection hummed and pulled pleasantly between their palms.

"You said..." she hesitated, remembering his message. "You said going out tonight was an act. What did you mean?"

"I had to do that so no one suspects anything is different. Someone is trying to frame me. There was another girl found dead early this morning. My name carved on her."

Erin gasped. "Oh my gosh! Oh..." The weight of what he said fell on her. "When did you find out?"

"Midmorning."

She let go of his hand and hunched over, wrapping her arms around her middle. "I'm sorry, Maddox. I was hitting you so hard right then, too."

"You were. I was really sick. I've never felt that bad in my life."

"I'm sorry."

"Erin...what's going on? You told me you were going to hurt me. Why are you apologizing?"

She stood. "I'm really screwed up. I'm not built for revenge. It's not me. And right now, I'm just too tired to be pissed at you."

He stood up, too. "I know it's not you. You're not a cruel person."

"How would you know?" she would have snapped it, but it came out only somewhat testy.

"I've been listening to your heart for days."

"Oh..." she felt exposed. "I came to the club to humiliate you."

"I know."

She faced him. There was too much truth hanging in the air around them. She decided to just give up for the day. "You could have easily humiliated me instead...you didn't." she swallowed. "Thank you."

A small smile lifted his lips. "I really did want to dance with you."

"I like dancing," she admitted. "I do it a lot in the privacy of my room...I'm sorry about the dress. I don't know what I was thinking. I couldn't wait to get out of it."

He snorted. "All I could think about was *getting* you out of it. You looked...I don't even have the words. I won't ever forget the way you looked tonight. Thank you for that, even if it was meant to hurt me. I'm glad you changed though. I probably wouldn't be able to speak to you right now if you hadn't. I 'd just stand and stare."

She looked down and rubbed her arms. The pain buzzed like a high frequency in her nerve endings. She held her hands out to him. He didn't take them.

"I should go home now. Aren't you going to touch me?"

"I'm going to ask you for more."

"Maddox, don't."

"Please. Just let me hold you for a moment. That's all I'm asking for."

She exhaled raggedly and closed her eyes. "Okay."

"Okay?" his voice held disbelief and hope. He took a step toward her.

"Wait!"

He stopped. "Erin…"

"Just wait."

She glanced at him nervously for a second and then turned her back to him. She pulled her chin down to her chest and wrapped her arms tight around her torso. She was as closed physically as she could be. "Okay. It's okay now."

His hands were on her shoulders first. They slid down her arms to her hands. She bit down on both of her lips to keep from moaning as his chest pressed against her back. His breathing wasn't steady, and his heart beat hard next to her spine. He dipped his head and pressed his lips against the top of her shoulder. Then he held still, his arms wrapped around her.

All the pain untied and dispersed like steam. This situation was torture, and she suddenly hated it more than ever, but not for the same reasons as before.

"You want to know how you can really get your revenge on me?" he asked quietly.

"Yes."

"Since you're not a cruel person and you don't really enjoy hurting me the way you did today...Just end it now, Erin. I promise you there is nothing else you could ever do to me that will compare to that. I know you want to end it...So just do it already."

She pushed gently against him, and he let go. She faced him. "You don't want it ended?"

"No. The fact destiny chose you for me has been the greatest honor of my life. It will haunt me as long as I live, that you couldn't stand me. And that was my fault. And I did so much damage there was nothing to salvage."

Tears choked her. "All right, Maddox. I'm going to end it. Right now."

He reached out and wrapped his arm around the back of her waist, pulling her slowly to him.

Her eyes went wide, but she didn't fight. "What are you doing?"

"I'm kissing you goodbye."

She touched his face and shut her eyes as he closed in. A jolt went through her core as his lips came down on hers. How could anything so bitter be so sweet? His heart filled hers with agony and longing. Tears ran out from her closed eyes. His tears fell on her cheeks also. Her breathing hitched as he entered her mouth and pulled her tighter against him. She had to let go. She clung tighter, reaching up and crossing her arms behind his neck. He hauled her up to her toes.

I want you. She thought. Then she panicked. This couldn't happen again. Well, it *could*. She wanted it. She wanted him, so hard. Sanity fought to grab a hold. She shook her head and pushed him away, ready to scream and strike at him for trying to seduce her. Her ire died immediately when she saw the look in his eyes. He was heartbroken. There was nothing false in the moment.

She wiped at her tears angrily and ran from the garden.

He sat down, both his hands on his chest, trying to hold his heart together.

FOURTEEN

Erin ran home, her world flipping upside down. She just needed to be alone. She could reject him anywhere. It was a bad idea to be with him when she did it. Too painful. Too raw. She came into the house quietly. Her dad had gone to bed. She glanced in at him for a moment and listened to his breathing before turning all the lights out and shutting herself in her room.

She laid down on the bed and tried to relax. Her body raged, her soul twisted into knots. She curled up, holding herself tight around the ball of need in her core. Erin had never felt desire this strong. *Why not?* A little voice in her head asked. *Just go back. Offer yourself up to him. What difference does it make? He's yours. You've already been together anyway. What does it matter if you do him again? You want to. It doesn't mean you won't reject him. It doesn't have to mean anything.*

Ugh. She rolled her face into her pillow. She couldn't go back. No way. What the hell was she thinking? His damnable words came back to her mind. *The rain…and your perfect skin…under my hands.* She stood up. She'd been in too much pain. She knew how to make the pain go away.

Erin left the house as quietly as she could.

I'm coming back. She messaged him.

She waited a moment. He didn't respond. She went invisible and ran back through the shadows to where she'd just been. The physical exertion didn't ease her desire; it nudged it up a level. She slid right through the barrier and marched up to the front door and knocked loudly.

He opened the door, his expression confused.

"What do you want?"

"You. I want you."

"No," his voice was ice and he slammed the door in her face.

She stood there and just blinked a few times. Was this a joke? She backed up a step, unsure what to do. She didn't feel anything yet, she hadn't processed what just happened. He opened the door again and stepped out shoving his finger in her face.

"I'm sick of being used for sex! I will not be used anymore, and *especially* not by you of all people. You and I will have something real, or nothing at all!" he backed up and slammed the door again.

Erin wrung her hands, totally discombobulated. *Yeah, okay. That just happened.*

She turned to leave but couldn't. Instead, she sat on the front step. She certainly didn't feel amorous anymore. She pulled her knees up to her chest, thinking about his unexpected response. Then it hit her like a ton of bricks. It was the first time she'd acknowledged Maddox was a real person, with thoughts and feelings. And she could see what he was saying. He was used...all the time. And she had tried to use him, too.

She rubbed her face. Oh, man. The shame was fast and mean...Time slid past her, and she didn't move. The night matured, and her butt went numb. She thought about him from an entirely different angle.

He opened the door again after a long while. She looked over her shoulder at him.

"I'm sorry," she said.

"Go home, Erin."

"No."

He huffed and shut the door on her again. This time, he turned all the lights out in the house, and she was plunged into darkness. She didn't care. She wasn't leaving. Not yet. She didn't know what she was waiting for, but there was something.

Hours passed. No noise came from the house. For a long time, all was still, so she heard him as soon as he moved around the house again. He didn't turn on any lights.

The door opened. He came out beside her and draped a fuzzy throw over her shoulders. "I don't want you to get cold," he mumbled as he went back into the house shutting the door yet again.

She smiled unconsciously and snuggled into the soft fabric. Her thoughts and emotions finally seemed to settle into place. She waited another hour.

Are you awake? **She messaged him.**

No.

She snorted. Will you come out here and talk to me? I won't try to jump you. Promise.

It's the middle of the night. Why can't you just let me sleep?

Please come talk to me.

She stared at her watch, waiting. Nothing. Her heart sank. Sad, she stood and decided to finally leave. She folded the throw and set it next to the front door. The porch light turned on, and he opened the door. He reached down, grabbed the throw, laid it out flat on the stair, and sat down on it. She sat next to him. He sighed and pulled a joint from his pocket. He lit it, took a drag and handed it to her. She pursed her lips for a second. She'd never smoked anything. She took it and inhaled. Her coughed ripped loudly through the quiet. He chuckled and took it back.

They sat there in silence for a few minutes. She felt a wave of anxiety from him. He finished smoking and stubbed the thing out on the porch.

"I was in love once," he said abruptly. "I was eighteen. She crashed into my life and took over me, and I loved every minute of it. Bess—her name was Bess. Things got serious with us after we started having sex. She was my first. We were together all the time. We did everything together. She spent a lot of time here with my family. For a while, it all seemed normal and perfect. I thought we would be forever." He paused and rubbed his head. "Then I learned the truth, and it was freaking Jerry Springer level bullshit."

"Jerry Springer?"

"Yeah...sorry, I was raised on Earth stuff. Long story."

"What was the truth?" she prompted.

"The crazy bitch had the hots for my dad. She had a screw loose. Apparently, she'd obsessed about him for years, and she used me to try and get close to him."

"Oh my gosh! She really thought she could get him? I mean your mom and him..."

He laughed darkly. "Yeah. Screw loose, like I said. My folks haven't ever stopped being crazy about each other. Their bond is seriously strong. Anyway, that got ugly real fast."

"I can't believe your mom didn't kill her."

He laughed again. "No need. She's secure. She knows my dad isn't going anywhere. She did enjoy scaring the hell out of Bess though before she threw her out. I never saw her again...I swore I would never be deceived again. That no one would ever use me again. I would be the one who used. Of course, despite my resolve, I was used all the time. So I got meaner and meaner to protect myself. People see me. They look at me, but they don't know me. I don't show myself to anyone."

"Will you show me?"

He looked at her sideways. "I want to, but I think I need to protect myself from you maybe more than anyone else."

"Hmm..." she mulled that one over. "I can understand that...I've been out here for hours just thinking about what you said, trying to see through your eyes. I'm sorry for the way I came back here. I was only thinking about myself, and I thought since..."

"What? Since I'm a guy I'd just go for it?"

Her cheeks heated. "I wasn't thinking much of anything, Maddox. I was hurting. It's not like you haven't made some advances toward me, though."

"Earlier…holding you… Thinking it was over between us, changed things for me. Are you going to end it or not?"

"I don't know."

He raised his eyebrows at her. "Well, that's different. You're unsure?"

"I…why do you want me, Maddox?"

He looked away. "Lots of reasons…I can't trust new people. I can't have a real relationship. But you…you're supposed to be mine. I *should* be able to trust you because you'd never want to hurt me. Because you didn't come to me trying to consume some fantasy idea of a person. Because I feel your heart inside my own. My whole life, I've seen what my parents have. Of course, I want that. To be able to trust without restraint…to love you."

Her heart responded to his words, against her will. "Don't you feel resentment though, that there was no choice for you? That Melina or someone else that gorgeous and stylish wasn't picked for you? Instead, you get this?" she gestured at herself.

"You're insecure? That's fascinating…All right, I'm giving a lot here, so I expect you to begin to open up soon and let me know about you."

"Huh?"

He took her hand and held it against his chest. "I want you to know I'm not lying…I saw you before you came here to kill me. In the crowd, on a dance floor. Just the side of your face, that's all I could see. I immediately tried to get to you, but I lost you. I've never chased anyone. The loss I felt was abnormal for such a random passing situation. I was so angry. You possessed me. I was determined to find you."

"It was probably just our future connection driving you."

He turned to her and touched the ends of her hair. "Beauty is in the eye of the beholder. You can think disparagingly about your appearance, but you are the most beautiful woman I have ever seen, and I'm constantly surrounded by beauty. Everyone you passed earlier tonight was stunned. I want you so much. I've never wanted anyone as much as I want you. You could rule the world with this face…" his eyes roamed lower. "This body that makes my hands ache to touch. I'm insane with the memory of having you in the rain. Absolutely *insane*." He let go of her hand and turned his face away again. "That's all superficial. Under that, I feel all these things from you. I get this sense you're an amazing person, but you hold yourself away from me. I feel this potential for us. But you don't…or can't."

She twisted her hands together. "I still blame you for Selena's death."

"That's bullshit, Erin," his voice went hard. "Yeah, I used her, but guess what, she used me, too. I wasn't what she really wanted? Well, she wasn't what I wanted either. I'm sorry for what I did. It was cruel. You accused me last night of having no respect for women. I'm guilty of that on a case by case basis, but look how most women treat me. How can I have respect for someone who has no respect for themselves? But regardless, killing yourself over someone is *stupid*."

"She was my best friend!"

"And I'm sure she was a lovely person...It's still stupid."

Erin stood, stomped down the stairs, and was about to leave. She stopped, reality slapping her. She looked back at him. "I thought I was furious at you for saying that, but I'm not. I'm furious at Selena. Because you're right. If she did kill herself, that was the stupidest moment of her life. I've been so angry at her, and I didn't even realize it until right now." The tears began building behind her eyes again. "It's not your fault, no matter what you did...but it felt better to blame you."

He flinched and stood. He came at her quickly. She didn't move. He picked her up and kissed her hard. They clung to each other with a violence. He didn't ease off her, and she didn't back down. Both of them were burning up in seconds. He broke away, breathing hard and shaking his head.

"I want to be sure," he said as she gazed at him, confused why he pulled away. "I *have* to be sure with you."

She ran her hands through her hair and blew out a breath, trying to force her hormones to calm down. "Okay...will you show me your room?"

His eyebrows pulled down. "You've seen my room."

"No. Not really. I wasn't paying attention. There's a ton of things I can learn about you, just by being in your room."

"You want to snoop," he accused, but he sounded lightly amused.

"I do."

He smiled and shook his head. "No. I don't think so. Not tonight. I've given you enough for now. You have to give to me now."

"Hmm...I'll have to think about that." She yawned and began to back away. "I'll see you around, Maddox."

"Goodnight, Erin."

She turned to leave, took a few steps, and turned back. His eyes were still on her. "Um...my dad wants to meet you."

"You told your father about us?"

"Not exactly. He saw you and Jaris get into it on the front porch. He's met Jaris. He wants to meet you."

"Sure. When?"

"I don't know right now. I'll message you."

Maddox watched her go. When he was alone, he threw his head back. "Yes!"

He picked up the throw and took it inside. There wasn't much left to the night. He was really tired, but he felt too hyped to sleep. He climbed into bed and closed his eyes, thinking of Erin. Under his happiness was a nagging fear. It reached up and slithered through him. What if this was her way of truly destroying him? Get him to lower his guard and then she'd really know how and where to strike him. He hoped with his entire soul, that wasn't what was going on. Trusting her...if he did, it would be the greatest risk he could ever take.

His heart wanted to run ahead, but he had to dig in his heels. If she would give up Jaris... that would make him feel more secure. Time and testing. He ground his teeth. He didn't want to do either. He wanted her there now. He wanted to take her until they both dissolved.

His watch pinged.

I feel that. Are you thinking of me?

A few replies ran through his head then he typed. Seeing you is like seeing my dreams...the best ones...made flesh.

Kendrick rolled a coin through his fingers over and over as his mind turned on his dilemma. The story of the dead girl had been kept quiet. That wasn't a problem. He could fix that. The problem was Maddox. He was off. Melina hovered close and Mystery Girl...Maddox was sprung over her. And what was going on between them, anyway? Her brief appearance at the club was weird. He'd been seen twice with Melina. She moved up his list of next victims, but that angered him. He didn't want to kill Melina. He *really* didn't want to kill Melina. Perhaps Erin would be enough, and he could leave Melina alive.

And if he killed Erin soon enough, before Maddox lost interest, that might break him nicely. And if he was screwing her, the evidence would be easy, like Selena. He needed to do a little stalking to make sure he knew where Maddox was at night and just exactly who was in his bed. His rage blinded him for a second, as he imagined that Maddox was having both Erin and Melina.

Time was running out for him to deliver to his mother what she requested. He needed to keep his head on her goals, but that was difficult when all he really cared about was taking Maddox down. That bastard had things too easy. It was time he felt some pain. Kendrick was sick of feeling jealousy. Tomorrow, he would find out what was going on so he could escalate the situation accordingly.

FIFTEEN

"Fall, Erin. I'll catch you," Maddox said.

She pressed her cheek to his. "I'm scared."

"You're scared? I'm terrified." He backed up, unbuttoned his shirt, and pointed at his heart. "You came here to cut it out, right?"

She looked down, a knife shook in her hand.

Erin's dream gave her a headache in the morning. She overslept after her long night and woke to her watch pinging with a message from Jaris. She stared at the ceiling, unsure how she felt about last night. She grimaced, thinking about her behavior. The dress, the club, their appointment, her coming back the way she did...and yet, she couldn't bring herself to regret it. Not really.

She licked her lips, remembering what it was like to kiss Maddox. Yeah, it was good, phenomenal really, but what did she expect? Those lips had lots of experience. Her ego smarted again. He'd told her some things she really wanted to believe, and even knowing he was telling the truth, she wasn't convinced he thought she was that beautiful.

It was like she'd gotten a glimpse of his real face, behind the mask he wore. Just a flash of him. How did she feel about what she saw? She couldn't trust him, and he didn't trust her. His reasons for not trusting her were valid. He wasn't just a handsome face with a lean, ripped body, he was smart and shrewd...and completely jaded.

She looked up at the box on top of her dresser. A portal to him lay inside. She imagined opening it, going through just as she was, bedhead and boxer shorts in all, and climbing into bed with him. How would that feel? Just to lay next to him and sleep for a while?

Her watch pinged again. She read the message from Jaris.

I'm sorry about last night, Erin. I shouldn't have pushed you like I did, and I shouldn't have gotten angry with you after. You're too sweet for such a devious plan. But I like that about you. I can't wait till you've ended it with Maddox and we can really be together. I have to go to work. Will I see you this evening?

She thought for a moment. What did she want to do? She was a simple girl. Maddox was wrong for her. Jaris fit her. Her walk of life. What she was used to. Common things, that's what she wanted for her life.

I'd like to see you this evening. I need to keep my contact with Maddox to a minimum. Message me when you get off work. I'll meet you. She sent it.

Then she noticed the bruises on her forearm. Bruises from Jaris' hand. They were unmistakable fingers marks. She frowned. He hadn't meant to hurt her. It was just a tense moment. She got up and dressed for the day, wondering what she should do until the evening.

Unconsciously, she took more time than usual fixing her hair. She frowned at her freckles, but she wouldn't cover them up, so she just put a little stain on her lips and a touch of liner around her eyes. She looked at herself with a critical eye. Was she beautiful?

A loud thump startled her. She rushed from her room.

"Dad?"

"Erin..." his voice was weak.

She ran to his room. He'd fallen to the floor. She grabbed him and tried to lift him up, but he was dead weight. His skin was spongy and pale. What did she do? He was going to die right there in her arms.

"Dad, please," she pleaded, sobbing. "Don't leave me alone."

His eyes rolled back in his head as he dropped unconscious.

"Dad!" she cried.

"Erin?" She jumped and turned around as a portal tore open behind her and Maddox came through. "What's wrong? I felt…"

"Maddox! Help me! It's my dad! He's dying."

He rushed to her dad, lifted him up, and laid him back on the bed. He spoke urgently into his watch. "I need you right now!" he spat out her address like he knew it as well as his own.

Before Erin could ask anything, another portal opened, and Tesla came through. She gulped and stepped back from the legendary savior of Regia. Tesla looked at her dad and sat down beside him, placing her hand on his chest.

Erin was beside herself. Maddox reached for her and held her. "It's okay. Tesla will know what to do." He smoothed her hair and rubbed her back. His touch was so comforting, but still, she cried. Maybe it was too late.

Erin blinked as red light slid from Tesla's hands into her dad. Even through his skin, she could see the light moving through his body, along his veins. The next moment, he gasped and opened his eyes.

"Oh my goodness!" Nathan exclaimed. "I thought I'd bought it."

Everyone laughed at the breaking tension.

"Hold still a moment," Tesla instructed him. "I'm not finished with you."

He gazed at her with wide eyes and nodded his head.

A ribbon of red light slithered from her palm and dove into his chest again. His eyes bugged, but he held still.

"Breathe," Tesla instructed him.

He inhaled. As he exhaled, the light retracted. A small bulb like a water drop hung off the end of the light strand. Tesla rolled the bulb in between her thumb and forefinger then it disappeared in the air.

"Your full health will return in a few days. You had a parasite in your heart."

"The heck you say," he said.

Tesla gave him a direct look. "Probably contracted it the last time you drank human blood. It was contaminated."

"Dad!" Erin chided.

"I would never!"

"Sir, there is no doubt," Tesla said.

Her father's cheeks colored. "All right, you got me." He sat up and looked closely at Tesla. "I can't believe it. I can't believe *you're* here in my house, saving my life. How?"

"Oh, well, your daughter and my brother are—"

"Dating!" Erin almost shouted. "We're just dating. *Casually*." She pushed out of Maddox's arms and came to her dad, taking his hand. "You're going to be okay now, Dad. I can't believe you drank human blood. You're such a hypocrite."

"I know, sorry sweetie. It was a long time ago. I was just so lonely for your mom. I'm sorry."

She looked over her shoulder. Tesla and Maddox had left the room, giving them privacy.

"Why did you keep him a secret the way you did?" her father asked. "That's quite a thing. Dating in the first family."

"I don't want to talk about it, Dad...How do you feel?"

"Not bad. A little weak, but fine other than that. I'm hungry. Would you bring me something to eat?"

"Sure. I'm glad you're hungry. Just give me a few minutes."

She came out of her dad's room. The house was empty. Through the front window, she saw Maddox waiting on the porch. She came outside. He reached for her, and she didn't back away. She rested her head against his shoulder and sighed.

"Are you all right?" he asked.

"Fine. Coming down off the adrenaline." She thought she was okay, but the next second, she was sobbing hard. "Oh, gosh, I thought I was going to lose him. He was gone. I didn't know what to do. I could do nothing."

"It's okay now. It's okay." His voice was as soothing as his hands on her back.

"Where's Tesla?"

"I asked her to leave."

"I didn't get to thank her."

"You can whenever you like."

For a while they just stood there like that, holding on and quiet. When she felt steady, she pulled away.

"Thank you."

He shrugged. "You scared me...the panic I felt from you."

"Huh...our connection saved my dad's life."

He raised an eyebrow, his face hardening from the openness that had been there a moment ago. "So it's not totally worthless then?"

"Not today," her voice turned waspish in response to him.

"Is it just the stress of almost losing your dad that's making you act like a bitch?"

"I don't know! Maybe!" she half shouted.

After a moment, both of their angry expressions faltered, then they both laughed. He grabbed her around the waist and kissed her mouth.

"You're a pain in the ass, Erin," he smiled down at her.

"I'm sorry."

"No, you're not."

"No, I'm not," she smirked. "Now back off. I didn't say you could kiss me."

He narrowed his eyes and grinned at her. "I thought we were *dating*. I should be able to kiss you if we're dating."

"Oh, please," she rolled her eyes. "Don't even think about using that against me."

"I wasn't until you just told me not to. Now I'm plotting."

She frowned and pulled back from him. This was too close. Too open. And they were outside. Someone might see her with him. She reminded herself of reality and shook her head. "Thank you for coming. My dad would have died. I cannot repay you."

He searched her eyes and blinked a few times. "You're ashamed to be with me."

"You only just realized that?"

"I don't get you."

"What? What don't you get?"

"You act like Jaris is so great but..." he grabbed her arm and held it up, his fingers framing the bruises Jaris put on her.

She jerked her arm away from him. "That was an accident."

"Fine. I'm leaving." He backed up, rubbing the heel of his hand over his heart. "Hatred is…you know, I get it…Shame, that hurts more for some reason."

He turned and walked away. She frowned after him, feeling like she should say something, call him back, but she didn't. It was the truth. Harsh and cold.

She went back inside and made a meal for her dad. He ate a ton and then wanted more. His humor returned along with his color. Even the gray in his hair had faded back some to its original red. He pushed her for details about her and Maddox. She refused to talk about it. It was so good to be with her dad, and he was like himself again.

She wanted to cry again. Inside she was. If Maddox hadn't come, she'd be planning a funeral. She tried to shrug it off, but she couldn't. He'd only done what anyone would do. It was Tesla who saved his life anyway. All he'd done was call her. But he responded…Her heart cried out, and he came. If the situation was reversed would she do the same? If she felt something strong from him, would she go to help? Probably not. And she had the nerve to say she was ashamed to be seen with him?

She pulled her watch up, thinking she should message him, but she didn't know what to say. She left it.

At midday, a thump against the house startled her. She came outside, went around the side of the house, and almost collided into a ladder. "What are you doing?" she yelled at the two guys on the roof.

They looked down at her. "Fixing the roof, miss."

"Fixing...*what?* I didn't order this. I can't pay for it."

"It's paid for already. It will be a little loud, but we won't take long."

Shocked she went back to the front porch and messaged Maddox.

Seriously? The roof?

I noticed the water damage on the ceiling in the living room. **He wrote back.**

So you just thought you'd have it fixed?

Is there a problem?

Are you trying to buy me?

With a roof? That's funny.

That's really expensive.

No, it's not.

Money doesn't fix everything, rich boy.

It fixes roofs.

She sighed and shook her head, feeling idiotic and annoyed and somewhat charmed.

Forgive me for earlier. I acted wrong.

She waited, he didn't respond. She deserved that. She went back inside. Her father was up, looking confused.

"What is all that blasted noise?" he asked.

"It's okay, Dad. Just some guys fixing the roof."

"Oh. Well, that's grand. I know the house has started falling down around us. I'll start to fix it once I'm all better. I promise."

She hugged him. "You were sick. Don't feel guilty."

"I do though. Especially now that I know I did it to myself. How are we paying for this?"

"Er…we're not. Maddox took care of it. I didn't ask him to," she added quickly.

"Well, it's not a typical trinket or flowers, but I guess if there's water leaking on your girl, and you have the means to fix it, you do. I can see that."

"It's embarrassing."

"Don't make more of it than needs be. It's probably nothing for him. Pocket change."

"He gave me this, too." She showed him her watch.

"Flashy. So are you going to tell me about how you two met?"

Her cheeks heated immediately. *Oh sure*, she thought. *I went to kill him and we ended up naked in the rain instead.* "Yeah, no. Not telling you."

He chuckled. "I'll get it out of you eventually."

"No, you won't."

He took a deep breath and spread his arms wide. "I feel so much better. Not one hundred percent, but alive, you know."

"I'm so relieved."

Her watch pinged.

Her dad leaned over to see. "Who is it? Which one?" he teased.

She gave him a light shove away. He chortled and shuffled over to his recliner.

It was Jaris.

I'm almost finished with work for the day. Will you meet me for dinner?

All her conflict and confusion came back. What did she do? She held off answering and messaged Maddox instead.

Are you going out again tonight with Melina?

Yes. Are you planning on crashing in on me again?

No.

Good. I think I've reached my limit for now.

I'm going out with Jaris.

She frowned. He seemed angry. She tried to listen to his heart, and she had to acknowledge she wasn't good at it. Maybe it wasn't exactly anger. Frustration and sorrow.

Jaris messaged her again. Erin? You there?

"So? Making your plans for the evening?" her dad teased.

"Yeah. Unless you want me to stay here...you know what...I'm not going anywhere tonight. I'm going to stay right here with you. I'll make your favorite for dinner, and we can play poker after."

His smile warmed her heart. "Now you're talking."

She messaged Jaris and told him she needed to stay in.

She fussed in the kitchen over the meal, talking easily with her dad while she made it. He hadn't been very talkative in a long time, and she'd missed him. He kept badgering her about Maddox. She told him about Jaris instead. They played three hands of poker. He won two, and she obliterated him in the last round with a royal flush. Then he started yawning.

"I'm going to bed, sweetheart. Thanks for staying with me. You know the night is still young enough. You could go out."

"I don't think so. I need a break. I feel like I'm the rope in a tug of war."

"So choose a side."

He kissed her on the head and shut his bedroom door behind him. She locked the house and turned the lights off. She wasn't really tired, but sleeping seemed like a better idea than scrolling through the media to see what Maddox was doing. She stopped, her mouth falling open. Holy cow! That was totally what she was going to do, unconsciously even.

She shut herself in her room and tried to read a book. Her eyes darted to her watch from time to time. Finally, she caved and searched his name. Pictures of him and Melina rose to the top. Jealousy poked at her as she looked at Melina. What was going on with them? Was it just part of the act he said he had to go through right now? He hadn't touched Melina in a way that burned Erin at all since that first day when he told her he was testing it. Hmm...

She closed her eyes and dropped into an uneasy sleep.

Erin woke with a jolt. She could feel Maddox near her. She slid out of bed and walked silently through the shadows into the living room. A figure walked past the window. She went invisible and approached the window to see out fully. He moved quickly, setting a single flower on the porch, a rock on the stem, then he left.

No way. Her mind tripped. She pinched her forearm hard so she knew she wasn't dreaming. She watched him move through the darkened street and around a corner before she ventured outside. She didn't want him to know she was there. This just couldn't be the truth. Staying invisible, she followed him at distance. Maddox was the gift giver?

He walked slowly into the memorial gardens and sat down next to Selena's stone. What was he doing? Erin didn't dare get any closer, or he really would know she was there, invisible or not. He cut his hand with a small knife and bled onto the roots of the tree. Its leaves shivered, and gold moved along the cracks in the trunk and up through the branches. His shoulders slumped as he laid his uncut hand against the stone. In a second, he retracted his hand as quickly as if it burned him. She heard his heavy sigh then he touched the stone again and held it still.

"I'm sorry," he whispered.

She moved away silently as he got up and walked out of the gardens. He headed toward the low end of town.

She watched him stop at a shabby place and leave something. He turned quickly, his eyes scanning the darkness. She held still, invisible and behind the side of a building. He frowned and then moved away, on to somewhere else.

Erin swallowed, her throat constricting around a sob as she processed the truth. All this time...all these years, it had been him. The phantom she held onto for comfort. The shadow she loved...it was him all along. Her heart began to riot as tears ran down her cheeks. So much misunderstanding on her part. So much of himself he hid from everyone. She wanted to tear his mask off and burn it. She wanted to look at him and truly know who she was looking at.

Erin pushed off from her hiding place and ran home, the wind kissing her tears. She almost laughed aloud as she came back into her house and closed the door. She ran to her room and closed the door unable to contain herself. She did laugh then, covering her mouth with her hands. She cried and laughed and then cried again. Her heart jumped around. Surely she would burst open any second. Her watch pinged.

Erin? Are you awake?

Smiling, she decided not to answer. She took a deep breath and wiped her eyes. She changed out of her pajamas and fixed her hair before opening the box with the portal inside it. She hadn't looked at it before. It shimmered black and purple as she picked it up. It felt funny, like holding onto a ghost, then it opened. It didn't rush and pull like other portals. It was silent and it stood open, fixed on her wall next to her closet door. There was a section, like a shadow curtain. She pulled on it, and the portal closed. She touched it again, and it opened.

She checked herself in the mirror again, grabbed the rock off her dresser, and took it with her through the portal. She landed in his room. How long would it take him to come home? Her pulse jumped so fast. Her watch pinged again. He must be getting her excited, freaked out feelings.

Erin?

She still didn't respond. A portal opened next to the one she'd just used. She set her rock down and turned invisible a second before he came through. He took off his hoodie, threw it on the bed, and ran his hands through hair. He looked at his watch and then turned around, his eyebrows raised.

"Erin?" he looked right through her, but his eyes fixed on the new open portal. "Are you here?"

She dropped her invisibility. "I didn't think I'd be able to sneak up on you that easily. But then that's something you don't know about me. Stealth is my greatest strength despite the fact I'm only half elf."

He looked stunned then his face closed to her again. "Why are you here?"

She moved forward and reached for his arm. She took his watch off and touched the medallion on his wrist.

"You keep this hidden. I didn't know...For the first time, I feel like maybe we aren't a cosmic mistake."

"Why?"

She turned and picked up the rock and showed him. "I saw you. All those years ago. I've kept this all this time. I never go to sleep without laying it on my chest for a few minutes first. There's power inside it. Power you put there."

He just gazed at her desperately. She set the rock down again. "I missed our appointment. I need to make up for that."

He raised an eyebrow at her. "I'm happy you're here, but that sounds...I don't know how much I feel secure doing with you. You hurt me today."

"You can have me if you want me."

"Do you want *me*?"

Yes. She thought. *For years. The real you.*

"I want something real or nothing at all," she used his words. "There's something I want to do with you right now. Something I *really* want."

"What?" he breathed.

She could feel she'd pushed him to the edge just with her words.

"I want you to trust me for just a minute. I know that's asking a lot. I don't deserve it, but I'm asking anyway. Will you try?"

He looked torn. "I'll try."

"Turn around."

His eyebrows pulled down, but he turned his back to her. She reached around his waist and put her palms flat on his chest, resting her cheek against his shoulder blade. He tensed, and then sighed, relaxing. In a moment, he covered her hands with his.

"This feels nice," he said quietly.

"I want more."

"How much more?" his voice was wary.

"Trust. Just a little more trust."

Her fingers went to the buttons on his shirt. She slowly began to undo them. He inhaled sharply, but he didn't move away from her. She unbuttoned them all and slid his shirt off. He looked over his shoulder.

"Stay just like that," she said.

He nodded and continued to glance at her sideways over his shoulder. She took a step back, pulled her shirt off, and unhooked her bra, letting it fall to the floor. She came back to him, pressing against his back and winding her arms around his waist again.

It took a minute for their breathing to ease back to a normal speed.

"What now, Erin? Is this all you want?"

"Yes. It's enough. It's good...Is there something *you* want?"

He closed his eyes and groaned. Then he pulled away from her. "I want everything. You're killing me with wanting you, but I'm not going to touch you when you're ashamed to be with me."

He picked up his shirt off the floor and put it back on, avoiding looking at her. She left her bra on the floor, but she pulled her shirt back on quickly.

"So you learned something you like about me tonight. But it's something I keep secret. I'm glad you're here wanting things from me, but I hate it at the same time. I can't go public with the anonymous stuff I do. To the world, I'm just a womanizer, maybe a murderer. I don't care what anyone thinks about me, but you do. You don't want to be seen with me. You don't want anyone to know you're my mate because you're embarrassed by me. Do you have any idea how that hurts, Erin?"

She opened her mouth, but he held up a finger to silence her.

"I get it. It's my fault. I brought it on myself. I don't blame you. I just..."

"I want you," she said.

"Sure, in the dark. Just so no one knows, right? I can be your whore, is that it?"

She flinched and shook her head in protest, but he kept talking.

"I want to not care, but I do. I want to claim every inch of you over and over, but not if you're going to lie about us afterward. There's no trust in that. The idea of that being the reality between you and me breaks my heart. I want you to stand beside me in the light."

She moved closer to him. He couldn't trust her yet. "I hear you," she whispered. "I understand. I didn't have a plan when I came here. I just had to see you. I had to touch you. You made me so happy to learn that you did that for me all those years ago. I always held onto you, not knowing your identity, drawing strength and comfort from you and what you left for me."

"You still don't know what you want," he accused.

"You're right. But I promise I won't hurt you on purpose anymore. I'll stop trying to destroy you."

"Thank you. That's something."

"Are you really with Melina?"

He smirked. "Does it matter that much?"

She could see he needed her confession. "Oh, it matters."

"Jealous?"

She threw her head back. "Yes! Okay? I don't want her touching you. I don't want you touching her. Happy now?"

"Marginally. I'm not with Melina. She's my best friend. We've been friends our whole lives. Our parents are close, have been since before either of us was born. She thinks standing in publicly as my girlfriend is a good way to protect me from whatever is happening right now. She's my alibi for whatever. And even if something happens while we aren't together, she'll say we were."

"Have you ever slept with her?"

"No. I've kissed her but that's it…Did you spend the evening with Jaris? You didn't burn me at all."

"I stayed home with my dad. We played poker."

It was the first time she saw Maddox smile, *really* smile. It was innocent. Beautiful. She moved to him again, reached around his neck, and kissed him. He was hesitant for a second, then he took her under and made her head spin.

"I want you with me, Erin," he said quietly moving his mouth to her neck. "I want you to say it. Say you're mine. I want you to stop seeing him. I want you to let me in. Show me who you are. I'll take my mask off if you take yours off."

She exhaled raggedly. She didn't want to but she pulled back from him slowly. She had to be fair to him.

"Okay. I feel like I can really think about it now. Really consider *us*. Let's spend the day together tomorrow."

"Are you leaving then?"

"Um…I want to stay, but I think my brain is going to burn up if I do."

"Mine's already there."

"I can't commit right now, and I see you need that."

He gazed at her mildly and put his hands in his pockets. "Goodnight then. I'm glad you opened the portal. Now I don't have to worry about you running home in the dark...regardless of how stealthy you might be."

"Goodnight." She left and was back in her room in a second. She looked at the open portal and smiled. That thing was dangerous. Instant direct access. Hmm...could be fun.

It was really late now. She climbed into bed, trying to stop thinking about climbing into bed with Maddox. She thought about messaging him but then decided against it. She'd never get to sleep if she kept the communication open.

She closed her eyes and smiled. Maddox was the gift giver. Her mind couldn't merge the two. The shadow she'd loved all these years—now she knew his face, his voice, all of him. Her mind refused to mesh the two into one, but still, peace and happiness moved through her. She focused on her feelings and tried to send them to him.

Erin dreamed a lot. Her mind blurred with amalgams of Jaris and Maddox. She woke while it was still dark, not on a jolt, but the second she woke, she was fully awake. Instinct told her to be still and listen, there was a reason she was awake.

A faint thump sounded outside her window. *Very* faint. Her gut sent her a fast, stern warning. What did she do? She didn't have a weapon. A shadow passed over the drapes. Her heart jolted. Were they going to try to get in? An eye peered at her through the tiny gap in the curtains. She gasped just as Maddox landed in her room, a sword in his hand.

She pointed at the window, her hand over her mouth. He was gone the next second through another portal. She ran to the window and looked out. Maddox was there, moving through the shadows, then she couldn't see him anymore. She paced. *Be safe. Be safe. Be safe.* Her mind chanted over and over. The moment stretched out taut, every second an eternity. What if something happened to him? What if...What if...panic ran it's long moist fingers around her heart and tugged on her lungs.

Maddox landed back in her room. She crashed into him and held on as hard as she could, blowing out the breath she'd been holding. Erin pinched her eyes shut tight, relieved and terrified at the same time. Nothing had happened to him, and yet the fear she'd felt just a moment ago... The magnitude of that fear startled her.

"Did you see anything?"

"No. Nothing," he said. "What happened?"

"I woke up...kinda weird you know, alert. There was someone outside, looking in my window. I saw their eye through the gap in the curtains. Then you came. Who do you think would do that? What for?"

"I really don't like the thoughts I have to answer those questions...You might have picked up a stalker. Lots of people saw you at the club the other night. It might have been Jaris..."

She stiffened in his arms when he said that. He ignored her response.

"It might have been the person who's trying to frame me."

"Oh gosh."

"Yeah. Your house is not protected. We need to fix that in the morning...do you want to come and stay the rest of the night with me?"

She did, but she shook her head. "What about my dad?"

"Right. I guess—"

"Will you stay here?" she asked.

"Okay. Should I crash on the couch?"

"If you want...you can stay in here with me."

"Well, that's an easy decision." He smiled and kissed her lips quickly.

He set his sword down and stretched out on her bed. She grimaced, realizing how small her bed really was and he was taking up almost all of it.

"Where are you going to sleep?" his smile was cheeky.

She climbed up next to him and elbowed him in the ribs. "Scoot over."

He shifted to his side and pulled her close. Tangled up, they made it work enough so at least she wasn't going to fall off the edge. She looked into his eyes, his face next to hers.

"Here you are again," she whispered.

"You keep sending me feelings I can't ignore. You were in danger."

"I never thought of myself as a damsel."

He played with the ends of her hair. "I never thought of myself as a knight."

They grinned at one another.

"Is your dad going to go nuts in the morning if he finds me here?" he asked.

"I doubt it. He'll probably shake your hand and thump you on the back."

"Interesting man."

She rolled her eyes. "Yeah. He..."

When she hesitated, he squeezed her gently. "Let me in. It's your turn."

"I don't want to talk about my parents. He's a romantic, and he wants me in a relationship. I'll leave it at that."

"Stingy," he complained.

She mulled it over for moment. "My parents were destined life mates. He was from Paradigm; she was from Kyhael. My mom's family is still stuck in the old ways and don't like the races mixing. I don't have anything to do with them. They don't want me anyway. I'm just a Halfling to them. My parents moved here before I was born because Anue is more diverse...Your mom has done so much to end racism in Regia, but of course, it will always exist... I was twelve when my mom died. All these years, I've seen the depth of that loss in my dad, but he swears one day with my mom was worth a lifetime of pain after."

Maddox stared at her for a moment. "Thank you." He closed his eyes and exhaled, relaxing against her.

With his eyes closed, she felt free to stare at him. He was gorgeous. She had always thought so, even back when she would have rather cut out her tongue than admit it. She leaned forward and brushed her lips along his brow and then down his jaw. He looked at her as she pulled back. There was a startling intensity behind his gaze and it looked like he was fighting it back.

"What?"

"You're mine." His whisper was so quiet as he closed his eyes again.

"We'll see."

"Stubborn...and occasionally stealthy. I'm learning you."

She nestled down more and closed her eyes. It felt better than she imagined it would, and she dozed off.

Erin woke up alone in bed to the sounds of male voices talking from the other side of the house. She listened for a minute. Her dad sounded in good spirits talking to Maddox. He told him his favorite, cheesy, worn out joke. Erin rolled her eyes, but Maddox laughed. The sound caught her sideways. It was genuine and relaxed. She slid out of bed, stood in her bedroom doorway, and looked out at them.

The two men sat at the kitchen table together, drinking coffee and just chatting. Maddox glanced up as if he sensed her looking at him. Their eyes connected. He smiled and winked at her. She backed up and shut the door. She groaned as she looked in her mirror. That needed to be fixed ASAP. Heading to her shower, she reminded herself she was spending the day with Maddox. She needed to look hot, but not like she was trying to look hot.

The water splashed over her head and shoulders. She leaned her head against the shower wall and closed her eyes. The shower was the rain. The beginning. The first touch and every touch that followed. The memory enveloped her like steam, alighting on her skin. His hands were on her again, his eyes holding hers, impossible to look away. The light, such a beautiful light tying their hearts together. Her knees weakened, and she sank to the shower floor, wrapping her arms around herself. She knew he could feel this right now from her. Agony and ecstasy lived in the same breath as the water pelted her fevered skin, then inexplicably she went cold, even though the water was still warm.

The shower stopped being the rain and turned into tears. The tears of grief. Tears for Selena. The tears of her family. Erin wiped her tears, a salty overflow of the well of pain inside her. Her hands shook as she held them up in front of her face. Why were her hands so weak? Why was she unable to hold onto Selena when she'd loved her so much? Why was she powerless in the moments that turned the direction of everything?

She shook her head. She couldn't go backward. But she could live in the past if she chose. She knew people who had. She could let herself root in one moment, one memory, and never leave it. Or she could forgive.

Forgive Maddox...or had she already?

What if she just embraced it? Accepted him? She was far from his first, but she would be his last. She thought about all the women before her, and it still angered and twisted her heart. She hated his memories, whatever they were...How could she ever measure up to all of those willing, beautiful, sexy partners? How could he ever be content with *just* her after all that?

She didn't want to live with her worth and self-image always a doubt in her mind. She thought about Jaris and looked at the bruises on her arm. They were almost gone. She frowned and finished rinsing her hair. She'd said she was going to spend today with Maddox. That's what she would do.

The time poked at her as she got ready for the day. She was taking too long, and she knew it, but she wasn't leaving her room until she felt confident in the way she looked. She put her best jeans on again and a plain white top she dressed up with a long necklace. She finished her look with a fat belt that accentuated the flare of her hips. It was the best she could do with what she had.

Blowing out a breath, she finally came out of her room. Maddox and her dad were still sitting at the table, talking like no time had passed. He looked up at her, his eyes flashing, betraying desire. *Yes! You like what you see.*

She sat down at the table with them, hooked her finger through Maddox's mug handle, and took a drink of the cold coffee. He raised one eyebrow at her and smirked, but he didn't say anything.

"Good morning, sweetheart," her father said. "You took your time getting ready, didn't you?"

"Dad."

He chuckled. "It gave me a chance to have a nice long chat with Maddox, and you look beautiful. Doesn't she?" he prompted.

Maddox looked at her seriously. "She does."

"Dad, you're so weird...how are you feeling today?"

"Pretty good. So, Maddox tells me you two are planning to spend the day together. What are you going to do?"

She looked at him. "Uh, I don't know." She panicked. "We're not going somewhere people are going to take our picture and ask us questions, right?"

"I thought we could go visit Tesla for a while if you want. Then we can go wherever you like. Or we can stay here. I don't care. I need to run home for a few minutes and change."

"I'll go with you." She stood up as he did.

He raised his eyebrows again, but he didn't say anything to her. "Sir," he held out his hand to her father. "The protection for your house we talked about will be ready this afternoon."

Her dad shook his hand and nodded. "Thank you. Don't be a stranger."

"My presence, or lack of, is entirely up to Erin."

Her dad gave her a hard look. "Be nice," he ordered.

"Yes, sir."

Maddox headed to her room, picked up his sword, and went through the open portal on the wall. She followed, landing in his room right beside him. He stared openly at her, his eyes turning more grey than green as they roamed slowly over her whole body.

"You look so hot, Erin. Are you trying to torture me?"

"A little, you know in a normal way. I'm not trying to hurt you. Do you want to kiss me?"

"Yeah, but I better not...I might not stop if I start."

She smiled and headed out of his room. "I'll wait for you to change then." She closed the door behind her and bit down on her lips. Her lips really wanted his, but she also didn't want to start something they weren't going to finish.

Erin took the moment alone to look around the house. It was so nice. Not too big, not too small. All of it was livable space. No useless rooms for show. Nothing pretentious. The house was happy. It had the life of the people who lived there imbued into the walls and furniture. Maddox grew up loved. She was happy for that. Happy for him.

He came out and stood beside her as she looked at some family pictures on the wall. She was captivated by one in particular. He noticed her fixation on the picture.

"Tesla's wedding," he said.

"They were bound together by the Heart?"

"Yes, but even before that, they were soul mates. X is the only human to have ever been able to survive here. He's really human in name only. One of a kind."

"Like her."

"Yeah. There's no one like her," Maddox said with affection.

She smiled at him sideways.

"What?"

"You love your sister."

"Yeah, so? Her wedding started a new trend in Regia. But despite the desire to copy their ceremony, The

Heart refuses to do it again. It doesn't talk to just anyone."

"Were you at the wedding?"

He pointed at another picture from the wedding, and she giggled. "Aww. You were a really chubby baby."

"Yes, I was. Can we quit this now?"

"All right fine." She faced him and scowled.

"What? Why are you looking at me like that?" he asked.

"Geez, you're so...so...posh. Do you always have to dress like a model?"

"You don't like my clothes?"

"Oh no, they're very nice. Too nice. How much did your outfit cost?"

"I have no idea."

"It's just such a waste of money."

He crossed his arms. "Class warfare? Is that really where we are, Erin? You took your time trying to look nice for me. I was trying to do the same for you, but if it pisses you off..."

He turned to head back to his room. She grabbed him by the arm. "I'm sorry. That was stupid of me. I just feel awkward next to you. Everything on you is worth a fortune, at least a fortune for me." She spread her arms out. "This is the best I have."

"You could wear a torn rag and still outshine every woman in Regia. No one is even going to look at me with you at my side."

His watch pinged. He looked at it. "It's Melina."

He responded to her quickly and looked back at Erin. "I told her I'm unavailable to play today."

"Did you really say that?"

He showed her the message he sent. She snorted.

"I noticed your sword last night. Can I see it? Will you tell me about it?"

"Sure. There's not much to tell."

She followed him back to his room. He took the sword off the wall and handed it to her. She slid it slowly from its scabbard and gripped the hilt in both hands.

"I've never seen anything like it," she said quietly.

"It was a gift from my parents. It's kind of a family thing, to have a blade made from the obsidian of the mountain."

She held it up and moved it from side to side. Maddox grabbed her wrist and took the sword out of her hands.

"What?"

"You have no swordplay experience."

"You can tell?"

He nodded. "I don't want you to accidentally cut off my head."

"I wish I had fighting skills. I didn't have a flashy education at the Academy, like you."

"Sure they teach some stuff at Academy, but my real training was always at home. Or when I tagged along to work with my Dad."

"That's awesome. Will you tell me about it? What's it like on the Obsidian Mountain?"

"I'll tell you, but…" his expression morphed, his eyes sliding out of focus. "My dad is my hero. I wish I was more like him. It's really something to watch him fight, and he's the only mage in Regia, the only one in like a hundred years. He trained me in the Kata since I could walk. I thought one day I'd be able to be a mage, too. When I hit my adolescence, I realized that wasn't a possibility for me."

"Why not?"

"I've climbed up the ranks in the Kata, but I can't even break through to the level of master. My dad says I hesitate, and I won't get out of my own head when I fight."

"Is that true?" she asked.

"I think I've never had anything to fight for. Training is all well and good, but I've never been in a real battle. I've never had to fight for my life or the lives of those I love. I don't know what I'm made of. I can't until I've been through the fire like that...no one who wasn't a full blood vampire has ever become a mage anyway. I'm too mixed to achieve it, even if I was a master."

He held his sword up and gazed at it. "It's my power, inside this glass. I don't know what that means. I don't have any power, but when my parents made this sword for me, they put my blood inside it. Tesla's swords are filled with lightning, my mother's too. I don't understand this patterned gold light, or what it means if anything." He sheathed the sword and shook himself. "You want to go to Tesla's now? She makes the best coffee anywhere. Particularly for half vampires like us."

"I'm nervous, but I want to go."

He framed her face and kissed her mouth. She sighed into him. When had this become natural? Their mouths were keeping company more and more.

"You've got nothing to be nervous about."

He opened a portal, took her hand, and they went through together.

Sixteen

Kendrick handed the dead girl's watch to his mom and waited. He paced along the wall like a caged animal.

"Sit down," she said. "Good night. You're so nervous."

"Yes, ma'am." He sat, but he twisted his hands together.

Her smile grew as she scrolled through everything he had. The pictures. The fake messages. All of it.

"Very good work, son. Was she easy to kill? Did you enjoy it?"

"Parts of it."

"You kept your head throughout the whole thing. I'm proud of you."

"Thank you, Mom. All you have to do is hit send, and it will break everywhere."

"Have you picked the next one?"

"Yes. And she will be more painful than the others. Maddox actually cares for this one. He's territorial with her. And she has a sweetness the others lacked. The public will want his head."

"She sounds good, but don't lose focus, son. This isn't about Maddox."

"Yes, ma'am."

Erin gaped at the house for a moment. "Wow. They live in that?"

He chuckled and pulled on her hand. "Cool, huh?"

"I like it. It's weird. A good weird."

Her watch pinged. A message from Jaris.

I MISS YOU. WILL I SEE YOU TONIGHT?

I'm busy. Talk later.

"It's Jaris," she told him.

"Did you tell him you're unavailable to play today?"

"No. I wasn't that cute. I just said I was busy."

The big door swung open for them. Erin's heart sped up—face to face with Tesla. When she'd seen her before, she was so absorbed thinking her dad was dead that she didn't get the chance to talk to or even really look at her.

"Come in," Tesla smiled and moved aside.

She was rooted where she stood. Maddox pulled her in.

"Hi," she managed. "I'm Erin."

"I know. I'm glad you came to see me. Maddie's told me about you."

"Please stop calling me that," he whined.

Her nerves bounced in her stomach. "I...thank you for saving my dad's life."

"No problem. Is he doing better?"

"Much. He almost looks normal again." Erin tried to come up with something to say. "Um...I saw a few pictures of your wedding. Your dress was amazing."

Tesla smirked, and it looked just like Maddox's smirk. "That was a long time ago now."

"You look exactly the same though."

"Thanks. I'm actually only three years older than Maddie."

"What?"

"Long story. I'll tell you sometime if you decide you're going to be my sister after all."

Erin just swallowed.

"I promised her you'd make coffee," Maddox interjected.

Tesla smiled. "Oh, all right. I'm going to have to teach you how one of these days."

"Yeah, but if you teach me, I'll lose my best excuse to just show up here," he said.

They followed Tesla into her kitchen. Erin sat next to Maddox and waited quietly for her coffee. She observed the way the two of them spoke to one another. It made her sad she was an only child.

"Oh!" she shrieked and pulled into Maddox as the black smear of a nightmare stalked into the room.

It turned its red eyes on her and smiled terribly. Her blood ran cold. Maddox chuckled and rubbed her arm.

"Relax. It's just Fluffy."

The monster laughed an evil, demonic sound. "*Just* Fluffy? I resent that."

Dumbfounded, Erin continued to cling to Maddox. Then X walked in.

"Hello," he said casually to Erin.

"Hi," she squeaked, staring at X. He was quite freaky and totally beautiful. Not as gorgeous as Maddox, but it was close.

X held out his hand, palm up to the monster. The next second it vanished.

"Wha…where did that thing go?" she asked.

"He's in here," X said showing her his hand. A clear stone, like a crystal, was strapped to his palm. He sat down across from her and pinned her with his ice blue eyes. "So you're her? The reluctant life mate."

"Um…"

"Do you really hate Maddox?"

"Yes."

X laughed. "Are you scared to be here?"

"No."

"You're not very honest."

"Stop it, X," Tesla said.

"All right. All right." He got up from the table and wrapped Tesla in his arms. "You're making that nasty stuff again?"

"No one's asking you to drink it."

Everyone's watches pinged at the same time. Scrambled words and images blurred the headlines. Incoherent flashes came through, then it was gone.

"What was that?" Erin asked.

Maddox's watch pinged again. He stood and walked into the other room before answering the call, but his voice carried through anyway.

"Hey, Redge. I'm at Tesla's house right now…I saw something. It wasn't clear…Do you need me to come there? Okay…Yeah… Bye."

Before Maddox came back, X got a call, too. He didn't leave the room to answer it. "Kindel…Nope. Nothing was clear. Yeah, I'll talk to him…Let me know." He ended his call and sighed.

"Is there another dead girl?" Erin asked.

X gave her a hard stare. Maddox came back in and sat down next to her again. "It's okay, X. I trust Erin."

She looked at him, amazed. He said it so easily. Was it true? Did he trust her?

"Lots of ugly stuff leaked to the media. It needs to be sorted through. Kindel stopped it from breaking."

"I deleted all my old contacts, but they're still on my other watch that I left at Fortress. Those girls need protection, or at least to be warned." Maddox said. "I'm worried about Mel and Erin the most. Someone was outside Erin's window last night."

"The dome for Erin's house is ready," Tesla said. "Mel's already well protected and informed, but you're right. What did Redge say?"

"That I need to be ready to make a public statement if the news actually does get through."

"If you and Erin could go public with your relationship, that would—"

"She's not ready for that," Maddox cut Tesla off.

"I'm just thinking of things to protect you," she argued.

"It doesn't matter," his voice made it clear the topic was closed.

"I'm sorry. I think I should go," Erin said. "I don't want to add to the stress." She stood. "Could you open a portal for me, please?"

Maddox stood, too, and put his hand on her lower back, directing her gently out of the room and through the front door.

"I'm sorry," he said once they were outside. "I saw that going a bit differently in my mind. I thought you would like them."

"I do. It's not that. I just don't know what to do…I feel weird. Like I've encroached on something too personal. I don't feel comfortable being a part of…I'm the outsider. And your family is in turmoil right now."

"You're right. This isn't fair to you, and I'm trying really hard to be fair to you, Erin. I'm trying to not push. I'm trying to not charm you when I want to. But this whole business is scaring me. I'm worried you're going to be targeted. Just last night—I can't even let myself think about it because I get all freaked out and furious at the same time. And I don't know what is going to be required of me in the next few days, or hours, in that case. But I have to know you're safe."

She took in his voice as he spoke, his eyes, and what he was feeling transferred from his heart to hers. Taking a deep breath, she made a choice. He needed her help.

"I won't be *that* girl. The one who insists she's fine and can take care of herself when she's really just a helpless dumbass who causes more trouble and puts herself and others in danger. I won't be that girl. I'll listen."

"Wow. I think I just fell in love with you." He leaned in and kissed her lips, but just briefly.

"I am pretty awesome," she teased, using snark to hide behind. "What can I do so you don't worry about me?"

"Stay close. And when you're not, stay under the protections on your house or mine."

"Sounds like I need a guard to go anywhere."

The door opened behind them, and X stepped out. "There already is one. Well, sort of."

"What?" she asked.

"Fortress is already tailing Maddox. It's not foolproof, and for the time being, they're only a shadow in the distance, looking for the perp to slip up. But there are eyes. They're only there when he goes out in public."

"So what are you saying, X?" Maddox asked.

"Don't do anything differently. If you start to look over your shoulder, so will the perp. It will screw everything up. Keep Erin close, but keep things looking status quo. Okay?"

"Okay," they both agreed.

X handed a small box to Maddox before going back inside and shutting the door.

"What's that?" she asked.

"The protection for your house. We should go back there and get it up now."

He touched the mark on his wrist, opening a portal for them back to her house. They landed back in the living room.

Nathan jumped in his chair and put his hand over his heart. "Good grief!" he exclaimed.

"Sorry, Dad. Didn't mean to startle you," Erin said sitting on the armrest of his chair.

Maddox set the box on the floor and opened it. Pale light vibrated inside. It rose up and coated the air like the membrane of a soap bubble, spreading more and more. Erin gasped as it slid through her. It felt like a warm shiver and then was gone. The air sparkled, and then everything looked normal again.

"It's done," Maddox said. "No one meaning you harm will be able to get through. If you want it to shut out door-to-door salesmen, you should have mentioned that before."

Her dad laughed. "I like this one," he said to Erin. "The other guy seems like a kiss-ass to me."

She patted his arm and stood up. "Okay, Dad, thanks for your input."

"I have to second what he said," Maddox added.

"Okay, thank you for your input," she repeated in the same tone she used on her father.

"What are you kids up to now? You haven't been gone that long."

Her watch pinged. "I uh...hold on." She went into her room and shut the door.

"Jaris. Hi." She answered the call.

"Hey. What are you doing? I miss you. Your last message was abrupt. Are you mad at me?"

"Not mad. No."

"Why did you break our date last night?" he asked.

"My dad. He's so much better. Better than he's been in so long. I wanted to spend the evening with him," she explained, feeling increasingly uncomfortable by the moment.

"Oh. Why didn't you say so? I was worried you were with Maddox."

"Um...well, I was after a while. For our appointment, you know."

Jaris was quiet for a minute. "Is he getting forceful with you? Pushing you for more?"

"No," she said quickly, thinking how she had been the one last night to want skin to skin contact. She'd told him he could have her if he wanted...*Something real or nothing.* Was she being real? She wasn't being open with Jaris. She blew out a breath. "Look, I'm spending today with Maddox. There's some stuff going on. I can't talk about it."

There was another silence, an angry silence. "I see," he said finally. "I thought you were smarter than this, Erin. I didn't think he'd be able to fool you, but it sounds like you're starting to believe his lies."

"You don't understand."

"Where's your loyalty to Selena?"

Insulted, she hung up and closed her eyes, taking a deep breath. Curious, she tried to tell Maddox to come to her through their connection. *Come here, come here, come here*, she thought, even though she knew he couldn't hear her thoughts. She smiled at the soft knock on her door.

"Come in."

He looked around the door, curiously. "Did you...*call* me?"

"I did. Come in and close the door."

He closed the door, but he didn't get any closer. "Are you okay?"

"That was Jaris. He's angry."

Maddox frowned. "So?" he asked slowly. "Was he mean to you? You want me to go kick his ass?"

She snorted at him. "Are you kidding?"

"Yeah...no...I totally am...I'm not."

She wanted him to hold her, but he just stood there. Erin crossed her arms. "What X said about everything needing to look the same, does that mean you need to go out with Melina again tonight?"

He sighed. "I guess it does. Sorry."

"Can I come, too?"

"Sure." He smiled. "I'd like that, but..." his smile fell. "I don't know if you'd be safer with me, or somewhere else."

"You told me to stay close. Are you going to worry more if you can actually see me, or not?"

"Hmm..." he seemed to think it over for a second. "Please come with me."

He came closer and reached for her. She let him fold her into his arms.

"I don't know why I even hesitated, because the truth is, no one could ever protect you the way I can. Or the way I would. You're my mate, acknowledged or not. I would die to protect you. I want you where I can see you, and not just because I love looking at you."

She leaned her head back and closed her eyes so he could kiss her…only he didn't. She blinked as he let go and stepped away from her.

"What?"

He ran his hands through his hair. "I'm sorry if that was too much. I'm not trying to *persuade* you. My mouth just ran away with me."

Erin felt oddly let down and relieved at the same time.

His face pulled in a sour expression. "Maybe you should invite Jaris to come, too."

She looked at him in shock. "Um…you want me to bring a date?"

"No!" he said quickly. "I just don't want the person trying to frame me to focus on you. So maybe they won't if it looks like we're nothing to each other. You're just a girl I danced with once and that's all…maybe you shouldn't go after all."

"*Maybe* I feel the need to keep an eye on you as much as you feel the need to keep an eye on me."

He cocked a brow at her. "Is that so?"

She shrugged. "Maybe. So where are we going tonight?"

"The venue will be the same. I'll call the club and make sure they're expecting me, and I'll insist on more security than usual. I'll check with Redge, too, and see what he says."

"I need something to wear. Can Melina help me? Do you think she would?"

He grinned and touched his watch. "Mel?" he said.

"Hey, M." Her voice rang out.

"I've got someone who wants to play dress up with you. What do you say? Help Erin fit in with us tonight?"

"Fit in or stand out like the last time she showed at a club?" Melina asked.

"Fit in, *please*. I need to be able to focus."

Melina snorted. "I have my doubts about your ability to do that regardless of what I—"

"She can hear you," Maddox cut her off. "Can you attempt to not embarrass me? And she knows we're not together."

"I see. Hi, Erin."

"Hi."

"I'll meet you at your house, M, around sunset."

"Sounds good. Bye." He ended the call.

"So what do you want to do now?" she asked.

"We could go out to eat, but that's a problem because we'll be seen together."

"I am hungry, but I can just throw something together for us and my Dad."

"You want to just stay here and hang with him?" Maddox offered.

"You wouldn't mind?"

"Why would I? Your dad's funny. I like him."

She liked the idea, but she suddenly felt off, overtired, or something she couldn't account for.

"What's wrong?" he asked.

"I don't know. I feel a little overwhelmed I think. Jaris said I wasn't being loyal to Selena by spending time with you."

Maddox's eyes turned cold. "Do you agree with him?"

She rubbed her head. "No. I told you I don't think it's your fault. He's...I don't know..."

"He's worried you're slipping away from him."

"Yeah. I guess. I feel so tired all of a sudden."

He looked down. "I'll leave you alone."

He moved toward the open portal on the wall. He couldn't leave like that. She gripped his arm. As he turned back to her, she grabbed his collar and pulled, pressing her mouth roughly against his. He closed his eyes and groaned in the back of his throat, holding her tight. It was fast and desperate, and both of them had to catch their breaths as they pulled away.

"I'm going to rest for a while," she said. "I'll be back at your house when the sun sets."

He put one hand on the side of her neck and tilted her chin up with his thumb. "Say it, Erin. Say that you're mine," he whispered.

She shook her head and took a step back from him. "I haven't decided yet."

He looked down again and left. She lay down on her bed and curled into a ball. Her tears were few, but she cried nonetheless before crashing into sleep.

Erin slept hard. A soft caress began to rouse her from sleep. Fingertips grazed her lips and smoothed her hair away from her face. "Maddox," she murmured, not quite lucid. She rolled over, her eyes opening slowly.

"Oh!" she was fully awake instantly. Face to face with Melina, smiling deviously at her.

"I thought about kissing you awake, Sleeping Beauty."

Erin sat up eying Melina warily. "Why are you in my room, touching me?"

"Just curious what you'd do, and I thought it was time you and I came to an understanding...You did what I suspected you might when I touched you."

"What was that?"

Melina continued to smile. "You said his name."

Erin pushed her hair back and took a deep breath. "Well...I...that's not..."

Melina snorted. "You are stubborn, aren't you?"

Erin crossed her arms. "Let's have it then," she said aggressively.

"Have what?"

"Give me the run down on how if I hurt Maddox you'll bring swift and painful retribution on me and I'm a fool for not just caving into him cause he's the best thing ever, and whatever else."

Melina blinked at her, then she threw her head back and laughed loudly. "Oh, hell. There's hope you and I can be friends."

"Who says I'd have you?" Erin demanded.

Melina laughed louder, and in a second, Erin dropped her attack stance and chuckled.

"I didn't come here to threaten you, Erin. I came here to really talk to you for the first time, now that you know me and M are not together. And despite what he might tell you about the rundown on tonight, you're going to need my perspective on what it will be like. Girls gotta stick together."

"Sorry for the attitude. That's very nice of you. I appreciate it."

Melina crawled up on her bed and sat cross-legged next to Erin. For a moment, they just looked at one another, an odd kind of examination and understanding happening between them. Erin relaxed.

"You've known him your whole life?"

Melina nodded. "He hasn't been himself since that hag, Bess. That's when I lost him. That's when he changed, and unfortunately, that was the same time his fame ratcheted up to what it is now. The combination twisted him."

"He told me about her. He must have really loved her."

"He did. He fell hard and didn't try to hold back. He'd have given her the world. He tried to. And she was false."

Erin frowned. "I feel weird about it...you know? Like I want to track her down and kick her ass."

Melina smiled deviously again. "I did. M doesn't know."

Erin returned her smile. "He won't hear it from me...Did you make her cry?"

"Oh, yes. And scream and beg. She wasn't quite so pretty after I broke her nose and blacked her eye. I took some of her hair, too."

"Damn...I wish I knew how to fight."

"You'll learn. Forest will see to it...well, if you stay in their family."

Erin looked down. "You're not going to try and sell me?"

"No. I really don't see the need, but that could be because I'm biased. I'm interested in your hang-ups on it though, if you'd tell me."

Erin grimaced for a moment, thinking it over. Then she opened up and found it was really what she needed to do. Melina listened as she told her about her feelings on Maddox before she connected to him. The night Selena died. Jaris. Everything she felt as she'd spent more time with Maddox. She almost blurted about him being the gift giver, but she didn't know if Melina knew about that.

"So when it's just you and him, what's the problem?" she asked.

Unbidden tears began slicking Erin's eyes. "Absolutely nothing and everything at the same time...I feel like trash with him. I'm poor. I feel so plain and ugly even. How could I ever be enough for him after all the women he's been with? I hate that. I hate that I feel like I would need to compete with all these dirty memories."

"Hmm..." Melina nodded, her expression thoughtful. "I can understand that."

Erin wiped her eyes. "Thank you."

"I really do get it, Erin. I'm going to give you a pep talk anyway."

She snorted. "Okay. Let's hear it."

Melina moved forward and took her hand. "You are not plain or ugly, first of all. I'm jealous of how beautiful you are. That's the truth. M told me about the first time he saw you and what it did to him. That was before your connection, so you can't use that as your excuse."

"I totally was, too."

"I figured. Anyway, your beauty is not in question. You're beautiful. You are not trash. You shouldn't think that, and M doesn't think that...If I was you, I'd be pissed about all the other women as well, but there is no competition. None of them mattered to him. And none of them had him either. As much as they might have tried to get a hold on him, they couldn't. I'm not excusing him. I think it's good he feels the pain of it now. I'm glad you've punished him over it. But his memories, whatever they are, have to compete with you, not you with them. See? You've been thinking about it backward. And here's something else. Maddox is one of the most insecure people I've ever met. You're worried you won't ever be enough for him, and he's worried he won't ever be enough for you."

"How could he be insecure about anything?"

"Look closer, Erin."

"I'll try. I need to think about what you've said."

"You do that. Now we're on the clock. We need to eat, and then move on to what you're going to wear tonight and how you should handle yourself."

Melina went through the portal on her wall and was back in a few minutes with a garment bag slung over her shoulder. She laid it down on the bed and ordered food to be delivered.

"Go shower. The food will be here by the time you get out."

Erin obeyed, her stomach beginning to jump with excited nerves. Melina was making this a fun prospect and taking the fear out of it. She showered at top speed and came out into the living room in her bath robe, following the smell and the sounds of Melina talking to her dad.

Her dad looked up at her as she sat down at the table with them.

"I like your new friend. Although I'm not quite used to people just popping in the way they have been," he said.

"I should have told you there's a portal in my bedroom," Erin said.

"That's quite the thing. Tesla herself comes here and saves my life, you've caught Maddox's attention, and now there are portals in my house." He blew out a breath theatrically and helped himself to more food.

Erin ate quickly, not really even tasting the food, her mind wandering onto the approaching night. After dinner, she and Melina shut themselves in her room again. Melina went over to the portal and closed the shadowy curtain over it.

"We don't want any snooping boys coming through right now."

Erin snickered. "Definitely not. So what's first?"

"Hair. Keep it simple. Leave it down. Tease it a little. M is obsessed with your hair, by the way."

"He is?"

"Yeah. You know he's never been with a redhead. Not ever. Ha! Look at you. You're smirking. You like that."

"Might be the only first I can be to him."

Melina helped her do her makeup in the current trend before opening the garment bag and laying out the contents on the bed.

"I'm not rich like M. These are the best dresses I own. It's all on the level we need for tonight, but I'm sorry I don't have more choices for you."

All three dresses were amazing, but she didn't know which one to choose. "What do you think? Which one will help me fit in best? What color are you wearing tonight?"

"I was planning on blue. You wore black the last time you came out to a club. That was over the top. I mean it was awesome, but you're not going to fit in if you pull a stunt like that again. And that's how you start fights."

"I don't want to start fights. I like the grey one."

"Try it on."

Erin slid into the short, one-shoulder dress and looked in the mirror, instantly unsure. "I don't know. This is really sexy."

"Sexy is the point of clubbing. But you're right, M is going to blister me for this. Ah, well, I think that makes it perfect. He's not in charge. Make him crazy; it won't hurt him none. And remember the past has to compete with you, and it's going to fail, hard."

Erin licked her lips and looked at herself closer. Melina stood behind her and put her chin on her shoulder.

"See how beautiful you are?"

"I see my freckles."

"They aren't a flaw, silly. Pay attention to M when he sees you. Look at yourself through his eyes."

Erin nodded. "I'll try. So where are the pitfalls tonight?"

"Kendrick is a big one. Don't talk to him much if you can avoid it. I blame him almost entirely for the asshole M became. He's a *really* bad influence. He likes to use M to promote himself in the spotlight."

"I've met him once, at Selena's funeral. He made my flesh crawl."

"I think I've almost convinced M to cut ties with him, but since we have to go through this public charade right now, Kendrick stays."

"Does he know about me and Maddox?" Erin asked.

"No, not about life mates. He thinks your M's side hustle right now. It needs to stay that way. If he knew about you guys, he'd tell the world. But he will probably make a few passes at you because that's who he is. Just ignore him. If he gets over the top with you, come to me, and I'll handle him."

"So who am I tonight?"

"You're just a part of the group. I'm M's girlfriend. Don't answer any questions thrown your way. Let M answer if he decides to. Go along with whatever is said. Hang back. You can keep behind me."

"Can I dance with him?"

Melina smiled. "That's fine, just don't monopolize him. Cause you could, and he would forget why we're going out in the first place."

"Okay. I think I got it. Anything else?"

"Don't drink anything Kendrick offers you. He's a drug pusher, and he always has something new. He'll try to slip you things if you don't take them willingly."

Erin wrinkled her nose.

"Yeah. That's how I feel about him, too," Melina said in response to Erin's facial expression. "All right, you're ready to go. Help me get into my dress for the night."

Seventeen

Maddox cracked his knuckles and paced while he waited for Mel and Erin. Kendrick sat on the couch, his head leaning back and his eyes closed, already high. Then he laughed for no reason.

"What are you on?" Maddox asked.

"New mix. It has shadow sand cut into the cocaine with a touch of some off-world meth type stuff. So happy making. You really need to try it."

"No thanks. The girls are my drug of choice tonight. If you're going to act like the court jester, I'm not taking you along."

"Relax. I'll be my usual charming self in a few minutes." He laughed again. "I only took a little, and it zips you up fast and drops you almost as quickly."

"You better drop fast. I've got Mel and Erin tonight, and I don't want you scaring Erin or flapping your lips about the shit we've been in before. She hears any stories from you, and I will let Mel cut you into tiny pieces, like she's been asking to."

Kendrick snorted, and then he grabbed himself. "Mel and I are going to damage each other so hard one of these days. I don't care if she kills me afterward. I know it will be worth it."

"Keep tripping. I want your word."

"*My word?* The hell are you talking about?"

"To not tell Erin shit about me."

"Oh, sure. No problem. You'll screw it up on your own fast enough. And then Mystery Girl will come running to my open arms. And I know she must be a real firecracker cause you don't have your usual *once is enough* attitude toward her."

"Shut up."

"Ha! She must be a *very* bad girl under that sweet exterior."

Maddox stopped pacing and narrowed his eyes at Kendrick. "Why do you always want what's mine?" he asked seriously.

Kendrick raised his head and gave him a dirty look. "*Yours?* The whole world is *yours,* isn't it? What the hell has happened to you? You're acting all weird. This new you sucks."

Maddox blew a breath out through his nose and scowled. *Status quo*, he reminded himself. Erin knew all this was fake. He'd ask Mel to quietly remind her of that throughout the night.

"Sorry. You're right. I need a drink. I've been in my head too much the last few days. Kinda screwed up over Selena."

Kendrick's expression relaxed, and he leaned his head back again. "Not over that yet? It's old news. You just need to get back into things. Stop sticking to one girl. The more you have, the happier you'll be. Whoreing soothes the soul, brother."

Maddox turned away from him so Kendrick wouldn't see him roll his eyes. Mel was right. He needed to cut Kendrick out of his life for good. He just couldn't do it tonight.

He continued to pace, a strong sense of unease in his stomach. What was he thinking bringing Erin to this? She wanted to come, he reminded himself. But she was his princess. He wanted to put her in a tower away from everything to do with his life before her.

They were getting somewhere, he could feel it. She'd changed dramatically toward him since she learned about his anonymous activities. They'd turned a corner. He really hoped tonight wouldn't be a setback or worse.

To the world, she wasn't anything to him except maybe a passing interest. He had to make sure it looked that way tonight to keep her safe. Would that jerk Jaris show up? Had she asked him to come? Did he still matter to her? She hadn't given him up, so he must still matter. How could he change that? He knew. His mind blurred with images of the two of them in the rain, her body's response. The intensity just in touching her bare skin and the way she rushed under his hands. He knew how to change it...

He shook himself from his thoughts of having her under him. Not until she said it. Not until she stopped being ashamed. He had to stick to that, no matter what.

He heard the girls come through the portal in his room. They both giggled, and then they came out of his room. His eyes locked on Erin. He blinked. Why had destiny been so good to him? She was a fantasy. The dress she wore showed off a great deal of her legs and clung to her curves like a second skin. *Fit in*. That was a joke. She would draw every eye.

Mine. No one is going to take her away from me.

He needed her. She was killing him looking like that. And he had to limit how much he touched her and the way he touched her tonight. It was all wrong. She was his mate. They should be alone. Dead to the world for weeks or months, doing nothing but enjoying each other.

She looked at him funny, like she was searching for something in his face. Then she smiled. He *really* needed her, but he hadn't moved an inch. Kendrick moved past him.

"Ladies. You take my breath away."

Erin's smile became fixed facing Kendrick, and Melina scowled.

"Save it," Mel said. She hooked her arm in Erin's and pulled her close, away from Kendrick.

"Are you ready to go, M?" Mel asked him.

"Yeah."

Still lightheaded from the way Erin looked, he opened a portal, and the four of them went through it to Paradigm. The main square was filled with people, and like before, they were swarmed as soon as they were spotted. Mel clung to his arm and smiled for the cameras like usual. He glanced over his shoulder at Erin. She looked down and discreetly held Mel's other hand. He needed to get Mel another present soon for being so wonderful.

He didn't answer any questions and led them into the club. Security was up inconspicuously, as he'd requested of the owners earlier in the afternoon. The music was loud, and smoke hung in the air over their heads as they moved through the people dancing on the floor. This was his time. Right then, before the focus of the club was on what he was doing.

He leaned to Mel. "Go to the booth."

She nodded and let go of him. He turned on Erin and grabbed her around the waist, moving her back into the heart of the dancing crowd. Her eyes flashed at him, and her lips curved up. She didn't ask him what he was doing, she just flowed into it. The bass of the music was hard, and she moved her awesome body along with it. The last time, she'd been scared. Now she surged under his hands and against his body as they danced.

Hell, yes! She could *really* do this. She was sensual grace. Not one inch of her was awkward or frightened now. She was a great dancer. He hadn't expected her to jump into this like she did. He wanted to catch her off guard so she wouldn't say no, but she smiled at him as she swayed, like it had been her idea.

His hands slid lower, his mind blank except for the beat and the way her hips hit along with it under his hands. The song changed, the tempo going up. She raised one eyebrow.

"Whatcha got, Maddox?" she challenged.

He spun her in a circle, showing her how he could rule her. She went with it and let him lead. He'd never danced with someone who moved with him like she did. It was so hot. Then she turned her back to him and blew his mind. She leaned her head back against his shoulder, held the back of his neck with one hand, and moved her hips back against him. What was she doing? Had she forgotten she didn't want to be seen with him? Had she just lost herself in the music?

What was *he* thinking? He had to get her off the floor before everyone started looking at them. She was too hot. Eyes were going to start sticking to her. He grabbed her hips and turned her around again, catching her lips with his for a second.

"We need to do this again. In private," he said in her ear.

"Agreed. Nice moves, player."

He directed her off the floor, his hand still possessively on her hip.

"Mel told me I could dance with you once tonight. I guess I have to hand you back to her now."

"Not if you don't want to," he smiled.

"No. We have to remember why we're here. Mel's your girlfriend. I'm just a drive-by."

They almost made it to the booth where Kendrick and Mel waited.

"Maddox!" someone shouted.

They turned. Jaris stood there, looking murderous. People cleared away from him.

"Oh no," Erin said. She pulled away from him and moved toward Jaris.

Maddox's heart tore as he watched her go to him. He forced himself to hold still.

"Jaris, let me explain."

"Explain what?" he shouted. "That you lied to me? Come with me, Erin. You belong with me, not him. You have to end it with him now."

Maddox froze inside. He couldn't breathe. Was she going to listen to him? She looked over her shoulder, her gaze locking on his, and he couldn't read it. Then she looked back at Jaris. Was this the moment she would end it? Was he about to lose his soul? Right then and there?

Jaris held his hand out for her. Erin looked at it, then she shook her head and backed away from him.

"No. I'm sorry, Jaris. It's over between us."

Maddox couldn't believe what she said, what she did, as she moved back to him and took his hand. It looked like Jaris was as shocked as he was.

Jaris' shock shifted into rage. "I thought you were better, Erin. But you're just another stupid girl, ready and willing to be used."

"That's enough," Maddox warned him. "She's made her choice. Just leave now."

Jaris decided to step forward instead.

Maddox moved protectively in front of Erin. "Don't force me to hurt you. Just leave."

"You just didn't have enough, did you? Not enough women to whet your appetite. You had to take the one woman who was different, and you brainwashed her. And now you've reduced her to just another whore."

Maddox saw red. No one would talk about Erin like that. His right hook landed on Jaris' jaw and sent him sprawling to the floor. Security moved in and picked him up off the floor. All eyes were on them. He turned to Erin. She looked up at him like a scared animal. He took her hand and pulled her back, past the bodyguard next to the entrance to the VIP section where Mel and Kendrick both stood, watching.

He felt like he was going to burst out of his skin, but he thought it was better to stay for a little while and act like nothing was out of place. Let the buzz around Jaris die down a little. Erin kept her head down as they all sat and ordered drinks. He could feel her trembling next to him. He didn't touch her.

Mel leaned close to him and whispered. "She chose you."

"No, she didn't, not really. She just didn't choose him," he whispered back.

Kendrick's eyes kept darting back and forth between Maddox and the two girls. "Well," he said finally. "That will be all over the news soon. It's been a while since Maddox had fighting headlines. Should make a nice change."

"Shut up," he mumbled at Kendrick.

They all drank when their drinks hit the table, even Mel. Maddox really needed to get Erin alone now and talk to her, find out where her head was. He decided they'd been out long enough and was about say they could leave when the *real* shit hit the fan.

Every watch in the club pinged. His stomach dropped as he read the headlines. Somehow, the person trying to frame him had gotten their story through Kindel's wall. It was worse than he imagined, and it all painted him as a murderer and the whole family as corrupt. He sighed as everyone looked at him.

"Time to go," he said.

They all slid out of the booth, and he opened a portal, taking the four of them back to his house. Kendrick plopped on the couch and leaned his head back again. Mel paced. Erin stood still, scrolling through the news on her watch, frowning as she read.

"What are you going to do, M?" Mel asked.

"I have to go to Fortress."

Erin looked up. "Now?"

"Yeah. I'm sorry there's—"

"Do you want me to go with you?" Erin cut him off.

He took her hand, led her into his room, and shut the door.

"What can I do?" she asked.

He pulled her against him and kissed her mouth. She gave softly, but there was worry behind her response.

"We need to talk, but I have to go now. Will you stay here with Mel, so I know you're safe?"

"Okay. How long will you be?"

"I don't know. I'll be back as soon as I can." He kissed her again.

"If it's really late, will you wake me? Please."

He touched her cheek. "Why are you doing this? What changed?"

"I..."

His watch pinged. It was Redge.

"Go," she said. "I'll be here."

"Thank you."

Maddox opened a portal and left. Erin stared at the space where he'd just been, his words in her head. *What changed?*

She worried her bottom lip between her teeth. This trouble would blow over. He would have the best advice on what to do or not do. The falseness of the story in the media would be exposed. And she would do what she could to help him through it because he'd helped her when she needed him. He'd protected her, and he'd saved her dad. The last thing she would give him right now was attitude.

Mel's raised voice drew her attention back to the living room. Erin came back out.

"It's not happening, Kendrick. We just need to do what we can for Maddox right now. Are you his friend, or not?"

Kendrick sneered at Mel, then his face smoothed. "I know you resist me so hard because you're scared of how much you really want it."

"That must be it. You caught me."

Mel looked ready to burst. Erin came up to Kendrick and stood a little too close to him. His eyebrows lifted as she put her hand on his arm.

"Can I speak to you alone?" she asked quietly.

He smiled wickedly at her. "Sure, sweetheart."

He followed her back to Maddox's room. Mel looked at her confusedly. Erin winked at her and shut the door.

"What do you want?" he asked.

"I'll help you with Melina."

"Oh?"

"Yeah. She's around too much. She ruins the time I get alone with Maddox. I'll pour honey in her ear about you. She'll listen to me."

"What do you want in return?"

"Could you leave us alone for the rest of the night?"

"That's all?"

"That's it."

He shrugged. "I had somewhere to be anyway."

She gave him a sweet smile and put her hand on his shoulder. His eyes betrayed how much he liked her touching him.

"Thanks, Kendrick."

"You and I need to spend more time together. Alone."

"I guess we'll have to see about that," she said suggestively.

He glanced over at the open portal on the wall. His smile flashed. "Okay, sugar. I'm leaving. I'll see you soon."

He opened the door. Mel stood there frowning, her arms crossed over her chest. He walked over to her, circled her closely, and then moved toward the front door. "Goodnight, ladies."

As soon as the door closed behind him, Erin locked it and shivered. "Beast."

"What did you do to make him leave so easily?"

"I told him I'd talk him up to you if he left. And I am a woman of my word. You should let him in your pants, Mel, cause he's wonderful. There. Has that convinced you?"

Melina laughed. "It has! I've been a fool, not seeing the treasure right in front of me. Thank you for opening my eyes!"

They both slumped on the couch and took their heels off.

"Thanks for everything tonight," Erin said.

"Has it hit you yet?"

"No. I feel the weight of what happened at the club and whatever he's having to go through right now, but I'm coasting. It will hit me soon, I'm sure. Then I'll probably cry a bit. Just warning you. I'm a big cry baby."

Mel snickered and patted her knee. "I won't tease you if you cry. So are you with M? You rejected that other guy."

"My head's not clear. All I can be right now is here for him. I can't decide something so big in the middle of all this drama."

"Okay," Melina smiled broadly.

"What?"

"It looked like you two really clicked on the dance floor."

Erin smiled too and blushed. "Yeah. That was...good."

Mel laughed. "M likes to dance."

"I do, too."

"Wanna watch a movie or something while we wait? Take our minds somewhere else?"

"Sounds good."

Mel chose the movie. Erin tried to get lost in it, but she couldn't help but check her watch every few minutes.

An hour later, both of their watches began buzzing like they were about to blow up.

"He's on."

Erin enlarged and projected the feed up into the air. She held her breath, her heart racing as Maddox began to speak.

"The tragedy of Trish's death, along with the recent death of Selena has both disheartened and enraged me. I had nothing to do with either crime, and I fully believe someone is attempting to frame me. I have given Fortress my full cooperation, and I will do whatever is required of me to assist in the investigation. This is one of those times that words utterly fail, but I wish all possible solace to the hearts of the families of these young women."

The next moment, Redge filled the feed. "Maddox is not a suspect. An investigation is underway. Fortress will find and bring the individual or individuals responsible for these crimes to justice. I'll take three questions only."

Erin blew out a breath and turned it off. She didn't care what questions were asked.

Melina scooted close and rubbed Erin's shoulder. "It's okay."

"It was fast...He did good, right?"

Mel nodded. "Yeah. He did good. He was open, you know. His face, his eyes. I could see him."

Erin exhaled and leaned against her. "Thanks for everything tonight. Thanks for staying with me."

Kendrick slid another drink toward Jaris. He took a sip and set it down, his head beginning to slump. He was wasted.

"I just didn't think this would happen."

"Hey, man, lots of us have lost our girlfriends to Maddox. It sucks. If you want her back, he never keeps anyone long."

"Yeah, if only she wasn't his destined life mate. He's never letting her go."

Kendrick pushed the drink back into Jaris' hand. "Say that again."

"What?"

"Erin is Maddox's destined life mate?"

"Yeah," he mumbled miserably.

"Are you sure of that?"

"Of course I am. She was mine first. Then she made eye contact with him, and that was it..."

"I'm sorry. I'm just a little confused. If she's his destined life mate, why is this not common knowledge and why did she continue to spend time with you?"

"Because she hates him, or she did. She swore to me she was going to reject him after she punished him for everything he's done. For Selena...Erin's too soft for that, and he must have exploited her sweetness. And now he really does have her."

Kendrick smiled to himself and took a drink. "Well, I'm very happy I tracked you down, Jaris. You've given me a great gift."

"Huh?" he asked drunkenly.

"Never mind, buddy. You just drink your troubles away. I'll take care of everything."

EIGHTEEN

The house was dark and quiet when Maddox finally got home. The whole ordeal made him feel wrung out, but he wasn't scared. He exhaled, trying to let go of it all. There was nothing else for him to do right now.

He gazed at Erin, asleep on the couch. She was here. Safe. She'd waited. She hadn't acted the way he expected the entire night. Especially when she told Jaris it was over and came back to him, where people could see, too.

He stared at her for a moment. He should leave her alone, but she'd asked him to wake her. He crouched down next to the couch and rubbed her shoulder. She sighed and opened her eyes.

"Why are you on the couch? You'll get a kink in your neck."

"Mel took your folk's room. I stayed up, scanning the news for a while. I don't think I've been asleep very long."

"You should be in my bed."

She smiled and stretched a little. "Innuendo?"

"Fact."

He scooped her up and carried her to his room. She leaned her head on his shoulder. He could feel how tired she was. He laid her down. Her gaze stayed on him as he took off his coat and shirt. She hadn't said it, he reminded himself, and Mel was in the other room. He took off his shoes and threw on a T-shirt before lying down next to her.

She snuggled next to him, her head pillowed on his arm and her hand rested over his heart. It was so easy. So natural, as if there was nothing between them and never had been.

"Was it terrible at Fortress? Were you scared?" she asked.

"It was fine. What I expected. I wasn't scared. I *was* a bit nervous. I would have said more, but Redge told me to keep it quick."

"You did great. I watched it. I think people will believe you."

"People always believe the worst," he sighed.

"I know that. It will work itself out."

"I only care what you feel. What you believe."

"Then you have nothing to worry about."

He looked at her. He wanted to push her to say it. He felt he could, and it would work. Because of that, he didn't.

She yawned and closed her eyes. He had her with him, and Jaris was out of the picture. That was enough. For now.

He woke early to clattering noise in the kitchen. He kissed Erin on the forehead and pulled his arm out from under her. She rolled over but didn't wake. He closed the door quietly as he left the bedroom.

Mel was pouring herself a huge mug of coffee. Her hair was all over, and she was rumpled from sleeping in the dress she wore to the club.

"Morning, sunshine," he smiled.

She gave him a dirty look over the rim of her mug. "Don't talk to me until I have at least three more gulps of this," she ordered.

He sat at the counter and continued to grin at her. She drank half of her coffee, then her eyes started to grow alert. She poured another mug and set it in front of him.

"Thanks."

"Helluva night, M. You okay?"

"I'm fine. Actually, I'm better than I've been in a long time."

"Because of Erin?"

He nodded and took a drink.

"Quite the girl you've got there. You should have seen the way she maneuvered Kendrick out of here. I didn't even have to resort to violence."

"I'm sorry to hear that," he chuckled.

"Are you done with him finally?"

"Yes. And now that things have changed, we don't have to pose as a couple anymore."

"Good! It's exhausting hanging off your arm. You're really quite disgusting."

"I feel the same way about you, hag."

She laughed and winked at him. "You know I love you, M."

"I love you, too. I can't thank you enough for everything you've done for me the last few days."

"You have to lend Erin to me sometimes for girl stuff. We've made friends."

"I'm glad. Your approval of her makes my life easier."

She finished her coffee and put the mug in the sink. "I'm going home. Call me if you need anything. I'm still on standby till things are all good again."

"Stay alert. The killer is still out there. You're probably on their list."

"I'll just hide behind my mommy's big, scary arm."

He laughed. "That works."

"Open a portal for me. I don't want to walk."

Mel hugged him before going through the portal he opened for her. So much was all wrong. But he was alone with Erin now. He should make her breakfast, he decided. He wasn't as awesome as his father in the kitchen, but he could manage.

As he started cooking, his mind moved to the future. What should he do with his life, besides share it with Erin? He needed to work. And if she decided to stay with him, they needed their own place. He needed to get to know her better. What did she like? Where would she want to live?

She came out, rubbing her eyes and yawning, right as he was setting the table. She blinked at him, then she focused on the table. "I love waffles. Did you make that?"

He nodded and pulled the chair out for her. She sat and pushed her tousled hair back from her face.

"I'm starving. Thank you."

"You're welcome." He sat across from her, immediately plunged into a fantasy of doing this every morning together.

He smiled as her eyes popped and she wiped a trace of whip cream from her lip with her finger. "Wow. This is awesome. You really made this?"

"It's not a big deal."

"I love it. It's so good," she continued to eat.

"Will you spend the day with me again?" he asked.

"Umm...okay. What did you have in mind?"

"Will you show me where you work? You haven't even told me what you do."

Her smile filled her eyes and struck at his heart. He'd never seen her smile like that.

"We can totally do that." She finished eating and headed back to his room. He followed her. "I'm going to run home and change. I'll be right back. Don't over dress, okay? Be as casual as your flashy wardrobe will allow, please."

"Okay. And stop hating on my clothes."

She kissed him quickly. "Not a chance." Then she went through the portal on the wall.

He looked in his closet and pursed his lips. He had casual clothes. He threw on some jeans, a T-shirt, and a pair of sneakers, and left it at that. He messed with his hair for a minute and waited for her to get back.

She was faster than he anticipated, coming back through the portal, a happy energy coming from her. His heart swelled. She was happy, that's how he wanted her, always.

"Am I casual enough?" he asked.

"Yes. Thank you. Are you ready to go?"

"Where are we going?"

"Halussis. I work in the Onyx castle."

"You're kidding."

She shook her head. "Nope."

"How did I never see you there?"

"I don't know. Fate?"

He shook his head, amazed, and opened another portal directly into the castle. They landed in the entry hall. She led the way to the west wing and up to Journey's area. His mind clicked into place as he followed her. Did she work with Journey?

She opened a door and jumped into the room. "HA!" she said loudly.

"Erin! Erin! Erin's back! Get her!" Little voices yelled, and she was swarmed by kids.

He followed her in and closed the door behind him. He stood against the wall and watched her get on the floor with the kids, who obviously adored her. A little hand tugged at his leg. He looked down into the darling face of a little girl gazing up at him with wide brown eyes.

"Maddox, Maddox..."

She knew who he was regardless that she was probably only five. He squatted down next to her.

"Hi, beautiful. What's your name?"

"Alora. Will you marry me?"

He chuckled. "Oh, I would, but I've already found my girl."

Her little mouth formed an O. "Who?"

"Erin."

Alora looked over at Erin, her eyes getting wider. "You love Erin?"

"I do." It was out of his mouth before he could think.

"That's a good choice," the tike said wisely.

"I think so, now I just have to convince her to love me back."

"You think she doesn't?"

"I think she might like me a little, but I want more."

Alora leaned in conspiratorially. "I'll help you," she whispered loudly. "I'll talk to her. She listens to me."

"Thanks."

Erin crawled over to him on her hands and knees, two kids on her back, giggling. He'd never wanted to kiss her so badly.

"All right, get off. You're killing me," she told the kids.

They tumbled off.

"So this is where I work."

"It fits. So you wrestle with them all day?"

She got to her feet and pushed her hair out of her face. "No. I wish. I do that during my breaks. I review case files and try to pair them with adoptive parents."

He looked over the room, his face falling. "They're all orphans?"

"Yes."

The little girl Alora grabbed onto Erin's leg then. "I need to talk to you! It's urgent!" she said.

"Urgent, huh?" Erin smiled down at her.

"Oh man," he chuckled. "I think that's my cue to go see my grandfather for a while or something."

"Good idea," Alora told him. "Girl talk."

He snickered and backed out of the room. He leaned against the wall for a moment, listening to the sounds of the kids coming through the door. Erin stuck her head out a minute later. She came out and stood beside him.

"Slick, getting Alora to talk to me," she chuckled.

"I did not orchestrate that," he said emphatically. "Don't tell me what she said. I'm embarrassed enough."

"I've got something I need to look at here. It might take me a few hours. Why don't you take off, and I'll meet you later? I know I'll be safe here."

"Okay. Message me when you're done?"

"I will. Sorry. I just need to do this."

He shook his head. "That's fine. Thanks for showing me a little of what you do. I hope you'll tell me more about it later."

He took her hand and raised it to his lips. Her expression sobered. It jerked him up short.

"What?"

She shook herself. "No, it's nothing. I'll see you later." She pulled the door open again and was swallowed back into the mayhem of the kids.

Why had she looked at him like that? His heart flinched. Was he going to lose her after all? He rubbed his hand over his heart. What had he done wrong? He hung his head and stalked off down the hall.

"Maddox!"

Her voice stopped him. He turned to see her jogging down the hall toward him.

Before he could ask her anything she plowed into him, fusing her mouth to his. She pulled back pressing her hand to his chest. "Don't' feel like that. Okay?"

"Whatever you say."

She kissed him again and headed back the way she came. "I'll see you later."

He stared after her. She was paying attention to his feelings. Only he didn't feel better. He hadn't realized how uneven they were until then. She took care of orphans, giving them love and finding them homes. She really was too good for him. He couldn't be enough for her... This was taking too long for him. He needed to know more about her. There was only one place he knew he could get the information he was after.

Maddox opened a portal back to her house. It was time he really got to know her father.

Erin finished the paperwork. She'd done it. The twins' adoption would be finalized tomorrow. They would have a home and parents. They would be loved again. Journey came up behind her and placed a hand on her back.

"Here," Erin handed the file to her. "All that's left is your signature and seal, and it's official."

"Good work. I'm proud of you."

"Thanks."

"Get out of here, Erin. I can tell there's somewhere else you need to be."

"Normally, I'd argue with you, but you're right."

She left the castle and sat down on the front steps and closed her eyes in the afternoon light. Her mind wandered. She needed to get home, but she needed to stay safe, too. Walking to the hub was too risky, and she'd promised she wouldn't be that girl. She went back into the castle to find an obliging ogre to open a portal for her.

She landed back home in the living room, unprepared for what she saw. Maddox was on his back, his head and torso under the kitchen sink. Her dad sat on the floor next to him and handed him a wrench.

"I need the bigger one," Maddox said.

Her dad handed him a different tool.

"I think I've got it...no, it's still dripping."

Erin came into the kitchen. Her dad smiled up at her.

"What's all this, then?" she asked.

"Well, Maddox came to visit me while you were at work, and the pipe sorta exploded. So we've been trying to get it fixed."

"I see. How's it going down there?" she asked Maddox.

"Fairly uncomfortable," he said wiping his hand on his shirt. "And dirty."

Erin felt like her smile would crack her face just as she felt the onset of tears. "Hey, Dad, you want to hear something cool?"

"What's that, sweetheart?"

"Maddox is my destined life mate."

When his head came up swiftly and connected with the pipe with a resounding crack, she tried to cover her laugh. He scrambled out from under the sink and got to his feet, staring at her and rubbing the top of his head.

Her dad chuckled. "I know honey."

"You know? How do you...Did you tell him?"

"No one told me anything," Nathan said. "I could see it, although why you kept it a secret is a mystery to me."

"It's a long story. I'll tell you later."

Maddox looked at her dad. "Sir, would you excuse us. Erin and I really need to talk."

Her father chuckled. "Oh sure. Go *talk* and don't come back for a long time."

They headed to her room and straight through the portal in the wall. They landed in his room, and she faced him as he took her in his arms.

"Why?" he breathed. "What made you change your mind?"

"I changed my mind a while ago, but I didn't fully realize it until I saw you with your head under the sink."

"Seriously?"

"There was a problem, and you did something with your own hands. You didn't just throw money at it...I dunno, it made me hot." His eyes layered with tears as she put her hands on his face. "I see you now. I know what I'm looking at when I look at you."

She moved closer, grabbed the hem of his shirt, and lifted it up and over his head. He closed his eyes as she kissed his collarbone and ran her hands over his back. He put his hands on the sides of her neck and tilted her face up.

"Say it."

"I'm yours," she whispered. "Now treat me like it."

"You're in trouble. I just wish it was raining."

"Hmm…Shower?"

His mouth fell open, then he smiled wickedly. "Oh, that works." He scooped her up and carried her to the bathroom.

They wrecked each other over and over all through the afternoon and into the evening until they were both starving. Erin didn't even taste the food or care. It was fuel, and she needed to get it out of the way as quickly as possible. They ate dinner, went to bed, and had each other some more before finally crashing into sleep.

She woke in the middle of the night, tucked into his side. She looked at him, while he slept. He breathed easily, his face perfectly relaxed. Hmm…he was hers. Odd. She'd claimed him in every way. There was no going back. Not that she wanted to…but life was going to be very different now.

Making love with him was almost scary, it was so good. Her body still felt all warm and shimmery. But then, all of her beautiful feelings shut off hard and fast, and she was suddenly choked with tears. Had it been special for him? Or just typical? Was he with her in his mind when he was inside her? She'd seen his eyes. They were with her. On her. Burning in hers. His heart, too. She knew it, so why did she doubt what she knew?

Stop it! She ordered herself. His memories had to compete with her not the other way around. Her tears came harder. She slid out of bed, pulled one of his shirts on, and sat on the floor across the room, her knees pulled up into her chest.

Her shoulders shook, but she remained silent. How could she doubt what they'd shared? But still, the things he'd done to her. How many others had he touched like that? Was any of it new for him? Did he love her? She was angry and jealous.

He sat up. "Erin!"

She felt his fear. "I'm here. It's okay."

She could see his frown in the dark. "What are you doing?"

She wiped her eyes. "Sorry. Just being stupid."

"Come here."

"Maybe I should just go home."

"Erin, please."

She caved and came back to him. He pulled her under the blanket next to him and held her against his chest.

"Why do you feel like this? What did I do wrong?"

She shook her head, but her tears continued to fall.

"Was I too rough? Did I hurt you?"

"No."

"Then what? I thought everything was perfect. Beyond perfect."

"It's just," her voice broke. "Was there anything we did that was new for you?"

He ground his teeth together and swore under his breath. "I wish I could change the past, but I can't. I really don't want to talk about this..." he sighed. "There's a lot we did that I've never done before."

"Like what?"

He grimaced. "Do I have to?"

"It would make me feel better."

"Everything we did in the shower. Never done that before. When you took control, never had that before. It was awesome, by the way. I want more of that. When we connected, I've never been with someone outside, let alone in the rain, in the middle of the day. Being with you is not even the same thing as what I did with anyone else, even if some of the mechanics are the same. All that was about it being fast and over and cheap. Not. The. Same. Thing. You are my soul. You own me."

"I'm sorry I've ruined our time together. I just didn't know..."

He sat up again and pulled her up, too. He slid his hands up the shirt she wore. "Take this off," he said lifting it over her head, careful not to pull her hair in the process. The moonlight highlighted them in the dark. She shivered as he touched her.

"Why don't you know how beautiful you are?" he whispered. "Haven't I told you? Don't you understand that I've never seen anyone as exquisite as you? And you're so warm. You burn me up inside. Intoxicate me more than any drug I've ever had. Stop doubting."

His hands continued to skim over her skin. Her eyelids fluttered, her breathing uneven. He pulled her against him and brushed his lips across hers. "You said you were mine."

"I am."

He moved his mouth to her ear. "Surrender," he breathed.

She licked her lips and pinched her eyes shut. She hadn't. Not really. She clung to him and nodded. "Okay."

His teeth broke through her skin for the first time and he drank from her, as he loved her again, *very* slowly. She fell through herself. Through her defenses, and found trust.

To say he was reluctant to let her go in the morning was an understatement. Every time she almost wiggled free, he caught her and brought her back.

"You're going nowhere, babe."

"I have to. I need to get to work. How do you even have the energy for this again?" she asked as he rolled her under him.

He shrugged and went to work on her. She could have protested, but it would have been false, so she let him have her again and enjoyed it all.

A while later, she headed to the shower and made sure to lock the door, otherwise, she knew he would join her, and she'd never get to work. She couldn't quit smiling. She didn't even realize she was smiling until her face started to ache with it.

She wrapped herself in a towel and thought about not going to work. He'd asked her to stay more than a few times. But she wanted to make sure that everything was going to go through with the adoption for the twins. Since it was her first completed process, she was nervous that she'd missed something or done something wrong, and she didn't want the kids to have to wait any longer. She didn't have to stay long at work. She could just go and come back.

Maddox was cooking again when she came out. She snuck past the kitchen so he didn't catch her and delay her anymore. Her clothes were here and there on his floor. She'd put them on, go home, change, and then go to work. Her stomach growled as she smelled whatever that was he was making. He could cook. She was a lucky girl.

"I don't know if you'll like it, but I made you an omelet," he said as she came out.

"Thank you. It smells perfect."

She sat down and began to eat. "It's already noon. I won't be gone long. I'll be back in time for dinner. Do you want to go out?"

"No. I want you all to myself. And I want to throw you on the bed at the slightest provocation. Can't do that in public."

She giggled and finished eating. "I promise to be careful."

He kissed her hand. "Thank you."

She started to leave, but he grabbed her arm and pulled her back. "Wha—"

"Shh…" he said quietly.

He held her like she might break any moment. She was confused for a second, then she exhaled and relaxed against him. His heart spoke to hers. There was a desperation and disbelief in him, and for the first time, she felt the weight of his insecurity. He had it worse than she did. And for a moment, he just needed to hold her.

She kissed his cheek and ran her hands through the back of his hair. "I'll be right back. I promise."

"I miss you already."

"Hey," she pulled back so she could look in his eyes. "I'm yours."

He kissed her lips. "And I'm yours."

"Can I go now?"

"Fine. Leave me all alone to pine and obsess over you till you get back."

She yelped as he slapped her ass as she went through the portal.

Checking in at work took only a few minutes, and then Journey booted her out, seeing whatever it was she could see in Erin's heart with her canny storyteller eyes. She didn't go straight back to him though. She sat in the hall at the castle and scrolled through the news.

Opinions flew around about Maddox. She stopped looking after a few minutes. It didn't matter, she told herself. People could say and think what they liked. It didn't change the fact that he was innocent. She wondered if he was looking, too. Closing her eyes, Erin leaned her head back against the wall and thought about their night together.

*Surrender...*she had, but had he? She thought about her tears in the middle of the night and the source of them. There would be times she felt insecure. Every time that happened, would she think about all the lovers before her? Would she always wonder about what he remembered and how she measured up? And would she get angry at him every time, that he'd given himself so freely over and over? It wasn't so easy to let go of...at least not for her.

A crazy idea zipped through her head. She laughed and dismissed it. Then it came back and rooted firmly in her mind. Hmm… she was going through with it she decided. She got up and headed to the castle library, hoping no one was in there, so they wouldn't see what she was looking at.

An hour later, with her head full of new and fascinating *adult* possibilities, she found an empty room and called Melina.

"It's Erin."

"Hey, you. What's up?"

"I need a little help. Could you meet me in the Onyx Castle? I promised Maddox I'd be safe, so I don't want to go anywhere on my own, and I don't know where I'd find what I'm looking for anyway."

"What are you looking for?" Mel asked.

Erin sent her a picture. There was a brief silence then Mel chuckled. "So you quit fighting your fate, eh? You're a bad girl. M doesn't deserve you. I'll help. I know just where to buy such an outfit."

"Thanks."

"I'll meet you in five."

 Maddox cleaned the house to stay busy and to keep from looking at the news. His mind stayed on Erin. He needed her to come back. He hardly believed she'd actually said it, that she'd really committed to him. It didn't seem possible. Time moved *so* slowly as he waited for her. Yesterday had caught him off guard. But tonight he could plan everything for her. He'd do what he could so she wouldn't be able to have second thoughts about them.

He thought about what he could make her for dinner, seeing as that was a skill of his she didn't hold against him. It took him a while, digging around the kitchen, to find his mom's nice place settings. He set the table, but he had to keep retelling himself not to be too smooth. She didn't like that, and it would remind her of the past.

He cringed, thinking about her crying last night. That was horrible. Horrible that she could think what she had. It wasn't anywhere near the truth. There was no one in his head or heart except her. She was everything. There was not one corner or shadow in him that she hadn't filled with her light. His heart groaned for her. He needed her back. How much longer would she be?

His watch pinged. He frowned at it and answered the call.

"What's up, brother?" Kendrick asked.

"Not much."

"Wanna take the girls out again tonight?"

"Can't. Gotta stay out of the public eye for a while after that shit last night."

"I've got some great stuff. I'll bring it over. We can have a private party with Erin and Melina."

"No. Mel's busy, and I want to be alone with Erin. I'm done using, anyway."

Kendrick was quiet for a second. "Good for you. Going clean. I should, too. I know it."

"I'm sorry, but I need to go. Erin will be here soon, and I'm not ready for her."

"You're so whipped. Not that I blame you. I'd reform for her, too. Okay. You're going to have to tell me how you swung her one of these days," Kendrick said.

Maddox half smiled. "One of these days, I will. Later."

He ended the call and headed to the shower. He got clean, dressed, and decided it was time to start making dinner. The sun was about to set. Surely Erin would be back soon. He was about to message her when his watch pinged. It was Mel.

I wish I could see your face. Mind you that's all I would want to see, but still, I know it's going to be priceless.

What are you on about?

You'll see as soon as Erin gets there.

Oh, hell. What have you been doing?

You'll see. I'm totally snickering over here. Just FYI.

Hmm...he narrowed his eyes at his watch. What was going on? He was about message Erin, but she messaged him first.

Sit down. Now.

He snorted, going to the living room and sat down on the couch. What was she doing? The lights cut off. His eyebrows shot up. His bedroom door cracked. Haze and floating lights filled the space around him. Then Erin came out.

He almost dropped dead in a mix of shock and lust. She had her hair in pigtails, a pleated mini skirt that barely covered her ass, and a button-up shirt tied in a knot right under her breasts. He stood up but she put her hands on his chest and shoved him back down on the couch.

"Erin?"

She put her finger over her lips in a shushing motion and tapped her watch. Music filled the house. She smiled wickedly and winked at him as she started to dance.

"Oh my gosh!" he said, putting his hands over his mouth.

Erin moved like a dancer right out of a hip-hop music video. He watched, trapped and helpless. Had he died and gone to bad girl heaven? Over and over, she moved in ways that made him want to whimper and beg. Her gaze snagged on his and there was so much there. So much power and she wielded it over him without mercy.

Finally, when he felt he couldn't breathe anymore, she grabbed his hand and pulled him to his feet, but she didn't stop dancing. He put his hands on her and moved with her. The dirtiest dirty dancing had nothing on them. But she had total control. And she moved him where and how she wanted him.

"I think you broke me," he panted as they crashed on the bed a good while later.

She laughed, taking her pigtails out, letting her hair down. Sweat glistened beautifully all over her naked body.

He swallowed and worked to catch his breath. "I don't know what I did to deserve all that, but you have to tell me, so I can make a habit of it. Where did you learn that stuff anyway?"

She blushed. "Well, there was this one book in the castle library."

"Oh man, it's probably the same book I snuck out of there when I was thirteen."

She leaned on one arm and looked down at him. "Were those your notes on page forty-seven?"

He laughed and covered his face. "Yes."

She drilled her finger into his ribs. He caught her against him and kissed her. He smoothed the hair away from her face.

"You are more than any fantasy I've ever had. What possessed you to do this?"

"I did this for me. To own you in a way no one else ever has. I wanted to give you something that I knew none of your memories could compare to. I want to be queen... Was I successful?"

"Unequivocally," he said seriously.

"That's good, cause I think I pulled my hamstring."

"I will carry you everywhere you need to go until it's better."

"Where could I possibly need to go?" she smiled, gesturing to his bed.

"Where, indeed."

She put her hand over his heart, her expression sobering, and she trembled. "I love you, Maddox."

"Oh, Erin...I love you, too."

She smiled. "I said it first."

"I thought it first," he countered.

"No, you didn't. I've loved you since you first left a flower on my doorstep."

He let out a heavy breath and closed his eyes, taking her lips. This kiss was devastating, and it held the world of his heart inside it. His love for her, the pain, the passion...and now the joy.

He moved his lips to her neck. "I want to mark you."

Her whole body purred. "I want that, too."

"When? What kind of a ceremony do you want?"

"Hmm...Give me some time to think about it." She yawned. "We can talk about it again tomorrow."

Erin smiled as she fell asleep fantasizing about their marking ceremony.

Voices woke Maddox. *Very* familiar voices coming from the living room. He shook Erin gently. She squinted at him.

"What?" she asked.

"We need our own place, like yesterday."

She rubbed her eyes. "Oh?"

"My parents are home."

She gasped and sat up, grabbing at the blanket to cover herself. "Where are my clothes?"

He pointed at the door. Her eyes widened, and her cheeks turned pink.

"Oh no. That bad school girl outfit is out there, ah, and my lingerie...Are your parents out there right now?"

He nodded.

"Well, I'm going to make a good first impression," she groaned.

He chuckled.

"It's not funny!"

"Well, you can laugh or cry, babe. Put something on. I'm going to go talk to them. Come out when you're decent."

He tossed one of his shirts at her before finding one for himself and putting it on over his pajama pants. He winked at her as he went to face the music.

"Hey! You're back! Great!"

Standing in the middle of his and Erin's discarded clothes, his mother and father gave him stony looks. His mom picked up Erin's black lace bra and raised her eyebrows, giving him that hawk look.

He held his hands up before his parents imploded. "She's my destined life mate."

That took all the wind from their sails. Their faces shifted from indignation to happiness. They both grabbed him and pulled him into a group hug.

"Oh, congratulations!" Forest said.

"Where is she?" Syrus asked.

"Umm...she's in my room, feeling embarrassed...I have a lot to tell you guys."

"I should expect so," Forest said. "I want to know all about how you and her found each other."

"Well, there's that, but then there's some other stuff. Really bad stuff. This is going to take a while."

Erin poked her head out of his room, her cheeks still beautifully pink. He held his hand out for her. She came toward him wearing his shirt, a pair of his boxers, and a sheepish expression. He tucked her under his arm.

"This is Erin."

"Hi," her voice was shy.

Forest reached for her and pulled her away from him and into a hug. "Erin," she said quietly.

Maddox watched, amazed as his mom looked into his mate's eyes. The two women seemed to connect immediately on some mystic female level.

"I...I can't tell you what an honor it is to meet you," Erin said to her.

She shook her head. "The honor is mine. And now so are you. My new daughter."

They clung to each other and cried, making him confused. His dad clapped him on the shoulder, smirking.

"Don't ask them why they're crying," he told Maddox sagely. "It's a good sign... So, did she knock the stupid out of you?"

"Absolutely. At least some of it. I have a feeling she's not done."

"They never are, son."

His dad moved forward and grabbed Erin's hand. "My turn," he told Forest. "Erin."

"Sir." She looked up at him nervously.

"Welcome to the family."

"Thank you. I really look forward to getting to know you both, but I think I should go home and, um, get dressed first."

His mother chuckled and handed Erin the clothes Maddox had happily removed from her last night. She wadded it all up, tucked it under her arm, blushed brighter, and headed to his room. He followed her and closed the door.

"Oh my gosh," she breathed. "I'll be back in a little bit."

"Don't take too long, and don't even think about getting rid of that stuff," he pointed to the naughty clothes under her arm.

She smiled wickedly. "Wouldn't dream of it."

She kissed him and went through the portal on the wall. Now he had to tell his parents all the ugly news.

NINETEEN

Forest sat on the couch and listened as Maddox told her and Syrus all about what happened while they were away. She scanned through the media as he talked, looking over all that he said. She needed to talk to Redge and Kindel to get the full picture of the situation and whatever information Maddox didn't know about, and she was sure there was plenty.

She wanted to cry and pitch a fit like anyone would whose son was being framed for terrible crimes, but she needed to keep her head cool. She was Hailemarris. If she felt she really needed to lose control, she'd go see Rahaxeris to do it. Her father always let her storm, and then he brought her focus back sharp.

She looked at Syrus. "We weren't supposed to be back yet. I think we should keep it quiet we're in Regia."

"I agree."

"Erin couldn't have come into our lives at a better time."

"Why do you say that?" Maddox asked.

"Because I can't be your mom right now. I can't look at this problem as your mother. I have to look at it from a cold, removed place. But it makes it easier on me knowing your heart is being cared for. I know you're a grown man, but you'll always be my baby. I can't coddle you. I can't give you any favor. The public will cry corruption harder than they already are if I do."

He nodded. "Sure, I get it...Thanks, Mom. I love you so much."

She pulled him into a tight hug and lingered. The feel of him, the way he smelled, he was her only son, and she would rip the world open for him. But he wasn't hers the same way anymore now. He belonged to Erin. She was grateful and sad at the same time. But best of all, he was Maddox again, and not the shell he'd become to face the public. They would get through this darkness and find the real source of it.

Forest sent for Kindel and Redge. They arrived together an hour later.

"How was your vacation?" Kindel asked.

"Super. I'll tell you about it later. Give me everything you have."

They laid their files out on the table for Forest to look at and waited silently. She scoured through all of it twice, then she sat back and crossed her arms over her chest.

"The whole damn thing is political," she said.

"For sure," Redge agreed.

"So who's behind it?"

"I've been searching," Kindel said. "Whoever is behind it has no ties to my usual informants. The murderer is a puppet, we know that much. The fabricated story leaked to the media was done with the dead girl's watch. I stopped the first attempt. I still don't know how they got it through after that."

Forest pursed her lips. "The dust used on the second body is illegal and seriously expensive. There's a deep pocket behind this. Are there assassins in play?"

"No. We haven't ruled assassination attempts out, but I think they just want you out of the way. Discredited," Redge said.

"So who's on your list?" she asked.

Both Redge and Kindel rattled off names on their suspect list. She didn't doubt them, but none of the names they mentioned seemed to catch in her mind as a real possibility.

"Are you going in?" Redge asked.

"Yes. But no one is to know I'm back. I'll be ghosting around Fortress invisible for a while, until I step in something. X, Fluffy, and Ena are the only others who can know I'm there. No one else. Spread it around you've had word from me and I'll be back next week. Hopefully, that will push an action we can catch."

They stood and tucked their files under their arms before leaving. Syrus put his hands on her shoulders. She stood and let him hang on to her a for moment.

"What do you need from me?" he asked.

She smiled. "Make me something rich for dinner. I'll be home late."

"Is that all?"

"Help Maddox figure out what he needs to do so we can get him moved out ASAP. Sharing a roof with a newly mated couple is a little too much for me."

He chuckled. "Truth. Hey, you know that means we'll be alone again."

"Sounds good," she kissed him, turned invisible, and used her portal ring to go to Fortress.

"Dad, I'm back...for a few minutes anyway!" Erin called from her bedroom, searching through her dresser, trying to decide what she should wear.

"Dad?"

No answer. Something moved behind her. She turned, her nose and eyes burning as dust was thrown in her face. She fell. The room vibrated, colors melting into one another. A shadow grabbed her with gloved hands and hoisted her up as she fell unconscious.

Kendrick dropped the note on her bed, closed the portal, and set a charge on the end of it. The charge sparked, swirled in a circle for a second, and then exploded, destroying her end of the portal altogether. Maddox wasn't coming that way again. He smashed the end of the bridge he brought and took Erin out of there while his small window of time was still open.

Maddox paced. What was taking Erin so long? She should have been back by now. Was she obsessing over her appearance? How much time did she feel she needed to primp? Was she just still nervous about being around his parents?

His heart sought hers, trying to read it. Nothing. He felt nothing as if she was asleep. He smirked. They hadn't slept that much last night. Maybe she did need a nap. Still, he needed to check on her. He tried to go through the portal. It let him through a foot and then he hit a black wall. It wasn't just shut, it was broken.

He backed up, his heart in his throat. He grabbed his sword off the wall, touched his wrist, and opened a portal to her room. Something smelled weird. He blinked and coughed, covering his mouth and nose with his shirt collar. It was some type of hallucinogen in the air.

His eyes fell on the note.

I hate you, Maddox. I'd rather be dead than mated to you.

The handwriting was a dead ringer for his own.

"Erin!" he yelled, rushing out of her room.

He slipped and fell in a pool of blood next to a body. He scrambled up, looking down at Jaris. His wrists were cut, and like the girls, *Maddox* had been carved on his arm. He ran to the other room. Nathan was on his face on the floor, his head bleeding.

He rushed to him and turned him over. He was still alive, barely.

"Where's Erin?" Maddox shouted.

"I don't know," Nathan hissed. "Leave me. Go find her."

He tried to focus on her. She was alive, but still, he felt nothing from her. She must be drugged. A pulse like a sphere of energy formed in his chest directly over his heart. He went down on his knees, unable to breathe. Erin had been taken. They were going to kill her.

A spark lit inside the sphere. A spark of power ignited by rage. Rage distilled, hate purified. The power inhaled, pulling down into a pinprick that stabbed his heart. Then it exhaled, breaking the sphere in his chest. The shards raced through his veins to his hands and into his head, bursting out of his eyes.

Maddox got to his feet. He held his hands out—they were charged. He *was* like his father. He could weaponize his rage, and it had transformed him. He'd bypassed becoming a master and jumped straight into becoming a mage. Gold electricity slithered along his fingers, through his hands, and up his forearms. Maybe he couldn't be a living elemental like Tesla, and maybe he couldn't heal or strike people dead with lightning like his father...but whatever the extent of this new power was, he was about to learn. He closed his eyes, focusing his whole being on finding her.

Kendrick laid Erin out on an old table. The basement of the club was the perfect place to kill her. He had hours before the sun set and Paradigm's night life started up. If he kept her unconscious, he could do things to her, mess with her in a way Maddox would feel and understand, but still keep her feelings shut off so he couldn't find them. He would take pictures of everything he did to Erin and send them to him.

He got hard thinking about it. There was no better way to inflict pain on Maddox. He'd done as his mother asked, so it didn't matter if he went off-script now. He didn't give a damn if his mother became Hailemarris anyway. Forest didn't mean anything to him one way or the other. He just wanted Maddox to suffer.

He shook himself, remembering he couldn't actually do anything to Erin sexually. That would leave his DNA on the body, and she was perfect as she was since Maddox had her under him all last night anyway. He'd enjoyed watching some of that. They'd been so wrapped up in each other they hadn't paid attention to anything else. He hadn't even had to be that stealthy to creep past them as they slept and through that handy portal to her house.

His memories of voyeuristically watching them made his blood boil. Maddox was so lucky. Why was he always so lucky? He looked down at Erin, her fiery hair cascading over the edge of the table. She was too beautiful. If only it didn't ruin the scene he was trying to construct, he'd smash her skull in. He'd break the bones of her face into pieces. She wouldn't be so gorgeous then.

He needed to decide what he was doing, get it over with, and get the hell out of there.

He spun the knife in his hand around his fingers. She wouldn't be left any dignity. Taking her dignity would take Maddox's as well. He slid the knife into the shirt she wore and began cutting it off her. She grabbed his wrist suddenly. Ribbons of gold light covered her hand. She wasn't awake. Her eyes were shut, her body limp, except the hand that had a vice grip on his wrist.

The hell? He jerked his hand out of her grasp. Her eyes opened but she wasn't the one looking at him. Gold light swirled in her irises. He had to finish her now. Something was happening he didn't understand. He lifted her limp arm to cut her wrist.

A smile spread his lips and pleasure swept over him as her blood swelled out through the open line he'd just sliced. He would carve her all over, quickly, but thoroughly. He jolted as the air around him changed. A rushing filled his ears. He spun around as a blast sounded behind him, a portal opening, and Maddox charged out.

Kendrick grabbed Erin and put his knife to her throat.

"What's up, brother?" he smiled at Maddox. "You look different."

"I am different. Let her go."

"I don't think so. Back off or I'll slit her throat."

Maddox took a step forward.

"I mean it!" Kendrick shouted, his eyes darting to the sword in Maddox's hands.

"You don't have anything against her." Maddox reasoned. "This is about you and me, isn't it? You always want what's mine."

"You have no idea. You don't know what I am."

"Maybe not. Until now. I see you, and you're not worth another breath."

Maddox advanced. Kendrick pressed his knife into Erin's throat. Gold light wrapped around his wrist like a rope, holding him back. The blade never broke her skin. He struggled against the force with all his might. The light jerked his hand up and held it immobile as more bands of light snaked around his body, lifting him inches off the floor.

He cried out as Maddox's sword slashed his left wrist. Gold light danced along the edge of his split flesh for a second, then vanished.

"That's for Jaris."

Then his right wrist was cut.

"That's for Trish."

The sword sliced diagonally across his face.

"That's for Selena...And this... is for Erin."

Kendrick's lungs froze as the black glass tip slid slowly at the junction of his ribs. Maddox held his gaze as he pushed the sword deeper, straight through his heart.

Maddox exhaled, his breath expelled in little jerks. Blood spilled from Kendrick's mouth as his eyes rolled back in his head. He dumped him on the floor, sliding the body off his sword, and rushed to Erin.

Tremors pulled and snapped in his muscles. Tears burned his eyes as he felt her breathe against him. Relief slammed into him with a violence. So close to losing her. Her life almost extinguished before his eyes. Terror had never been more real to Maddox than in that moment. He knew he'd never shake the memory. It would haunt him the rest of his life.

His hands shook around her. He had her. She was alive. He'd made it in time. He took her out of there. She would wake soon. She didn't need to see that.

He carried her upstairs and sent a message to his mom.

The killer was Kendrick. He's dead now. He took Erin. I have her. I'm taking her home now. Send Redge to the main street club in Paradigm. The body is in the basement.

He opened a portal back to her house, laid her down on her bed, and sent for his dad.

Syrus was there in a second.

"Go see to her dad. He's in the other room. He was barely hanging on."

Syrus didn't ask questions, he just turned and went. In a few moments, he was back, looking in at Maddox.

"He's fine. I fixed him up."

"Thanks, Dad."

Syrus came closer and reached for his hand. Then he tipped his chin so he could look into his eyes, his smile growing broader by the second. "Look at you. How?"

"Rage."

His dad laughed, touching the gold light on Maddox's arm. "You *are* like me. But your power is different. It's not wild like lightning. It's a drift... a current."

"It came in a rush when I needed it."

"I didn't get to choose my mage title, and neither will you. You are The Torrent."

Maddox grinned. "I can live with that."

Syrus looked down at Erin. "Is she okay?"

"Yeah. Drugged. She'll be okay soon."

Maddox told his dad quickly about Kendrick, and he sent for Kindel to come and bring a team to deal with Jaris' body. His father loomed around and talked with Nathan.

Erin was still out, and Maddox realized she was going to have a hard time surfacing. This was still the wrong place for her to wake up, with Jaris dead in the next room. He opened a portal and took her out of there.

TWENTY

Forest waited and watched, invisible inside Fortress, her watch on silent. Something was happening. No one knew exactly where she was, but she could see Kindel was looking for her, surreptitiously. She followed him down the hall toward her office and had to side-step to avoid colliding with Catarina.

"Kindel, I need something from Forest's office," she said. "There was a file she left for me to handle while she was gone, and I forgot about it till now. And since you said she will be back in a week, I need it today if I'm going to get it finished for her by the time she returns."

"Okay," he said vaguely. "Do you know where she put it?"

"No."

She followed him into Forest's office. Ena wasn't there. Kindel checked a message on his watch, his face pulling in anxiety. "I have to go. Ena will be back any minute from her break. She'll help you."

"Thank you," Catarina said as Kindel rushed out.

Forest would have followed Kindel, but she stayed still, watching Catarina. She was lying. Forest hadn't asked her to do anything while she was gone. Ice swooped into her stomach as intuition sparked. Surely not...

As soon as the door shut behind Kindel, Catarina moved around Forest's desk and began rifling through the files on top. She grabbed Maddox's file and scanned through it. Forest didn't breathe. Then Catarina spotted the bag from the lab with Maddox's watch inside it. Her eyes lit, and she slid it into her pocket. She made to close the file and straighten the pages so they looked undisturbed.

Forest grabbed her letter opener and stabbed it straight through Catarina's hand, pinning her to the top of the desk before dropping her invisibility.

"Forest! I..." her face blanched in pain, and she spluttered. "Why would you do this? I was just—"

"Save it. You're under arrest."

Catarina tried to lash out at her. Forest sucker-punched her in the face. She went down to her knees, awkwardly, with her hand stuck to the desk.

"It's too late for your precious baby boy. He'll never recover from the damage I've done to him. And neither will your family's reputation."

A message pinged Forest's watch. She looked at it and then sneered at Catarina. "No, it's your son who'll never recover, not mine. Kendrick's dead."

Erin felt her lungs fill, but she knew she was gone. Thunder rumbled. She felt her body, cradled in his arms, but she knew she was dead. She had to say goodbye. Would he be able to hear her? She didn't want to leave. Rain drops kissed her face. She looked up into his eyes. His strikingly beautiful eyes, not grey, not green but both colors mixed. *Hers*. Her generous shadow. His heart of gold encased in a fantasy of masculine beauty and strength. It was a dream. None of it was real. She floated, her soul adrift. This was a trance. He wasn't holding her. She was dead, their connection destroyed. How could she let go? It was impossible. She would never let go. She didn't know how, and she didn't want to know. She had to tell him.

"I can't stay. I don't want to leave."

"You're not going anywhere."

"I love you, Maddox. It turns me over and breaks me all the way down...makes me something new. I never thought I would feel this. I surrender to it. To you. To us. I'm sorry I have to leave." Her voice was weak and sleepy.

"I've got you, Erin. It's over."

She sobbed, her vision wavering like ripples on the water. His hand held her cheek, gold filling her eyes.

"You took me over…" she breathed. "Don't ever doubt your worth or what I would have done for you… Don't forget me and don't hide your real face again."

Thunder rolled louder all around, rain falling harder on her. She blinked. They were in the garden. Where they began.

"You'll wake soon," he said.

"Wake me, Maddox…If I'm not dead, wake me."

He kissed her, so soft it couldn't be real. She jolted as his blood filled her mouth. All she could see was gold light. It raced under her skin, lighting her up. He lifted her up so her head was on his shoulder. Her fangs throbbed. She needed more. She sank her teeth into his neck. More heat, more light flowed into her.

She broke away, her head thrown back to the rain, gasping. "What *are* you?"

He held her head in his hands and searched her eyes, then he smiled. "You're awake now."

She was. Erin had never felt so awake. All her senses sharpened. "What are you?" she demanded again. "How could your blood do that?"

"I transformed when I thought you were going to die. I'm a mage now."

She touched his hands and ran her fingers over the light on his forearms. "I like this."

"I like it, too. I wouldn't have been able to save you without this power."

The connection was tearing her up inside. She'd never needed him like she did right then. She needed him to touch her everywhere, and she had to touch him. A thirst built in her throat and burned in her mouth. She had to consume him, absorb him, dissolve into him so they could never be separated again.

"Are we alone?" she asked.

"Yes."

"I want to mark you. Now. Here. Just you and me."

"You don't want a ceremony?" he asked.

She shook her head. "Not like most have. I just want you. And it *is* a ceremony. Every second of it will be sacred. I don't want to wait. I want it now."

"You really don't care that no one is here? You don't care what you're wearing?"

She looked up at the sky, rain falling on her face, and smiled. She slid out of the clothes she wore and began to grab at his.

"As it was the first time."

She winded him.

"I don't deserve you," he said.

"Whether that's true or not, I'm yours. You're stuck with me."

They made love again outside in the rain in a celebration of life and memorial of their first time. He filled her spiritually and physically before running his tongue along his incisor, filling his mouth with blood, and biting down into the top of her shoulder. She gasped as his blood ran into the bite mark, sealing inside her skin as her flesh closed, leaving a traditional, crescent, lovers mark behind. She shivered around him, looking into his eyes as she touched the scar he'd just put on her.

Her smile was warm and her eyes bright as she pulled tighter around him. She kissed his neck once and breathed, "Forever," against his skin before she bit down, repeating the same process on him. He touched his new scar when she pulled back. It was warm and added yet another layer to his commitment to her.

His heart sang in exultation. She wasn't ashamed anymore. She'd marked him and taken his mark. The scars were visible to the world. Erin was his, and she would stand by him in the light. Every second of their very private ceremony was sacred and beautiful, just as she'd said it would be. Their hearts and souls entwined along with their bodies. Their love unbearably soft and passionately savage at the same time.

Later, after they'd laid down in his room for a while, just talking, he told her all about what happened. She cried over Jaris a little as he thought she might. It didn't hurt him. He held her through it, and she grew quiet.

"Where do you want to live?"

"What do you mean?" she asked.

"Us. We can live anywhere you want. I want you happy. We can be rural like this, or further out like Tesla and X. We can live in the middle of the city. Or we could go to the coast like where Melina lives. I don't care, sweetheart. You decide."

"That's a big decision."

"I'll make sure your dad is somewhere new if that's what he wants. If you want him to live near us, I'll arrange that."

She touched his face. "Are you just going to throw money at this problem?"

"Absolutely. Do you mind?"

She smiled. "Not this time. I want to live somewhere nice. We need a *very* private garden for when it rains and a really killer shower in our house for when it doesn't."

He chuckled and snuggled into her. "Agreed...I've been thinking about what I want to do. Would you mind if I worked with you?"

"What? You mean crafting adoptions?"

"Not exactly. Maybe I could work finding the adoptive parents. I think more people would be willing and interested in bringing kids into their lives if they were just more aware. I could use my celebrity status for that. I could make people listen. I could show them...I want to find a great family for that little tike, Alora...My sister says I'm lucky. Maybe I can spread that around more."

Tears filled Erin's eyes.

"What's wrong?" he asked.

"Nothing at all." She grabbed his hand and placed it over her heart. "Destiny doesn't make mistakes."

They slept through the afternoon. Maddox roused slowly, faintly aware Erin wasn't next to him. He blinked and rolled over. Evening was fading into night, casting shadows all through his room. Her side of the bed was cold. Where was she?

His heart sought hers out, and all he felt was sorrow from her. He got up and dressed quickly. Where was she? He could feel the distance between them. His heart, that had been so light before, now pulled down with darkness.

He strode outside and let their connection lead him to her. He would have messaged her, but she was in a quiet state that stopped him. She wasn't far, but the closer he got, the more he worried. He found her sitting next to Selena's gave, talking quietly to the dead. He didn't know if he should just turn around and leave her alone or not. He frowned, looking down.

"Maddox." Her voice fell softly on his ears and he looked up at her.

"Come."

He strode over to her. She looked up into his face with a sad smile. "I was just telling her some stuff...I miss her."

"I'm sorry. I'd trade my life for hers if it would bring her back for you."

Erin stood, touched his cheek with one hand, and pressed the other over his heart. She shook her head.

"Let it go. I give you permission to forgive yourself. Selena was murdered. It wasn't your doing, and it wasn't hers. All the blame I assigned to you and then to her for what happened...all my rage and bitterness...it's all gone now. She was stolen from me, but the thief is dead. My memories can rest in peace now. I will always miss her, but I can let her go, as she would have wanted."

"How do you know?" he asked quietly, his heart still tearing.

She sank to her knees, pulling him down with her, next to the tree he planted. She pulled a small folding knife out of her pocket and opened it.

"Hold out your hand," she said.

He did. She laid the double-edged blade flat in his palm before clasping his hand with hers. She turned the blade to the side and sliced both of their hands at the same time. She never let go, their mixed blood falling on the roots of the tree. Gold light ran up the trunk through the cracks in the bark and out along the branches. The leaves shivered.

"The shadows of the past will no longer darken our love." Erin's breath caught. "Look. See it, Maddox...Forgiveness. And only peace follows in its wake."

A flower budded on the tree and opened before their eyes. The petals should have been white...They were gold.

EPILOGUE

Rahaxeris sat down and picked up his book, opening it to where he'd left off earlier in the day. He'd enjoyed the family gathering and getting to meet Erin. She was easy to like, and he looked forward to getting to know her better. Having Maddox settled was a great relief.

His mind began to slide over the words on the pages, slipping away from the here and now.

Something moved in his peripheral vision. Startled, for the mere fact that he *was* startled by something, and that it was able to creep up on him. He turned his head very slowly and looked at what was looking at him. He set his book down just as slowly and stood up.

The female figure looked like a flat cutout, a silhouette. She was all darkness, like the heart of a shadow, only her eyes glowed a strange green light. She breathed, causing her defined edges to blur. He'd never seen an entity quite like her, that fact alone was chilling. Then she smiled.

"Hello, grandfather."

His cold blood ran a bit colder. It spoke with Sophie's voice.

THE END

DON'T MISS

FERAL and FORSAKEN,

THE NEXT BOOKS COMING SOON IN
THE SHADOWS OF REGIA TRILOGY!

ABOUT THE AUTHOR

Reading my bio, huh?
Real life sucks. I bet you feel like that sometimes, maybe even right now. That's why I write fantasy. I need to escape depression, bitterness, bills, illness...I could go on, but you get it. In the pages of fiction, I can slay the dragons, triumph over the bad guys, be immortal, and never struggle with love handles. For a short time, I can let it all go, and be everything I can't be in real life. Maybe you're hurting right now. Maybe you're in the waiting room of the hospital, or just stuck in traffic. I've brought a portal. Come with me...Let's ditch this crappy popsicle stand and go somewhere great, where we can forget all this, at least for a while.

That's why I write. I'm not an author, I'm an escape artist.

If you want to come play with me, visit
www.tenayajayne.com

Lightning Source UK Ltd.
Milton Keynes UK
UKHW010430160223
417042UK00010B/1406

9 780998 674131